RUM PUNCH REGRETS

ABBY GEORGE BOOK 1

ANNE KEMP

For Dad.

CHAPTER 1

EVERYONE IN THE MAIN CABIN LET OUT A SURPRISED SHOUT AS the sputtering, tiny, too-old-to-still-be-flying biplane lurched suddenly to the left, then dropped about 100 feet in the air. Abby had closed her eyes as she tried to calm herself with quiet happy thoughts. She refused to believe that this was how she would go down.

I finally get to go to the Caribbean, she thought apprehensively, and I'm going to plunge to my death in a plane crash? Abby felt like a character in Alanis Morissette's "Isn't it ironic?" song. We're probably over the Atlantic still anyway. I won't even make it to the Caribbean.

It felt like light-years away but it was truly just a few weeks earlier that Abby's sister Leigh had shown up on her doorstep, revealing her newest plot. Abby had just been laid off from her job as executive coordinator and VIP relations manager for the CEO of an Internet start-up in Los Angeles, and was swimming in confusion and loss, when Leigh arrived, making the offer of a lifetime: Abby could lick her wounds in the Caribbean and Leigh would pay for her to get there.

"Abby, I need you to go down to the islands for a few months to help me wrap up the sale of . . . well, the sale of my house there. I can't go, and if Daryl found out, it would kill him." Leigh took a deep breath. "He can't ever know this is happening." Abby had been completely confused. House in the islands? This was all very dramatic. And why didn't Leigh's husband know about it? Shouldn't he know?

"You. Have. A house. In the Caribbean. And it's for sale." Abby nodded once for effect after each word, making sure she was getting the details right. She reached toward the pack of cigarettes to light one. As she did, she looked at Leigh out of the corner of her eye. "How do you have a home there?"

"I just do."

"Like a time-share condo?"

"No. Not a time-share."

"Like a rental property that you dreamed about last night and then ya woke up crazy?"

"Abby, shut up and listen. I've had it since I was married to Ken, and I kept it, okay? It was his. When we divorced, I got to keep it. Mom and Dad knew about it, but Daryl doesn't. He would freak out that I never told him. And he's never going to know. You get that part? Never."

Despite all the secrecy and drama surrounding it, who could say no to a free trip to the Caribbean? Abby thought. Yet as with anything Leigh-related, there was always a catch. This time it was to do some work on the house. Abby's head began to spin just at the mere memory of the night Leigh had told her about her dilemma.

Of course she would have some hidden home in the Caribbean that needs some TLC. Of course she would need me to go down there to oversee the sale and some repairs. And how hard could it all be, anyway?

Leigh was the kind of sister who made other people's heads spin, especially poor Abby's. Twenty years older than Abby, Leigh had acted as Abby's mother over the years, when their mother just couldn't . . . right after their father passed away. But Leigh treated Abby as the perennial village idiot, almost without meaning to. Known for her caustic tongue (that frequently lashed out at Abby) and biting backhanded compliments (again, meant for her ill-fated younger sis), Leigh was that woman who, no matter what, could keep it all together and make it look as simple as tying your shoes. Or so she would have you think. Yes, most grown men feared Leigh. Abby was sure she had made many cry over the years.

As much as Abby wanted to be irked that her sister had never bothered to tell her about her secret Caribbean home, she was determined to push those thoughts to the back of her mind, opting instead to go to the Caribbean in order to help her sister out, and to take advantage of a terrific offer. After all, opportunities like this only happen once in a lifetime, and honestly, how often would she be newly laid-off and single? Abby scoffed internally at this last thought.

Single. Laid-off, broke and single, she thought sadly. I'm worse than a country song.

Yes, the last 365 days had not been Abby's finest. At least I didn't have to tuck my tail between my legs and move back home to Maryland from Los Angeles. Abby was still picking up the pieces of a lost romance-turned-engagement-turned-breakup-because-said-jerk-cheated. Before Abby had even had time to recover from the blow, her mother had passed away. It was too much devastation and Abby had closed herself off to the sadness and had put on her best stoic face, the way her mother had done years prior when her father had passed. It was a Southern tradition to smile through the pain, and Abby and

3

Leigh were both well versed in this ritual by now. Abby had been through this once before and knew that no matter what, she could not bring her mother or father back, so she needed to move on. But it was on a night like tonight that she wished she had her mom to call and cry to or her dad for answers and a shoulder to lean on.

Abby wiped her sweaty palms on her pink capris, reflecting on how the whirlwind trip had already changed. Oh, Leigh. The promise of a first-class flight was long forgotten, if it had ever been an option at all.

In order to get Abby to the island at a "reasonable cost," Leigh had flown her on three different legs before having Abby land on St. Maarten, the neighboring island. Then she was put on a twenty-minute puddle-jumper flight to St. Kitts. Now, Abby was in the air, the last ten minutes to go, wishing she had the ability to teleport.

The lurching was quickly replaced by a smooth ride and clapping from fellow seatmates as the plane righted itself and glided along over the water. Abby smiled to herself and said a silent thank you as she let out a huge sigh of relief. It was night, so Abby could only see the occasional light playing peek-a-boo with her beyond the view she had from the window. It was the telltale sign that there was an island down there somewhere and the promise of a new adventure that would be filled with . . . well, she really had no clue what it was going to be filled with.

Abby had done some research about St. Kitts before leaving and discovered there were three universities on this particular island. There was an American-based nursing school, an East Indian medical school and another American-based school, a veterinary college. Apparently, Leigh also had a tenant whom she had forgotten to mention, who was a student at the vet school and lived in the pool house.

This surprise news was information Abby had digested surprisingly well when Leigh had shared it with her. They were organizing Abby's boxes at her storage unit when Leigh had slid this tidbit into conversation.

Abby was leaning against an old shelving unit that housed boxes of memorabilia and listening to Leigh rattle off a list of things that needed to be accomplished before flying out.

As Leigh was ticking down said list, she suddenly interrupted herself to say, "Oh, Abby, I did forget to mention one thing in my haste the other day. I hope you'll forgive me."

There was that smile again -- the one that Leigh pulled out of her reserve when she really needed something. Abby narrowed her eyes at her sister.

"Of course you did, Leigh. Let me guess, the house is wired with explosives, but as long as I get to the blue wire in under ten seconds, I can save not only myself and the house but the island and civilization as we know it?"

Leigh breathed out a heavy sigh and shook her head. "You are such a pain in my butt. No. There's a tenant. He's a student in the veterinary program. Nice guy. You'll need to let him know that we are selling the house and he may only have a few weeks left."

"Does nice guy that is about to be homeless have a name?" Abby tightened her smile as she locked eyes with Leigh.

"Ben. His name is Ben, and he's from the U.S. but he's British. Like half or something. Or maybe Australian?" Leigh winked. "Eh, they all sound the same to me. He pays his rent on time and the folks down there who help keep up the property say he's a good guy."

5

"So Ben isn't aware his home may be going away while he tries to study for med school?"

"Vet school, Abby. And if you must know, I believe Ben is already in his last semester at Rhodes University, which is a pre-clinical school of veterinary medicine. What that means is that when he finishes up there, he'll come back to the States to complete his degree here." Abby couldn't help but notice the annoyance in her sister's voice as she spoke to her -- well, more like spoke down to her. Rather than argue about the tone of Leigh's statement, Abby chose to move forward.

"Okay, Leigh. Well then, I will be more than happy to give good old Ben the bad news. In fact, I will do it right when I get there. 'Hello, are you Ben, the nice little college student that needs to live here until you finish out your semester? Okay, that's nice. Get out.' Yep, sounds perfect, Leigh." Abby shook her head and looked at Leigh. Why do we always have to spar? "I mean, really?"

"Get off your high horse, Abs. Just tell him and then do what I need you to do. He'll figure it all out. The couple who help keep the house live on-site, so they'll be there to help with any other issues you may encounter."

Yeah, yeah, I got it, Abby thought. Here it comes, all the little surprises that had been "forgotten." Next thing you know I will be living in a house with four other people that -- whoops! -- Leigh forgot to tell me about. Or the first-class tickets will somehow disappear due to a computer glitch. Or there is no house and I get to stay in a tent. Ha ha, Abby, here is your version of Survivor. Joke's on you!

"Oh, and I got your tickets all handled this morning before Daryl had a chance to see me do it." Leigh smiled as she took a swig of her scotch and soda. "You are out of here on the 8th of January. I wasn't able to do the first-class ticket. Sorry." She took another swig of her drink. "There was some weird issue with me redeeming miles, and I had to play all kinds of games with different airlines to get you there."

What is this woman, a mind reader? "No problem. As long as I get there in one piece, I'll be happy."

Leigh laughed at this. "Don't worry, you'll be fine, I got you covered."

 ⁖

FAMOUS LAST WORDS. THREE AIRLINES AND ALMOST TWENTY hours later, what should have been an easy five-hour trip out of Charlotte, on an airline with a movie, some nuts and cool air, had turned into a nightmarish day of travel with broken air conditioning and flight delays. On one of the flights they even ran out of food for the Economy Class passengers. Not only was she running three hours behind her original estimated time of arrival, but Abby was now on a plane ride made of nightmares, and her stomach was growling. The cabin was hot, sticky and humid; everyone was packed on top of one another and gasping for air in the stale cabin as the jostling of the plane finally stopped. Abby couldn't get her breath and could only wish to feel firm, unmoving ground under her feet and to have her hand grasping a cold drink as she sat in front of some air conditioning.

Once landed -- finally! -- and through the sauna that St. Kitts called their immigration and customs line, Abby thought she would step into the cool, air-conditioned comfort of the luggage terminal. But no. The room was sweltering, like a July evening in New Orleans. The air was saturated with the smell of sweat and sticky bodies. As soon as she was able, Abby grabbed her over-packed luggage from the belt and hauled it out the door to the curb, dragging it and sliding it the whole way, even stopping to kick it a time or two.

There was a guy outside the terminal standing by the curb holding a dingy ripped-up sign that had the name "Jorge" scrawled on it. Did he mean "George"? He and Abby eyed each other for a moment, and then she finally broke, nodding and waving her hand to call him over.

"Hi! Is that for Abby George?"

The Rastafarian shrugged and smiled a big toothy grin. He looked like he had yellow Tic Tacs in his mouth. "Indeed, yes, yes. Are you Abby?"

Abby smiled as she realized that the tension was sliding from her body. Home must not be far off, and this guy seemed nice enough. This man was Ziggy, one half of the couple that helped Leigh by maintaining the property. Leigh had called and asked if he would please fetch Abby from the airport and help her get settled at the house.

"Yes, that's me. Abby George. Nice to meet you. And you are Ziggy, I presume?"

The Rasta man laughed and grabbed one of Abby's three bags. "Yes, mon. I be Ziggy. Master of all tings. Let's get you in da taxi so I take you 'round to your place an' get you dere. Then you sleep, mon. Good?"

This is going to be different, Abby chuckled silently. She was truly on the island now, her escort complete with accent and dreads. She suppressed a laugh and walked with him towards the white minivan that had "TAXI" in big bold letters (like the kind you would buy from a hardware store) emblazoned across the side. The front of the hood was painted in bright colors and zigzags (maybe this was where "Ziggy" came from?) and on the top of the front windshield, in the Rastafarian green, red and yellow, was painted big and bold: "ZIG-

GY." The back of the white van displayed a bit of island wisdom: "You got to GO to come BACK."

Where am I? Abby thought as she shook her head and climbed into the back of the beaten-to-hell-and-back minivan.

Ziggy tore out of the small parking lot and began the journey to the place Abby would be calling home for the next few months. As he flew at a race car's pace through narrow dirt lanes, Ziggy pointed out the things she would need to know, like Ram's, the grocery store that was not open on Sundays and closed at six o'clock in the evening all other days. There was a gas station, one of two on the island that was open on Sundays, but never open later than ten o'clock at night. Then came the bakery, a car rental lot, and a small stadium for rugby, cricket and soccer games. She could make out the lights at Port Zante, where cruise ships docked and the town would be overpopulated for a few hours while tourist dollars stimulated the local economy. Then there was Ricky's, Ziggy's favorite bar and a local spot for dive training. Ricky's was attached to the Frigate Beach Hotel and the property also boasted a small but quaint beach with a view of Nevis, the other neighboring island. Ziggy made sure to toss all of this information Abby's way like a machine gun, glancing in his rearview to make sure she was taking it all in.

And she was. Abby nodded blankly. Grocery store, bar, gas station, bar, port, bar, bar, yeah, yeah, bar, yeah. Abby needed a shower, not a sightseeing tour right now. She couldn't help but notice something else was lingering in the air of the vehicle. It was the smell of someone who had some serious pot in his or her pocket or possibly a skunk.

Ziggy slowed down after they went through a small roundabout, and without putting on his blinker he turned sharply to the left. Abby was thrown across the backseat and landed hard on the armrest.

Well, she thought, the good news is I'll be able to pass the driving test swiftly and with ease!

They stopped at a gate in a partially hidden driveway. The wrought-iron doors swung open as Ziggy tapped the remote he held in his hand. He turned around and handed it to Abby. "Dis one be yours." He smiled, showing her his sexy yellow teeth again.

They pulled up the winding driveway and made their way through the lush green foliage to the house. The South American guys who had originally built it had named the spread "La Cantina." They had lived there years prior, before selling it to Leigh's ex, Kenny. In not-so-typical island fashion, it was a Spanish masterpiece that was set back off the main road, surrounded by palm trees and other dense tropical plants. Being not so well versed in trees and bushes of the islands (or anywhere, really), Abby only knew they were green and gorgeous.

The South Americans were wise in the home design and landscaping. It had ultimate privacy, and there was plenty of land -- something that not many homes had here unless they were old plantations or sugar mills, as Ziggy was quick to point out. There were maids' quarters on-site, but not where they could be seen from the main house, in addition to the two-story guesthouse that had been built after the pool was added.

Abby was stunned when she saw it. The home was more of a manor than a little old cottage. There were balconies -- not just one, but two. The porch was massive, built with a Southern flair, stretching like fingers around to the back of the house, where it met with a stone patio. And the grounds were like those of a Beverly Hills home, perfectly manicured and neatly organized by color. Abby could tell that Leigh had had some influence on the landscaping as they pulled closer, recognizing some of the rose bushes from her hybrids.

Ziggy came to a sliding halt in the circular driveway and jumped out of his taxi. He grabbed the heaviest suitcase and took the steps two at a time to open the front door. Abby followed him in and stopped short in the foyer. She took one big, long sweeping look at her new place of residence, and almost passed out.

Nothing could have ever prepared her for this moment. Nothing. Her eyes were trying to take it all in and they just couldn't. She was so far from her little one-bedroom in her old run-down apartment building in Los Angeles. From the palette chosen to cover the walls to the art hanging on them to the beautifully enticing overstuffed couches, Abby felt as if she had just awoken in the middle of a beautiful dream. She had found herself in heaven, and it was her sister's hidden home.

To Abby's left was the formal dining room -- formal in every sense of the word. There was a gorgeous light wood dining table that was set for eight, but there were other chairs in the room to provide seating for twelve. That must mean there is an extra leaf somewhere, she found herself thinking. Why would Leigh have been entertaining this many people? And the South American influence was wonderfully married to the island feel. The colors were very relaxing, yet vibrant. The walls had a yellow tint that was highlighted with the artwork that had been chosen. Stunning.

Glancing to her right, toward the family room, Abby's eyes rested on a 72-inch flat-screen TV. Really? Leigh obviously had made arrangements to get that put in, as flat-screens were not around when she and Ken had divorced. There was an oversize coffee table made out of an old dock, and the fireplace beyond the sitting area was massive. It was flanked by book-shelves that were stuffed with tons of reading material. Anything from a good James Patterson read to the karma-focused "heal your life and find yourself" books that Leigh loved so much. Abby could feel her jaw sinking closer to the floor as she took in her surroundings. She had just hit the lottery.

Somewhere in the distance Abby heard a throat being cleared, and she was brought back to reality. Ah yes, the Caribbean answer for Dale Earnhardt was still in the room.

"I am so sorry!" Abby said, reaching in her bag for her tattered wallet. "I'm so tired and confused, and this is more than overwhelming for me." Ziggy watched her with amuse-ment. Or was that stoned confusion? "Here, how much do I owe you?"

Ziggy laughed. "No, mon. You don't. Leigh already took care of it. I live here, mon. But I got to leave now. So I got to go now to come back, okay?"

"What?"

Ziggy stared at Abby, hard. "I said dat I. Go now. To come. Back. You see? I go now. I come back. I got to go . . . to come back." He nodded his head and made hand gestures that said to Abby "follow along." It was put in a particularly patient way that was mildly amusing to her.

Then Abby smiled, realizing what it was he meant, and why it was on the back of his taxi.

"You go," she nodded, "so then you can come right back . . . . Okay. I totally get it. So, when are you coming back?"

He shrugged and pulled on a dread that was peeking out from under his cap. "I be here. Tomorrow I find you to see if you need to go anywhere. Maybe afternoon, but before six."

Abby looked at him and tilted her weary, fogged head.

"You can't give me a more 'set' time? Just afternoon, but before six?"

Ziggy looked at her and tilted his head, too. "Well, yes. Dat is when I find you. Afternoon, but before six." He shrugged, then laughed. "Oh yeah, you like Leigh. Welcome to St. Kitts' island time. It is what it is." Ziggy started laughing, and as he was doing so he reached into the breast pocket of his shirt and pulled out a rolled-up piece of paper. Or, a joint. His lips were curled back, sharing his yellowing teeth with Abby again as he lit his find. Nope, Abby was not in Kansas anymore. And she was beginning to understand why Leigh needed her to be here.

"Okay, Ziggy. Tell you what. I will be here tomorrow and I plan on seeing you when you get here. I need to sleep and get settled in, so maybe you should go outside . . . " She waved at him and his joint to go outside like she was trying to shoo a small child to the swing set for playtime. Maybe she could find some Febreze in the kitchen when he left.

He laughed again. "Okay, Abby, Leigh's sister. I go. You rest. Tomorrow we go to store or someting. Maybe go limin'."

Interesting, Abby thought. He wants to pick limes. "Okay, Ziggy. Sounds good to me." She reached for the door and held it open. "G'night."

"Yes. Oh, Abby, sister of Leigh . . . " He smiled and stood in the doorway, blocking it from being closed and blowing a steady stream of reefer into her nose. "Maybe tonight you watch for centipedes. Dey are not your friend." He turned to leave.

What the . . . ? "Wait, Ziggy! Centipedes? What are you talking about?"

Ziggy leaned back and drew another long pull off the joint. "Centipedes, mon. Little, lots o' legs, dey bite. Dey bite hard, and it hurts. Make sure you pull back da sheets, look all around. Tuck covers all around you after you look and try not to move. Dey like warm spots if it is cold, so be careful of de air conditioning." He smiled and blew out the smoke, all over her face.

Great, Abby thought. If a centipede attacked her now, she would have a contact buzz and be too high to do anything about it, except maybe dip it in chocolate.

"So, I just have to look for them in the sheets? What do I do if I do get bitten? Will I? Get bitten? Are there some here?" Great, she was freaking out now. She wanted to rip the joint from his hands and throw it into the bushes, or give him the kick in the butt she had so desperately wanted to give herself for so long.

"Yeah, mon. Just look. If you get bit, you cry. It's okay. And dey are everywhere. It's de island." He laughed and pulled the joint up to his lips for another long pull. As he blew it out he looked at Abby. "I get a soda, okay?"

He wants a soda, Abby thought, torn between being annoyed and amused. He's never leaving. He is either going to be a giant pain in my rear end or the best friend I never wanted. Doesn't he have a place right here on the property he can go hang out in?

"Fine, umm, kitchen?" She looked at Ziggy, shrugged, and then gestured with her right arm as if to say, "Lead the way." She didn't have to worry; he was already padding in his bare feet to the kitchen. Wait, she thought. Oh good lord! He has no shoes on?

Abby shook her head as she followed this funny little island man to the kitchen. As she walked in behind him, watching him root around in the fridge for a drink, she thought how funny would it be if this guy suddenly started talking to her like he was from the States, if he was not really an island native at all and Leigh had set this all up to mess with her after the long flight. She was smirking thinking about it, but as Ziggy began speaking, he snapped her back into the reality of the situation at hand and she realized that no, this was no joke. This was her new world.

"So, Abby . . . How is Leigh? She coming to see us soon, too?"

"Well, I don't think she planned on it. She sent me here to help get this place ready to be sold. You do know that she is selling it, right?"

Ziggy nodded his head emphatically up and down. "Oh yeah, mon, we got to start wit' da roof. She sent me a letter 'bout it." His whole face lit up as he looked at Abby seriously. "Email."

This man has a computer? Abby was blown away.

"Oh good! So you know what I'm here to do?"

"Yeah, mon! We like it here, Maria and me." Ziggy bobbed his head up and down to no one in particular. Abby knew that the Maria he mentioned was his wife; Leigh had said she was the other part of the property-managing duo she had hired to assist with the upkeep of the house. Maria was usually around during the day, sporadically, cleaning and making sure the house was kept nice. For what, Abby was not sure. Hell, Abby was not sure of a lot right now, but who was she to argue with a sheer stroke of good fortune?

She noticed that Ziggy had cocked his head toward the big glass doors off the living room. Across the pool and patio Abby saw a two-story building with a light on outside the door. That must be the pool house Ben lives in, she thought. Nice. I want to see it, too. If this place is so kick-ass, I can only imagine the pool house must rock. And it's two floors!

"You will meet him tomorrow or next day." Ziggy nodded

and smiled. What? Another mind reader? He was sitting on a bar stool that was by the island in the middle of the kitchen. Man, he looks more than comfortable there, Abby thought. He's probably used this place a lot over the years; he seems to know it really well. Weird. He's like the guy who comes over to help you do handyman work and never leaves, she thought. Like that TV show . . .

Abby took in the layout of the kitchen as she was pouring herself some soda as well. Immaculate and new, it was fit for a gourmet chef. It was stocked with Viking appliances, a huge island in the middle, butcher-block style. Julia Child would be jealous. Waffle maker? Blender? What is Leigh doing with a place this amazing on an island?

As she was looking around, taking in the room, she heard the soft splash of water as it was broken by human -- or maybe animal? -- contact. Was someone or something in the pool? She scooted over to the window and peered outside and saw someone gliding through the water, slowly and effortlessly. Obviously doing laps, back and forth, back and forth, the length of the pool. Abby could see the silhouette of the person's arms rising up methodically to the swimmer's body, then cutting through the water, and the turning of his head as he went from left to right to get air as he executed a flawless freestyle stroke.

"Dat be Ben," Ziggy said matter-of-factly as he put his empty glass down in the sink where Abby was standing. She had been so mesmerized by the motion of the swimmer that she hadn't even heard Ziggy get up and walk over to her. He was standing next to her watching Ben do his laps as well.

"I guessed that would be Ben," Abby said as well, to no one in particular. Well, it was too late to go meeting him tonight. Tomorrow she and Ben could meet, and then go from

16

there. Maybe she could have him over for dinner one night to find out more about this place and the island. And to break the news of eviction a little bit nicer.

"Okay, Ziggy," Abby yawned. "I'm usually not the party pooper, but I must sleep or I'm going to be no good to anyone tomorrow. I'll see you later, okay?"

Ziggy nodded and smiled at Abby. "Oh yeah, I be back. You sleep good, and I see you tomorrow. Good night, Abby, sister of Leigh." He giggled and went down the hall without a look back and teetered out the front door. Well, that was easy, Abby thought.

She went around the kitchen and turned off all the lights and made sure all the doors were locked. Front door, glass doors, and windows . . . Ahhh, her OCD. She grabbed one of her bags and trudged upstairs with it to the bedrooms -- the glorious, lovely bedrooms that were just waiting for her. She spied at least five upon her initial glance, causing her alarm bells to ring a little more, but not enough. Abby was so tired and excited from arriving on the island that she figured a good night's sleep was the first order of business. Tomorrow she could figure out why Leigh's house on a Caribbean island was more like a mansion.

As she was peering in the first couple of rooms, she was amazed at their size -- these two particular rooms had king beds in them and sitting areas to boot. One room had its own bathroom while the other appeared to have a shared bath or maybe it was attached to another suite or sitting area? Again, too tired too comprehend, Abby settled on the larger of the two bedrooms, the one with the bathroom in it, assuming it was the master suite. And hopefully these rooms were truly centipede-free -- NO! Why did she have to think about that now? She knew she would spend the rest of the evening jumping at the mere thought of a flipping bug crawling on her.

Abby hopped in the shower and then threw on her crisp, clean pajamas. She did her bed check for the centipedes, pulling off all the covers and looking under everything, even the pillowcases. Even though it was humid and she was sweating just making the effort, Abby refused to turn on the air since Ziggy had said the centipedes were attracted to warmth in cold places. Man, she thought as she put on socks, I am going to lose ten pounds as I sleep tonight just sweating from the clothes alone. She sighed heavily and lay down on top of the pillows and reached over to turn out the light. Then she jolted up to tuck her pajama bottoms into her socks so the centipedes didn't get in there.

Ben must have been doing his laps still because the last thing she remembered before she fell off into dreamland was the rhythmic sound of the water lapping from the motion his arms made as they glided smoothly through the water.

CHAPTER 2

ABBY OPENED HER EYES TO THE WELCOME SOUNDS OF THE ceiling fan above her as the morning light and humidity were finding their way into the bedroom. The monotonous hum of the engine mixed with the whirring of the blades as they circled round and round was a white noise so soothing that she was usually lulled into a state of instant relaxation when she heard it. However, there was an unnerving feeling that had found its way into the pit of her stomach.

In the stillness of the room, Abby thought she could hear someone breathing. That is, someone other than herself. As she lay there quietly, listening to what she thought was empty space, she heard the rustle of fabric, texture upon texture sliding over each other, like legs crossing and uncrossing. There was also a tapping sound -- maybe someone's foot or a knock on some faraway door? Abby licked her lips and quietly let out a slow breath between them as she began to gather herself, opening one eye to sneak a peek around the room.

As she squinted her eyes and began to raise her head out from under the sheet that covered her, she was greeted with a smile. A big toothy smile that belonged to a strange woman who was in the rocking chair opposite the bed. Who is this and why is she in my room? Abby's thoughts were racing as she jumped from the bed and landed on the side opposite this rather robust Kittian lady, placing the bed squarely between them.

"Abby George! Leigh said you'd make it one day," she said with a smile. Her teeth were bright white in comparison to Ziggy's.

Who is this woman? And where is her accent from? It's different from Ziggy's Kittian slang . . . Wait, that's it, Abby thought. Ziggy. Leigh said Ziggy has a wife. This must be Maria!

"Maria? Are you Maria?" Abby asked tentatively as she fumbled around for a light shirt to throw on over her pale pink tank top. Being caught asleep and braless made her feel unarmed, like a soldier sent to battle with a water gun.

A loud raucous laugh came from Maria's gut. The laugh of a very pleased woman, one who was not as uncomfortable with the present situation as Abby was. She nodded, rocked and stared at Abby.

Wow. This is really awkward, Abby thought as she smiled tightly at her, maybe a little too tightly. Maria just sat and kept on rocking and smiling and staring.

Okay, this is beginning to feel like a claustrophobic Caribbean standoff, Abby thought. She began fidgeting with her fingers out of nervous habit and trying to smile, yet her shoulders were hunching up closer and closer to her ears with each moment that passed. Abby was the one who finally broke.

"So, you're in my room. I guess this is an official good morning? The St. Kitts' wake-up call?"

Maria grinned and smoothed out the fabric of her pants as

she continued to rock. "It's a wake-up call, yes." Maria gazed at Abby. "I'm here to get you up and out of the house . . . before the company arrives."

She's drunk, Abby thought. It's what, 7 or 8 a.m. and this woman is already drunk? Kicking me out of my sister's home?

Abby smiled to herself, looked directly at Maria and said slowly, "I'm not trying to be a jerk or rude, but you wake me up after a long day of travel to ask me to leave my sister's home?" Abby waved her hand around the room. "That I'm here to take care of?"

Abby looked Maria in the eye, almost laughing at the thought that this was an issue. Yet Maria was not reacting. In fact, she was just rocking and nodding.

"No time for limin'. Leigh asked me to be kind in telling you since you traveled so far an' being her sister an' all. Just no way to wake someone up to say get out, really." The big pearly white smile was back. This woman needed to share her Crest Whitestrips with Ziggy.

What is the obsession with picking limes here? Abby thought. Are limes a main source of island income, and do I need to help pick them?

Abby crossed her arms. She could tell that her quizzical stare made Maria melt a little, wanting to explain further. Yet Abby felt like Maria was stopping herself.

"Abby, come. Let me make you some coffee. It seems to me that Miss Leigh may have left something out when she sent you here . . . "

Oh no. Oh no! Abby's voices were screaming in her head. Of course there is more to the story. She never, ever, ever can tell just the truth or tell something like it really is. Oh, no. She has to cover up something or . . . instead of lie, "I omitted the truth, Abby," she says. Humpf. Omits the truth. I always think

I know her. All I really know is that I never will know her like I think I do.

Abby was rubbing her forearms and realized her demeanor had shifted from "I'm the Queen of the Manor" to "I think I'm lost." Maria took note of this, too, as she lifted herself from the rocker.

"Abby, come. Coffee and food. It does wonders for the body and the mind, not to mention the surprise of all this. And then I can explain to you the things you need to be hearing. It's gonna be a bit to take in, oh yes. But Leigh wants you to know it for some reason. Otherwise, it would not be you doing this, right?" And with that, Maria began to walk out of the room, stopping at the door to turn around and wait for Abby.

Okay, strange Kittian woman with the bright smile, Abby thought as she slid into her flip-flops and shuffled out of the room behind Maria. You have a point. I need coffee. Let's do this.

☙

"LA CANTINA IS LEIGH'S BED-AND-BREAKFAST AND I HAVE TO move in with BEN?!?!" Abby shouted, slapping her hand over her mouth almost instantly when she heard her own voice hit an octave that had never been captured before.

"Abby, it's gonna be uncomfortable and a wee bit crowded . . . "

"'Wee bit crowded'? Are you kidding me?"

"But you can do it. He has an alcove that was meant as a place for a desk. Ziggy is bringin' an air mattress today for you. After he tells Ben that you're movin' in." Maria placed Abby's coffee mug in front of her. "Here. I just put milk. Like Leigh likes it, too."

Abby gripped her coffee mug tightly. So tight she was worried she might just shatter it. Maria continued to bustle around the kitchen, chopping vegetables and cooking as if getting ready for Thanksgiving. Well. At least I don't have to break the news to Ben, Abby thought.

Abby had to fight her sudden urge to video-chat Leigh so she could see her face as Abby slapped the computer screen.

"Maria, I'm going to repeat back to you everything you just told me to make sure I have this under control in my brain. Okay?"

Maria nodded, mumbling, "Okay, Abby," and kept busy prepping food in the kitchen for the mystery meal.

Abby took a deep breath, like the yoga kind her therapist always suggested to her, especially when she was trying to quit smoking. Or dealing with her mother or Leigh.

"La Cantina is a bed-and-breakfast. An inn. My sister owns an inn. A B&B. And it is La Cantina. Right?" Abby asked.

Maria turned and looked at Abby. "Yes." Then she returned to her work.

"Okay. And tonight, there are guests arriving so I am not to be in the house because the space is needed, therefore this truly is a classic case of 'no room at the inn'?" Abby stopped long enough to take a breath before continuing. "Again, La Cantina being the BED AND BREAKFAST MY SISTER OWNS?"

Maria turned and glowered at Abby. "No need to be shouting. I am right here."

Abby nodded and took another drink of coffee. "I'm sorry I'm shouting, but all of this," Abby began waving her hands around and motioning loudly, as if her hands could talk and they were the ones shouting, "is a bit of news to me. A big piece of info that my sister, the person I should know best in the world, has left out. That's what she does. She leaves things out." Abby was exasperated. "I even asked her . . . Okay. That she has a house is one thing . . . but a freaking inn on a Caribbean island? And I can't even stay in it? I get to room with a complete stranger for a few weeks while I help her fix her inn?"

Abby pounded her heart with the palm of her right hand and began breathing dramatically. "Forgive me if I am yelling or in any way offending you, Maria, but things as I know them keep shifting. Dramatically." Abby suddenly shuddered.

Abby was sweating profusely and her stomach was sick. "This. This is what a heart attack feels like. I think I'm having a heart attack . . . "

Abby got up and was really stroking at her heart now and couldn't catch her breath. Oh no, she thought. I'm going to die in this house of Leigh's right before her guests arrive to stay. Well, well. That's one way to totally get her back.

"Gas. It's gas. I bet you need to go number two."

Abby turned and looked at Maria. Is this woman joking? From Maria's deadpan, know-it-all expression, Abby could tell she was not.

"You traveled and are probably dehydrated. I am sure you just need to release a little stress. Maybe a massage for your bowels later? Now sit back down . . . "

Abby was stunned. "No one will be massaging my bowels today. And stress? Maria, really? Everything I keep discovering and now there's a you and a Ziggy and a house and a roommate and guests and you think I only have gas? I'm thinking an ulcer or an aneurysm."

Maria nodded, her face emotionless. "Ziggy gets it too. No worry. I make you a root tea later; everything will be," she winked at Abby, "regular again. Smooooth. You'll see."

Maria started to laugh raucously, and it echoed all through

the kitchen and dining room. It rolled over porches and into the yard. The neighbors probably heard her, if the wind was just right. Abby knew she would not escape the sound of this woman's glee. In fact, Abby knew she would not escape any of this. It was her new reality. Yet as Maria laughed, Abby started to smile as if she was infected by the sound. Slowly her own laughter joined Maria's. Here she was in paradise, Abby George, and she was about to stay with someone she had never met, much less had even been introduced to. It was all quite surreal.

Abby was still chuckling as she sat back down at the kitchen table.

"Okay, Maria. I'll play. I really have no choice, do I? I've never been here, and I don't know you or Ziggy." Abby looked at Maria, who was smiling at her again.

"So, Ziggy is telling Ben that he has a new roommate?"

"Yes, ma'am. He already told him Leigh is going to be selling the place." Maria watched Abby for her reaction. Realizing Abby was calm and listening now, she went on. "Ben's studying to be a vet and needs to get done this semester so he can go back."

"To the States, right? Leigh mentioned the vet school and finishing up back on the mainland." Abby asked as she dived into a plate of muffins Maria had placed in front of her. Mmmm, blueberry . . . Better than the Starbucks or coffee truck variety to which she was accustomed.

Maria nodded. "Maybe he gets done and the house will sell at the same time." She was prepping ribs with a sweet-smelling marinade. Abby's nose was tingling with all the new Caribbean spice smells assailing her senses.

She chewed her muffin thoughtfully, almost with a deliberate slowness because she was tired of speaking. "Maria, is

Ben going to be okay with me staying with him? I would not want a 'me' living in my house if I were a Ben."

Maria's laugh resonated through the room again. "Abby! Trust me. Tonight you two will have dinner and get to know each other. Ziggy is going to drop you off at Ricky's down the street. It's close and it's quiet. Rum punch and dinner make people happy. You and Ben are gonna be just fine."

"Oh I get it, you want me to just get really drunk every night so I don't care where I sleep, right?"

"No, girl. No. Your family raised you better than that. Now, you just help me get this place ready today. We keep you busy so you're not idle, okay?"

Abby ignored the family comment, especially since the way she felt about Leigh at the present moment was not familial at all.

"I'll be glad to help. Just please make sure to shield me when Ben comes in and unleashes the anger of the gods this way . . . Okay? Have him know it's not my fault?"

"Girl! Go get changed!" Maria was laughing and shooing her out.

"Just one thing . . . Ziggy's accent is Kittian. But yours, it's different. Where are you from, Maria?"

Maria and Abby locked eyes, and there was trust. Not that Abby could pinpoint the moment and say it then, but she felt good with Maria. "My mom was from London, and my dad was Kittian. I grew up in the U.S."

Maria began to speak, but once again stopped herself. "Just clear out of your room quick and I get Ziggy to put your bags out in the pool house. Guests come and so do Ben soon. We deal with each one as it happens." Maria started chopping some green onions very efficiently and with purpose. "First, we need to change sheets, open windows, fresh flowers in rooms. You need to be calling the roof repairmen so dey come dis week and get started. Lots to do!"

Abby could tell she would get nothing else out of Maria until later, and she honestly wanted some busy work to help her sort through all of the mixed feelings she had at the moment. Maybe jumping right in with repairs and doing some cleaning will help me unleash some of this irritation inside, Abby thought. I can scrub some tile and pretend it's Leigh's face. She watched Maria as she began chopping some celery and onion together. The way she moved was fluid and poetic. She was about to leave the room when Maria called after her:

"And, Abby. There is a lot to know here about a lot that you may not know. You can't be having expectations, girl. None. Day-by-day. Just remember, you are always taken care of."

Abby started to open her mouth to ask what it was Maria still needed to tell her, but Maria was chopping furiously. As if she had eyes in the back of her head, she waved her right hand over her shoulder toward Abby as if to say, "Get out."

Abby smiled at Maria's back. She slowly nodded and turned on her heel, unable to shake the feeling of familiarity she had with Maria. This woman was funny and honest: She had gone from being a jolting surprise to a blessing in a just a couple of hours.

All this and it wasn't even noon yet.

Welcome to the island . . .

CHAPTER 3

THE THICK CARIBBEAN HUMIDITY WAS BEGINNING TO TAKE ITS toll on Abby. Sitting at a table on the patio at Ricky's, she waited patiently for a very late Ben to join her for their get-to-know-your-roomie dinner. Already on her second rum punch, she was jiggling the ice cubes in the cup as she waited to order number three. Abby was nervous, but ready to meet Ben. All she could do was hope he was the understanding type.

ABBY HAD BEGUN THE DAY BY PLACING A CALL TO HER SISTER, which had promptly been sent to voicemail. She followed up by sending her the obligatory "What were you thinking?" email while wishing there were some way she could send a good ass-kicking instead of flowers to her doorstep. Obviously a conversation with Leigh was out of the question at this point -- at least until she decided to return Abby's messages.

Maria then had gotten Abby settled in the small office off the main kitchen, where Abby would be making her calls to schedule the repairmen. Being used to the "go-get-'em" attitude of the States, Abby was expecting to place a call and have the repairmen over for an estimate within a few hours. As she opened the Yellow Pages for the island, she found that there were only three roofing companies to pick from. The first two didn't have voicemail, much less answer the phone. The third try was her lucky charm, as someone named Buddy answered and agreed to come by. In three days.

"Three days? Buddy, is there anything I can do to get you to come sooner?"

Buddy's end was silent as he thought. Then, "No."

Okay. "I'll pay more. We can pay a little bit extra on top of the fee to get you here?"

Silence again. "Mmmmm. No. Sorry, Miss George. I got tings to do. Leavin' today for fishin'. But I see you in tree days."

So he was going fishing. Abby felt her frustration welling up inside of her, but decided that if it had to be "tree" days, then it would be. She agreed to his terms and opted to let it go for the time being.

She spent the rest of her day hustling around, jumping at the mere sound of Maria's voice and her delivery of orders to prep La Cantina. She helped polish, shine, dust, sweep, launder and replace linens. Maria allowed her one last lovely, luxurious long shower in the main home before having Ziggy grab her bags and help her get set up in the pool house, air mattress and all.

"An air mattress? Ziggy . . . I mean, really? I go from 'I'm living in this gorgeous home' to 'Here's your air mattress and a hole under the stairs'?"

Ziggy chuckled. "Miss Abby, you will not be sleeping

under the stairs. You have a roof over your head! What more do you need?"

Ziggy was already walking away from Abby, headed to the pool house with the air mattress tucked under one arm and one of her suitcases dangling at the end of the other.

The pool house was not as large as Abby had originally imagined. Granted, from the outside the size was deceiving; it looked small because the width was not grand. Yet the length was amazing -- it stretched back into the tropical foliage, almost disappearing as if into a miniature rainforest. From her first glance, she guessed the living room to be the size of the bedroom she had just slept in the night before.

Ziggy had begun rooting around in an alcove off to the side of the living room. It was a small area. It looked about 5 x 10, had curtains and was the size for . . . Wait, Abby thought, is he taking the air mattress out of the box and putting it there? Am I not getting a door at least?

"Ziggy, is that my place? Or are you adding some more seating?"

"No, man. I'm making your bed nice and firm now, Abby. Blow it up with the hair dryer and cap it for you." His head nodded and the dreadlocks bounced as he began to inflate her new bed.

Unreal! Leigh, you did it again. I always think things will be different with you, Leigh, Abby thought. They never are. I don't even have the pleasure of being able to shut a door to close out all of the complete strangers I keep meeting.

Abby found a corner behind the dining room table where she could hide her bags for the time being. May as well wait to see where Ben wanted her to store her things. She then made her way through the pool house, looking at pictures -- Ben had only a few present in sporadic locations. It was most certainly the home of a college student. There were some schematics of animals up on the walls as well, skeletal systems or diagrams of some sort, and shelves that were laden with books on anatomy, physiology and animal science. There was a pile of dishes in the sink and the coffeemaker looked as if it had seen better days about twenty years ago.

Abby moved slowly through the house, taking in the quarters she would be sharing for the next few weeks. The downstairs appeared neat, but when she looked upstairs, she was granted a glimpse into Ben's bedroom, which appeared to have suffered from a small explosion. She started climbing the steps and then opted not to go. It was, after all, someone else's living quarters. It was awkward enough without her rooting around any more of his space.

As she surveyed the surroundings, she noticed a litter box a few feet from the air mattress. Please don't let that thing stink in this heat, she cringed silently.

The sound of Ziggy's voice snapped her back to the present.

"Mon, all set. I'm taking you to Ricky's now," Ziggy said, looking ready to go.

Abby furrowed her brow. "I thought Ben was meeting me here first?"

"Happy hour, Abby. I need to meet some people at Ricky's for some tings." He was grinning widely. It was the smile that said, "I'm about to sell some of my weed that perfumes the air around me."

"Okay. As long as he knows I'll be there?"

"Yeah, mon. Handled."

With that, Ziggy sailed out the door, heading to his cab. Abby took a look around at her new digs one more time. She had a bad feeling in the pit of her stomach. *I hope Ben and I get along* was the only thought she could muster.

●●

ABBY TOOK HER CUP AND WIPED IT ACROSS THE TOP OF HER forehead, letting the condensation from the drink trickle its way down over her flushed face. It was harder to catch her breath here today, and sitting outside was turning out to be a dumb idea. But she wanted to "break bread" with Ben since they would be living together for the next who-knows-how-many weeks.

Ricky's Café and Bar was a comical little spot down the road from La Cantina. At the end of a pothole-infested drive, it was tucked in the underbelly of a hotel that was slowly rotting away due to lack of love from the owners and a hurricane that had hit seven years ago. Abby got the feeling that Ricky's was a home away from home, much like Cheers, to many of the folks gathered around its plastic patio tables and picnic benches. There was a dive shop, and the whole crew was at one end of the patio enjoying the sunset, knocking back the local beer, Carib, and hanging with tourists from a cruise ship. The bar had only four seats pulled up to the window, with two customers sitting with their heads together, sharing beers and cigarettes. One of the gentlemen was quite dark and weathered with bleach-blonde hair and seemed kind of dirty in that needing-to-be-washed way, while the other man was tall and rugged with dark hair and a great smile, emitting a "mysterious stranger" quality. The two were speaking in hushed conspiratorial voices, the blonde one gesturing wildly ever other word or so.

Behind the bar, the bartender was fanning herself with a

People magazine that was so tattered Abby thought it must be from at least three years ago. Abby knew she needed another drink to keep herself cool, so she slowly crept up to the bartender.

Abby was walking up behind her and was about to introduce herself when the robust woman made a grunting sound, like "Ahem, yeaaaaahhhh," and then turned to face Abby.

Abby stopped dead in her tracks, thinking that the woman was ready to yell at her. She braced for the biting words to come.

"Another rum punch, girl?"

Abby smiled and showed her the elegant plastic cup she held in her hand.

"Please."

The bartender eyed Abby like the drunk she was proving to be.

"Be careful with dose. Dey can bite you in de ass."

Abby smiled politely but held fast. "I just want to be numb. Please, another drink."

"What you needin' to numb, girl? No need." She slid off the stool and went behind the bar to mix Abby another concoction. "For every bar on this island, there are two churches. Not many people know dat. It's like we forgive the drinkin' everyone does and we ask them to go to church. My boy," she clutched a locket around her neck, "he loved the drink. He loved the church, too. Fitting he ran into a church when he was drunk and died instantly."

Abby was stunned. Her mouth dropped and she stared at the woman stirring the elixir.

"I don't know what to say. I'm really sorry that . . . "

The older woman laughed. No, she guffawed at Abby. "I'm

sorry, girl. Don't know why I decided to lie to you like that. I got a son, but he alive."

Wow, you really can't make this up, Abby thought as she stared at the woman as if she had three heads.

"Well, good then," said Abby a little sarcastically. "Glad to hear it. I'm going to take my cocktail and go back to staring out over the water and drinking myself into the sand." With that, Abby pinched a smile at the two other customers, raised her now-refilled cup to the woman and went to her table.

"Girl!"

Oh what now?

"Yes?"

The woman was still laughing as she came from around the bar and went up to Abby.

"They call me Miss B. B is for Benson. That was my husband's name."

"Hello, nice to meet you. I'm Abby. Abby George. My sister owns La Cantina."

"Leigh?" Miss B. exclaimed. "You Leigh's sister, all grown up, eh? Well!"

"Yes, Miss B. I am . . . "

"Girl, things just changed for me and you. Now we gonna get along! My name is really Charlie, for Miss Charles, not Miss B. I mess with people. Usually ones I don't know." She smiled at Abby and patted her head. "You? I kind of know. You're Leigh's sister."

Abby stared intently at the woman, Miss C. or B. or whoever she decided she was at the given moment. Abby wanted to ask her how well she knew Leigh, but as she opened her mouth she saw Miss Charles' eyes light up; apparently there was something more interesting beyond Abby's shoulder.

"Ben Stenson! Oh, baby boy Ben! How are you doing tonight?" she practically sang to the sunset.

Abby slowly sucked in a deep breath through her nose. Ben had arrived, bless his heart. She was fumbling with the rings on her fingers in her signature nervous fashion, glancing over at Ziggy working his pot-selling magic across the patio with some locals. He waved to her as he jumped a small wall next to the beach and walked off with the rugged dark-haired guy from the bar in tow, most likely to smoke some of his goods before the money was exchanged. What an entrepreneur, she thought.

Abby could hear Ben and Miss Charles talking behind her. She was clucking like an old hen, and he was laughing with her and the dirty man that had been left behind by his friend at the bar. Cutthroat? Did he really just refer to the man sitting there as Captain Cutthroat? What is he . . . a pirate? Abby fought the urge to shake her head and laugh out loud, opting instead to turn around and meet her new roommate.

Abby stood and watched the scene in front of her for a beat before interjecting. Ben was holding a Carib and toasting with this Captain Cutthroat person and Miss Charles was giggling and patting him on his head. It was Miss Charles who motioned for Abby to come over and join the group.

"Abby, you must come 'ere girl and meet my Ben. An' this be the Capt'n of our dive crew, Cap'n Joe Cutthroat, or Cutty."

Abby felt out of place and a little lost as she put her hand out and approached Ben. Standing among the group of castaways, laughing at an inside joke, was a blonde, tanned young man, in his mid-20s, standing six feet tall. He had the build of a construction worker, yet also managed to emit a boyish charm that was almost infectious.

"Ben? I'm Abby. Your dinner companion . . . " She stopped

suddenly, not because it was her choice, but because Captain Cutty decided it was time for him to be introduced.

"Abby, you're cute." The smile he gave her was yellowed and missing a tooth or two, which seemed the way of this island, but the grin was wide and sincere. Captain Cutty had a leathery, weathered look to his too-tanned face, but there was something in those eyes that made Abby like him instantly.

"Thank you. Nice to meet you, Cutty."

"Not Captain? I deserve to be called Captain, you know." The smile was still there as he lit another Camel Filter and took a swig of his beer.

"Nah. I like Cutty. Captain is too complicated. Makes me feel like you may be relied on to be in charge of something." Abby smiled and took a swig of her drink as well, then leaned over and took one of his cigarettes out of the pack. She was surprising herself with her boldness, but she felt the energy around her to keep up with these guys so she wasn't verbally tossed to the side.

"Touché." Cutty grinned and pointed a gnarled finger at Ben.

"Is there a reason you're called Cutthroat?" Behind her smile, Abby hid her surprise that such a menacing name was attached to such a non-threatening man.

"Well, I can be a real jerk if you -- " He never finished.

"Ain't no reason, girl," Miss C. interrupted. "He just decided when he came 'ere he should be Cap'n Joe Cut-troat."

Cutty scowled at the older woman, who was grinning from ear to ear, before turning his attention back to Abby. "You know this guy?"

It was Ben's turn to speak. "No, Cutty," he said in a tight British accent. "We are just meeting now for the first time. It seems we are about to become really good friends out of circumstances we cannot control. At the most inconvenient time possible."

Ouch. Abby felt the arrow of irritation land directly at her feet. Ben was not happy about this at all and would more than likely be taking it out on her. This was going to be nearly impossible, and she couldn't blame him.

"Ben, I'm sorry. I had no idea this would be the situation when I agreed to come down here on my sister's behalf. Leigh needed to -- "

"Leigh!" Captain Cutty was back and obviously acquainted with her sister as well. "You tell her the next time we bet on horses, it won't be for money. Your sister took $50 from me her last visit. Those were my tips from tourists, and I was going to use it to get my tooth fixed." This last statement, Abby highly doubted. More than likely he would have bought some more cigarettes and booze. Abby decided she may have just met her first Caribbean crackhead.

"I'll be glad to pass that along for you." Abby moved her focus back to Ben. This knowledge that Leigh and Cutty knew each other would have to wait for later as well.

"Abby," Ben raised a hand and interjected, "look, this is all a surprise. I knew it could happen, the inn being put up for sale; I just thought since I was so close to being done at school I was home free. I know your sister has to do what she has to do, but having someone I don't know live with me just sucks. You get that, right?"

"I completely agree with you. I was shoved into the alcove in your living room today." Abby looked at him with her best puppy-dog eyes to instill her own honest intentions. "I have no idea how to handle this or what to do. I just hope we can figure something out and make it so it works for everyone involved."

Ben was eyeing her, looking into her eyes as if trying to

read her mind. He seemed nice enough, but what if he turned out to be the roommate from hell?

"I know this isn't your fault, Abby," Ben said thoughtfully. "Look, I'm just under a lot of pressure for the next six weeks."

"You only payin' half price, mon. So no complainin'." Ziggy had suddenly shown back up and was plopping himself down next to Cutty at the bar, handing him a joint as he lit one for himself. Abby noticed he was minus one hot, mysterious, rugged stranger.

"Thanks, Ziggy," Ben sighed and stared at the beer in his hand. "Leigh has always treated me like I was one of her own, taking me to dinner when she was here visiting, or sending me supplies as I needed them from the States. I want to help, and I will. But I'd be a liar if I did it with a smile on my face and said it was going to be okay."

Abby nodded and threw back her third drink, getting her fourth from the cup Miss Charles was already refreshing for her. *Man, this rum punch is great!* Abby had made friends in the stickiest of situations. This one was tough since she had no true upper hand here, and she needed time to decide her course of action.

Ben had grabbed a menu off the bar and pointed to an item, asking Miss Charles if he could have "that." Abby, feeling light-headed and a little buzzed, thought she saw Ben play with his fingers nervously like she did in tense situations. Deciding she was seeing things, she recognized she needed to get something in her stomach and fast, or Ben would witness "Puking Abby" in a few hours.

She guessed Ben was a gentle enough guy, but not one to piss off. Everyone seemed to like him, too. They were like a dysfunctional family in the middle of the Caribbean. *If that's the case, I should begin to feel more at home any day now,*

Abby thought. Of course, Ben being pissed won't help my case, but I can win him over. I know I can. Plus, he reminds me of Leigh's boys . . . same age, same mentality. And I get along with them.

Miss Charles looked at Abby and nodded toward the menu.

"Girl, you want anyting before I throw de order in? Or do you plan to drink your dinner?" She grinned big and crazy at Abby, wiggling her eyebrows and laughing.

Seriously? Abby thought drunkenly, these people are either really happy about life or just plain nuts.

"What's the best thing on the menu? Do you have a nice salad?"

Cutty snorted with a laugh so hard that beer flew out of his nose, causing a ripple of laughter among the ragtag crew.

"No, girl. You Americans and your 'salad' . . . Conch fritters. You like dem. I get dose for you." With that, Miss Charles flounced up the steps to the kitchen that was housed in the main hotel perched on the cliff just above them, overlooking the same view of the Caribbean across to the neighboring island of Nevis.

Abby sat down at the bar on the other side of Cutty. The order at the bar now was Ben, Cutty, Abby, and Ziggy. Meeting of the minds, Abby thought sarcastically in her drunken state, as she leaned back to let Ziggy and Cutty pass their joint back and forth.

"You want any?" Ziggy asked.

"Ah . . . Nah. I don't really do that anymore. But thank you for the offer." Abby had no clue what they put in their weed and was not about to even begin examining it. Not when she was already feeling floaty and light from her rum punch consumption.

"Ben, may I talk to you alone?" Abby felt if she could get

Ben one-on-one for a bit maybe she could begin the slow charm of winning him over so they could make things right.

Ben nodded and pointed to a picnic table that sat on a deck overlooking the water. He grabbed his Carib and began to lope over the sand, not really looking back to see if Abby was joining him. She felt her legs moving a little faster beneath her in an effort to keep up.

"So," Abby began as she was fumbling to get her legs under the picnic table without falling over in the dark, "you sound like you're, ummm . . . British?"

Even though it was dark, Abby felt the blank, irritated look on the other side of the table.

"My mum is from London. So, yes. That makes me British."

"Ah." Abby smiled and tried to emit warmth to relax Ben's rigid body.

"Abby, I get it, okay? Maria told me Leigh is selling the place and she needs your help, but having you stay with me when I need to work my hardest is just crazy. The last thing I need is distraction. I'm used to living alone."

"Ben, don't you feel like you might just be acting a touch . . . overdramatic?" Abby asked as gently as she could.

"Overdramatic? There's a woman I don't know sleeping in my living room and I'm being called overdramatic?"

"Again, Ben, the over-the-top upset you seem to be feeling is really a little bit, too . . . I don't know. Maybe diva-ish? The way I see it, me and you? We have got to find a way to get along really quickly. Please. No drama, no irritation. And . . . "

Abby stopped short here to hold her hand in the air and close her eyes for a minute. Oh, this is not good. The spins. No, no, no . . . She let out a small drunken hiccup and then nodded and kept on going.

"Where was I? Oh. No drama. I don't want to be the source of any kind of anxiety. Look. You need to finish school, and I need to help with this stinking house and then go back home. Get a job and rediscover my love of air conditioning. Feel me?"

Abby couldn't see his face clearly, but there seemed to be a smile beginning to play on Ben's lips as he listened to her drunken ramble. Abby's gift for accidentally entertaining people was one that came in handy for her in moments like these; she could only hope that his apparent amusement meant she was starting to win him over.

"So, Ben. I propose that you and I have what they call in the South a 'come-to-Jesus meeting,' where we sit together and lay out our needs and expectations for the other person, so we can make sure that we get what we need from this situation. Cool?"

Ben watched Abby take a swig from her drink and sway just a little on the picnic bench.

"Abby, you don't drink a lot, do you?"

Abby slammed her cup to the table and giggled at the loud bang it made. "I thought that was going to be quieter. No, I don't drink a lot at all. Why?"

It was at this moment Abby felt her world getting woozy, and she realized the spinning was not slowing down. Oh, no . . . stop the ride. Stop it. It was like being on that plane, except this time . . .

Abby had about five seconds to get off the picnic table and get to the railing so she could set her drinks free into the Caribbean, so to speak. As she struggled to get up from the bench, her legs got twisted under her and she fell backward, landing with a thud so loud that Miss C., Cutty, and Ziggy all jumped up to race over and help her. Abby grabbed her lips to hold them together with one hand, pinching them tightly in an effort to keep any vomit back, and used the other to hold herself steady as she worked her way back up to the table with Ben helping to hoist her up.

As soon as she regained solid footing she paused, feeling that the pukey moment had passed. And she was so wrong. As she relaxed and pulled her hand off her mouth, her stomach made another flip-flop and everything inside it began to make its way out. She turned her head in just enough time to offer up her consumed beverages to the sea. Abby was not a quiet puker. As she threw up and moaned at the same time, her new island family all stood at the picnic table trying not to laugh at her misfortune.

When she was done, Miss C. made her way over and led Abby by the arm away from the deck. She guided Abby to the bar so she could give her a bottle of water and some wet rags to wash her face with. Abby nodded a quiet "thank you," and plopped down sheepishly on a barstool.

As if on cue, a food-runner came racing down the stairs from the kitchen to bring Ben his dinner and Abby her conch fritters. Miss C. intercepted them before the runner could put them on the bar in front of Abby, in the fear that she could have another episode. Instead, she found some crackers behind the bar and hurried around to place them in Abby's sweaty hands so she could bring her tummy back under control.

As Abby sat chewing the saltines and sipping her water, Ben grabbed his medium-rare cheeseburger and sat down on the barstool beside her. Abby glared at him over her water bottle.

"I just threw up, you know." She sounded harsh and didn't care.

"I'd have to be deaf to have not heard you." Ben took a big

bite of the juicy burger. It was dripping with blue cheese and had hunks of bacon on it as well. Abby thought she was going to be ill again. She found herself chewing her crackers harder.

"Well, this is all going just as painfully as I had hoped," Abby said as sarcastically as she could muster.

Abby slid her frosty water bottle across her face in a sad effort to bring her body temperature down to a more normal degree. She could feel Ben's eyes on her, taking in her every move.

"Abby, this is going to be tough for both of us. I've been living alone for a long time, so for me to suddenly have a stranger in my home is just weird." He wiped his mouth with his napkin, took another swig from his bottle and nodded to Miss C. that he was ready for another. "But I can't afford to say no on many levels."

"Trust me, I understand. I can't afford to go somewhere else. And it's not like I can stay with Maria and Ziggy, since they have the maids' quarters and it's not like it's the biggest of spaces either." Abby chewed her crackers thoughtfully.

Miss C. had shuffled over and was presenting another bottle of beer to Ben and a fresh bottle of water to Abby. She smiled at the two and patted them each on the head.

"You two will get along jus' fine. You'll see." She chuckled and went back to join Cutty and Ziggy in a card game at the bar.

Abby and Ben sat in silence for a few minutes, the only other prevalent sounds being the slapping of cards as they hit the wooden bar or the lapping of the waves as they splashed the rocks beyond where they sat. This has to be what it feels like to be on a reality show and everywhere you turn people are playing tricks on you left and right, she thought. The underlying animosity from Ben would eventually go away, or so she hoped, but in the meantime, she had a lot to do to prove herself, since technically she was the invader.

"I'm going home." Ben finally broke her thoughts when he pushed back from the bar. "Well, we can go home. I can drive you."

Abby caught a glimpse of something new in Ben's eyes. Not animosity or irritation, more of a thoughtful nervousness. Like he needed to impress or take care of her, maybe? That could be what this is all about, she thought. He may be freaked because I'm his landlord's sister and he thinks I'm going to ruin something for him. Abby had been forgetting that even though Ben seemed mature and experienced, he was also a kid on his last leg of college and still in the process of learning about the world.

Abby relaxed in her seat, letting her shoulders drop slightly, and could feel a small amount of weight coming off them. She knew her approach needed to be different, that she had to take her time and let him learn to trust her. But who knew how long that would take?

Her thoughts were again broken by Ziggy's loud cackle and the crash of an ashtray as it hit the cement floor. It seemed that Cutty had just lost his card game and was drunkenly stumbling home, flipping the bird over his shoulder to the group as they called out their good-byes. Abby could smell the booze oozing from his pores as he walked away.

"Good thing he's going to bed," Ben chuckled. "He has to lead a dive out near Nevis in the morning." He turned and grinned wickedly at Abby. "And he's driving the boat."

"You're kidding, right?" Abby was shocked, not even slightly amused. Just shocked.

"He's good at what he does. He pisses off tourists and provides local color. He's the shipwrecked American who came here to get away. No one knows his story, but everyone either loves him or just flat-out hates him. You'll see. Ready?"

Ben got up and went to settle up with Miss C. Abby had tried to give him some money, but he insisted on paying, so she let him so as to not injure what ego he had left at this moment.

Bidding goodnight to Miss C. and Ziggy, who was smiling even though he couldn't open his eyes, Abby realized she was beginning to understand the dysfunction of this little group here on the island. That in itself is a scary thought, she mused as she climbed into the passenger seat of Ben's car, heading off to get a good, drunken night's sleep on her new air mattress.

CHAPTER 4

THE SLAM OF THE FRONT DOOR WOKE ABBY FROM HER drunken slumber. She shot up, hitting her head on the corner of an old wooden bookshelf that was jutting ever so slightly from the wall. She couldn't understand who was in her home making noise at this hour and wondered how they got in. As the pain welled in her brain, reality began to make its way through the foggy, hungover gray matter. She was not in her home tucked in her comfy bed in Los Angeles, but on an air mattress in an alcove of a stranger's house in the Caribbean. She wanted to puke. It was hot, and it was really early. The kind of early where the sun is not even up yet.

The sound of a car starting outside snapped her to the present. That's Ben, she thought. School. And thank goodness he decided to slam the door so loud. As she surveyed the looks of the living room from her perch in the alcove, a smell penetrated her olfaction and turned her stomach into knots. Ammonia? Or crap?

Surveying the lay of the land from the floor, she looked over and realized there were two cats glaring in her direction from the kitchen table. That's the smell -- freaking litter box hasn't been changed since who knows when, she thought. Great.

The two kitties were stretched lazily on their sides, almost spooning each other. One was all black and the other was a black and white mix. Lazy and long, the two took turns -- as one was cleaning the other's ears and face, the other would watch Abby.

Abby stretched and slowly began to rise, even though her pounding head begged her to stay in a prone position on the floor. She stumbled to the kitchen, searching the cabinets for a glass. This proved to be tougher than she thought, as most of them had a film of dirt on them. She dry-heaved slightly as she noticed there were ants swarming the sink around what appeared to be an old bagel.

She finally found a package of plastic party cups (hmmmm . . . the college life) and, without paying much attention, turned on the faucet to fill up her glass. She was concentrating on the banging in her brain and the fact that she needed more sleep as she tossed back the water that was --

Oh my…Am I chewing my water?!

Abby hung her head over the sink and spit out the water as if she were releasing a demon. Looking in the sink, she saw a few weird chunks of dirt, but it wasn't until she turned the faucet on again that she could plainly see that this was not the best drinking water. Holding on to the side of the counter, she looked at the cats lounging on the table and could swear they were laughing at her. Furry little jerks, she thought snappishly.

There has to be water I can drink, she thought as she fumbled around the kitchen. Opening the fridge, Abby found -- voila! -- a whole crisper full of bottled water. You would have thought she had just won the lottery the way she grabbed the water and gulped it, devouring it as if it were liquid life. As she stood there letting the cool air of the fridge hit her legs, she took a mental inventory of its contents.

There was a package of Oscar Mayer bologna, various condiments, some kind of green vegetable, a packet of American cheese, some bread, full-fat mayo, and some milk. The milk, when she looked at it closer, was in chunks and the expiration date had passed about a month prior. Abby envisioned a trip to the grocery store in her immediate future.

She closed the door and looked at the cats, which were following her every move. Weirdos, she thought. Quit eyeing me. The room was silent, the hum of a box fan playing in the background like ambiance for a spa. First things first, Abby needed to get some coffee and then figure out the grocery store.

She pulled her long mane of chestnut-colored hair back, wrapping it into a bun, changed into a miniskirt and her favorite comfy shirt, grabbed another bottle of water and headed to the main house to see if Maria could point out the directions to the grocery store. Luckily, when she let herself into the kitchen, Maria was hovering over the stovetop. The smell of fresh coffee permeated the air and beckoned like a porch light on a dark night calling out for Abby to come to safety. Or at least to a kitchen that was stocked.

"Morning, girl! How you feeling today?" Maria was grinning from ear to ear and Abby could only guess that Ziggy had already relayed her drunken evening to Maria.

Well, she thought, every town needs a crier. Guess I'm here to be the village idiot.

"I've felt better, that's for sure. And the lack of things one needs to survive in that place," she nodded toward the pool house, "is killing me. Please tell me there's some kind of breakfast or that I can mooch some coffee?"

Maria was already pouring a cup of coffee for Abby. She put the mug down in front of her, along with a plate of home-made scones, scooping up containers of some sugar and creamer for her, too.

"Here you go. So, the real estate agent stopped by with some folks looking at the property. They are going over the grounds with me and Ziggy today so they get an idea of how the place works." Maria was studying Abby's face to make sure she was taking in all Maria was putting out. "Hopefully Buddy will be able to fix the roof, and quick."

"Yeah, as long as Buddy shows up." Abby took a sip of her coffee. "I think he is on what Ziggy called 'island time,' Maria. And I get the feeling that means he'll be here when he gets here."

"I have Ziggy going to the store later to stock up on supplies and food, as the boat be coming in today. I'll have him go by and talk to Buddy's wife." Maria winked at Abby. "She gonna make sure Buddy is here when he supposed to be. Anyway, we have some guests arriving over the next few days, so we got to get crackin'. As for the store, get a list together and I can have him get you some things, too, unless you want to go with him?"

"As tempting as it sounds, I think I may opt to just hand him a list and some cash today, Maria. There are a few things I need to figure out here, like Internet, cable, phone, ants . . . "

"Abby. The Internet is good here -- we got wireless." She winked at Abby.

"I'm impressed. Cable?"

"You get the channels that count."

"Okay. Leigh also mentioned I should get an island cell?"

"Yep. The store in Basseterre has it. You get a phone, and you pay as you call. Ziggy can drop you in town so you can go in and get one. Better yet, let me look around and see if we have a spare one here. Sometimes Leigh leaves them for guests."

"Leigh leaves her phones for guests? Maria, I don't think I'm going to get used to this life where Leigh is a double agent."

"Abby --" Maria sat at the table with her own mug of coffee and patted her hand -- "sometimes we do things that we wait to tell people why later. It's Leigh's life, not yours. So really, it's none of your business."

Abby sipped from her mug, helping herself to a scone. Chewing thoughtfully, she looked over at Maria and nodded.

"I know, Maria. It's her life and none of my business. Except by asking me to come down here and tend to all this for her, she's kind of made this my business."

Maria smiled, took another sip of her coffee and leaned forward to grab Abby's hand.

"Abby, people can be strange. Sometimes, our family? Well, they are the strangest of all. They do things to tell on themselves. Leigh is your family, Abby. We all love our family, but you don't have to like them."

Abby stared at Maria after the last sentence. Obviously, she did know Leigh, and well, since that was a phrase her family had used for years and years. Abby could still remember the day she first heard it. One of Leigh's boys had said it in a fit of anger, and it made Leigh and Abby laugh so hard that they used it now to describe almost everything, especially the way a family loves.

And Maria. There's something so comfortable in this space with her. Abby couldn't understand why she was okay with how close Maria had gotten to her in just a few days' time. With all the touching and the patting, Abby forgot that she was a creature who enjoyed her personal space. Yet, here she was, opening herself to this strange woman with the golden heart and wise words.

Abby traced the rim of her mug with her forefinger and had a flashback to her last day of work, when she was laid off. She smiled into the depths of her coffee, like a seer looking into the fountain of truth. If only I could see the future . . .

As if reading her mind, Maria squeezed her free hand. "Abby, no one knows what's in store as our days go on. Just be in this moment right now. Girl, you are on an island. How many people can say that they are on an island in the middle of the Caribbean because they can be?"

That made Abby laugh, and she toasted the air with her mug.

"You win, Maria. You win." She pushed back from the table and grabbed another scone for the walk back across the lawn. "Maria, will you please ask Ziggy to take me with him when he goes to the store? It's time I took my day by the balls."

Maria hooted with laughter and nodded, shooing Abby out of the room.

"Dat's it, girl! Go get on your bathing suit and embrace it. You're on St. Kitts!"

☙

THE GROCERY STORE, GRIMMS, WAS BUSTLING FOR A weekday morning. The aisles were being "filled wit' new product, fresh off da boat, mon!" as Ziggy had told Abby. People were lining up to get their supplies before they ran out. It was a menagerie of locals, students and tourists all jammed into one small store with an even smaller parking lot.

There were only two stores on the island, and with the lack of a Target or Wal-Mart, Abby knew she needed to stock up now. Ziggy had told her that if she did not hit one of the stores on the days the boats came in with the supplies, then she would, for lack of a better term, be screwed.

Abby tooled up and down the aisles, grabbing staples and trying to think of foods she could get for Ben as well. Pasta, chips and pretzels, tuna fish, all kinds of frozen meats, cookies and breads, sodas and beer. She made sure to get an equal amount of healthy and unhealthy foods to use as her peace offering for invading his home. Oh, and puking in front of him on the first night they met. Ever the planner, she'd already made out a menu of meals she could make and have available to him all week so he wouldn't have to worry about food. Crap, he could be a vegetarian! Abby thought, so she made sure to grab some veggie burgers from the frozen food section and some cheese pizzas as well.

When checking out, Abby almost pooped herself when the woman asked her for $655.

"Are you KIDDING me? I'm not investing in the store or buying stock. I only got some staples!"

The woman looked at Abby like she had two heads. "You don't be havin' any staples here, girl. Dey over in aisle tree."

"Not staples . . . staples." The woman stared blankly at Abby. Abby stared blankly back. She felt a twinge of frustration begin to play in her stomach. Abby also wanted to make her say "three" with her ten times over until she pronounced the h.

"Oh, whatever. Look, $655 is steep, don't you think? I

might have just gotten here, but I know when someone is trying to rip me off. Can we please look at the cost again?"

The woman rolled her eyes. Obviously, customer service was not a strong suit for Grimms.

"It's $655. That would be in EC."

Abby was confused. She thought she was on St. Kitts. "Where is EC?" she asked, biting back her irritation at the game this woman was playing with her.

The woman took a big breath and rolled her eyes. Again.

"EC, Eastern Caribbean. It's our money here. It's what you owe. You pay or you leave. Either way, I don't care. I'm not the one that is needin' to be eatin'," she said tersely.

"Oh." Abby felt her face go flush with embarrassment. "Uh . . . do you take credit cards?"

The woman nodded, and Abby handed over her Visa. As she looked up, she noticed the Captain from last night, Cutty, talking to Ziggy. He was smiling at her and making throw-up motions.

"What are you? Like fifty years old and you act like a teenage boy?" She signed her credit slip and was pushing her cart over to meet Ziggy, hoping to leave before this heathen sucked them into a conversation.

"I'm actually thirty-five. I just look fifty because I don't wash my makeup off before bed," he drawled. He smiled and nodded at her cart. "Groceries?"

"Observant. I see why you're in charge of driving a boat and taking people out to sea for diving. Let me guess, you probably drink the whole way out to the dive site?"

Ziggy laughed at that. "No, mon, he only drink when dey go under if he ain't leading da dive. Or smoke his Mary Jane."

Abby stared at them both in horror. "I'm leaving. You --" she pointed at Cutty -- "disturb me."

"Then we should get married now, 'cause I think I'm in love." He wiggled his overgrown eyebrows at Abby and smiled wickedly. Abby could not help but find she was smiling at this man, in all of his irritating glory.

"I have food that may thaw in this heat. Ziggy, can we please go?" Abby asked as sweetly as she could muster.

"Tell you what, Abby-cakes. You take those groceries home then come for happy hour. My treat," Cutty offered, putting his hand out for her to shake.

"I can't, but thank you. I have things that need to be done today. Lots of things. Things that if I don't --"

He held his hand up. "Just say no if you don't want to, but I doubt you have things to do."

"But I do! I have to make my list when I go home and --"

"And what? What's going to be on it? Let me guess: 'To Do Today. Number One: Get up. Number Two: Buy groceries. Number Three: Put groceries away. Number Four: Annoy Ben by being around too much. Number --"

"I get it. Just stop," Abby begged.

Why not? she thought. It's not like I have a lot to do today, and the repairmen aren't due for another day or two. So, one day at happy hour with this insane man would be fine.

"Okay, Cutty. What time is happy hour at Ricky's?"

"All day."

"No, really."

"All day."

"I want to hit you," Abby said unapologetically.

"I want you to hit me. I'm into that." Cutty grinned.

Abby shook her head, which seemed to be her new trait these days, and said, "I'll be there around 4 p.m."

Cutty nodded and grabbed his bag of groceries. "Good. Bring some playing cards. I think I burned the ones from last night." As an afterthought, he yelled over his shoulder, "And some cigarettes. I like Camel Filters."

And with that, he shuffled out the door of Grimms and began his walk back to Ricky's.

Ziggy and Abby got in his taxi and headed back to La Cantina to unload. She used this time to ask Ziggy questions about the captain with an affinity for Camel filtered smokes, alcohol and the "Mary Jane."

"Cutty? He been here for at least fifteen years. Maybe longer. Some say he was running from da mob back den. Miss C. says he just came and decided he wanted to be on the island, and the IRS wanted him."

"So, no one really knows his whole story?"

"Abby, this is why so may people like to come to de islands. You can come here and start over. No one knows who dey were in de other lives they have before dey get to us. St. Kitt's was de island where some people in da witness protection program would come many, many, many years ago. Den someone ran his mouth too much and dey figured it out. Mob showed up and dis guy and his big Cadillac he had shipped here? Dey was found at da bottom of a cliff on da other side of the island. So now, we just an island that people like to come to for vacation. Because you can go divin' and snorkel and be like us." He grinned widely. "You get to be Kittian. You get to lime."

Abby was slowly falling in like with Ziggy. It seemed Abby was the one with the knack of judging people not in the best light. She smiled warmly at her new buddy. "By the way, Ziggy, what the heck do you mean when you keep talking about liming?"

"To lime is 'to be.' When we just hangin' out and chillin'? Dat's limin', girl. Limin' is not an activity, it's a practice."

"I always thought it meant you guys wanted to go pick limes," Abby said through her laughter.

"You Americans find it hard to do. Lime. Just be. Dere is no need to get ahead here. We just like to wake up and have life, make some money to get our food and pay our bills. But it's life we love. It's de limin' dat makes it all balance."

That makes sense. And obviously something I need more of, Abby thought. Balance.

As they pulled into the driveway, Maria came strolling up to the cab to meet them and help unload the groceries. Ziggy hopped out of the car and grabbed his woman by the waist and spun her around in the middle of the yard. This took her by surprise, but she was laughing and enjoying the moment with her husband. Abby felt a little knock on her heart as she realized that these two were probably one of the happiest and most connected couples she had seen in such a long time. It must be 'cause they take the time to lime together, she thought. Something more people need to do, I guess.

"Leigh called while you were out, Abby," Maria said as she was reaching into the cab to get some bags.

"Really? What did she say?"

"For you to go get a cell phone so she could call you," Maria countered.

"I would, but I thought you were going to try to find me a cell phone in the house." Abby winked at Ziggy as she teased his wife.

"I will, I will. As soon as I put away the groceries, make us some dinner and then get the meals prepped for tomorrow . . . oh, and finish the laundry, I'll be glad to take a moment to search to find you a cell phone," was Maria's sarcastic comeback.

ABBY WAS STILL LAUGHING AT MARIA'S LAST ZING WHEN BEN came zooming into the driveway. He parked, nodded at the small group and rushed inside the pool house.

Abby turned to Maria and commented, "Well, that wasn't awkward at all, huh?"

"Time, Abby. Give it some time." Maria's smile was all-knowing and brighter than the blazing Caribbean sun. "He's a good boy, and you are a good girl. Eventually, this is gonna work out. You'll see." She shared a secret wink with Abby and then helped Ziggy begin the task of unloading the cab.

Abby entered the pool house expecting Ben to be in the living room. But he must have gone straight to his room because he was nowhere on the first floor, as far as she could see. Abby sighed and headed into the kitchen to unload her wares.

As she was bent over in the fridge, a voice behind her broke the stillness of the room.

"How are you feeling today?"

Abby turned around and faced Ben. She shrugged her shoulders and grinned.

"I'd be lying if I said I felt like I could run a race. You?"

"Not bad. I have to rush back now to help with some animals in the barn." Ben was watching her unpack the groceries in mild fascination. "I have a donkey."

Abby, still putting groceries away and trying to play it cool, asked, "Donkey? There's a reason you wanted to share that?"

Ben looked at her like she had just asked him how many feet it was to the moon. Then he realized she was genuinely asking him what he meant.

"I forget that not everyone around here knows about vet school. We get an animal that we monitor during the semester. My lab partner and I have a donkey. I have to get up early to go take care of him, and now I have to rush back to S.O.A.P. him."

"You go to school to learn how to wash ass?" Abby was fighting the urge to laugh in his sweet little face.

"No, Abby," Ben was showing his frustration now. "SOAP-ing stands for 'Subjective, Objective, Assessment, and Plan.' You take vitals and monitor the animals."

"Ahh, okay…I don't know. Or, I.D.K., as I like to say."

"I think you're being facetious."

"I think you just used a big word. Nonetheless, you are correct, sir." Abby curtseyed and grabbed the plastic bags the groceries had come in. "Where should I put these?"

"The bags?"

"No, the air around me. Yes, Ben, the bags. Do you keep them or recycle them?"

Ben looked more than a little confused. "I usually don't have the time nor the money to get that many groceries at once. I guess you can put them under the sink?"

"Good place to start." Abby put them away, asking over her shoulder, "What do you mean you don't usually have time to get groceries?"

"I'm always in class. In my free time I play volleyball, I run, I study. Or I go to the beach or out with friends. Not to the grocery store."

"So, none of the delicious food I got that is totally and completely fit for college-student eating interests you?" Abby asked.

"Well, I'm not saying that . . . "

Abby gave Ben her warmest smile. "Anything I picked up

today, I want you to please help yourself to. I wanted peace offerings, and I hope this helps some."

"Thanks, Abby. That's pretty cool," Ben said as he started to rifle through the fridge. He grabbed a cheese stick, and his eyes lit up when he saw steaks in the freezer.

"You cook?" he asked, surprised.

"Not great, but I get by. I'm sure if you wanted me to try to make you something, I could pass with an attempt."

Things seem to be going well, Abby thought. It's like a dance or a first date. Time for me to pull away and prove to him I'm easy to live with.

"Okay, then. I'm going to clean up a little and then go --"

Ben looked mortified. "Clean? You don't need to do that."

"Oh, it's okay. I really don't mind."

Abby's last sentence fell on deaf ears. Ben was shaking his head and Abby could swear he was playing with his fingers again, using her signature nervous move.

"I guess I need to be clearer right now. Don't do that."

It was Abby's turn to look mortified. Was Ben telling her not to clean? But, she thought, I bought litter for the cats . . .

"I kind of thought it might be nice to -- I don't know. Sweep, dust, maybe straighten up?" Ben's face was twisted in emotion and it was freaking Abby out. Uh-oh, she thought she saw the green creeping its way into those brown eyes again, the way it had the night before when he'd gotten angry with her. "Ben, all I want to do is make it so the common area smells nice and I can hang in it."

Ben's lips were pulled tight. Abby could tell his wheels were spinning.

"Abby. Things are organized here in such a way that I know where they are for when I need them. It's my stuff in my place. Like the books over there." He pointed to a shelf on the far wall, near Abby's bed. It was dusty and very obviously handmade. A few boards on cinder blocks, actually. Books were piled on top of one another and there were stacks of papers scattered on all the shelves, and some under it, covering the floor. "I know what's there, and what's not supposed to be. I've placed term papers and tests in spots where I can pull them out for studying. If I screw up at all this semester, I'm out. My career is over." He looked very serious as he pointedly said, "Do not clean my home."

This was a new twist. And it would be an issue.

Abby searched for the right words and hoped that whatever came out of her mouth sounded the way she meant it to.

"Ben, I get that there are things here I shouldn't touch. But, to not clean? For one thing, here's a litter box next to my bed that needs some serious attention."

Ben stared at Abby so hard it began to feel really awkward. Finally he spoke. "Fine. I will get the litter box and clean it out, but please let me handle anything else that is mine. I have too many papers here for school that I need to know where they are and too many projects to have you mess up the way I have things organized."

This made more sense to Abby, and she realized he wasn't just being a douchebag but he was being a territorial guy who just wanted to take care of his own home. She acknowledged it to herself, then realized she had said this out loud to Ben.

"Well, that makes a little more sense! You're just being territorial. Okay..." Uh-oh.

"The fact that you want to clean my home makes no sense. You're being a knob-head." Ben combed his fingers through his hair in frustration. "And of course I'm being territorial! You just got here and you're trying to take over my home. Look, I know you mean well, but . . . Well, no. Just no. Don't clean my house. I'll clean out the litter box and take care of my things my way. You'll just have to deal with it."

"You are so oddly passive-aggressive, do you know that?"

"I'm passive-aggressive? You're neurotic and passive-aggressive!"

Abby flinched slightly. "I'm neurotic? Maybe you should go and take a good long look in the mirror. Get an idea of who truly is the poster boy for neurosis!"

"Really? I'm pretty sure I'm looking at the poster girl right now!"

"Ben. We're not a couple moving in together. It's a weird merging of two people that kind of need to make it work or both of them will be screwed."

"That's my point, Abby. We're not a couple moving in together. I don't know you."

Abby was beyond frustrated now. "Ben, I can't argue like this. I'm not made for it. Have a great rest of your day." With that, Abby grabbed her purse and walked out of the pool house, slamming the door behind her.

She wasn't sure where to go, so she just started walking. When she reached the end of the driveway, she realized a drink would be good to have right then and decided to go have one with the mildly irritating Captain. Maybe he could take Abby's mind off her living situation with his oddness. Someone like him was bound to have good stories, or at least could make some up.

She was sweating bullets when she finally got to Ricky's. It wasn't a far walk, but the heat was insane and made her thirst for any kind of cold beverage. Sitting at one of the outside patio tables smoking a cigarette and drinking his Carib was Cutty. He smiled a big grin and called out to Abby.

"Well, you made it for happy hour." The Captain pointed at an imaginary watch on his arm. "Lucky for you, it just started."

Abby laughed and pulled out a chair to fall into. "I thought you said happy hour was all day, Cutty."

"That's what I meant. It just started --" he winked at her -- "this morning. What are you drinking?"

"Anything cold, and with a double shot. I need to make the last hour go away."

"How can you be in a foul mood? You just got here." Cutty was already walking to the bar to get her a cocktail. His T-shirt was tattered and faded, with the emblem of a university long since washed-out on the front, obviously a hand-me-down from one of the students, and he was wearing board shorts. As he ordered her drink, Abby found herself wondering if he had skin cancer, because there was no way he used lotion with SPF in it, judging by the dark brown color of his skin.

"I did just get here, but Ben is not making it easy on me to get settled in," she sighed. He plopped her rum punch down in front of her, and she took it like a baby grabbing a milk bottle. In fact, Abby drank it in one gulp.

Cutty took her empty cup and went back to the bar to get her another one. He didn't seem like a bad guy, just lonely. He got the bartender -- today it was a man named Mikey -- to make her a new drink. Mikey smiled at Abby and added a little extra rum.

"You here to have a date with this one today, girl?" Mikey asked Abby.

"Oh, no. Just drinks. And the way I'm feeling, there may be a few."

Cutty looked miffed at her comment. "'No'? RUKM?"

"Are you speaking in text, Cutty? Or do you go SOAP with

the students, too?" Abby stated with genuine surprise at Cutty's comment.

"No, I don't SOAP with those losers." He grinned. "And, yes. RUKM means 'Are you kiddin' me?'"

Cutty then crinkled his eyes and looked at Abby very seriously.

"Look, Ben's a good kid. You have to understand his situation," Cutty began. Abby, though, was on the defensive and she stopped him short.

"Cutty, please let's not talk about Ben right now. I have nothing nice to say. Tell me about you."

Cutty slid back into his chair, lighting up another cigarette even though he had put one out while he was at the bar getting Abby's cocktail. He blew it out lazily, yet in one big puff, and grinned at her.

"You want to know about me? That'll cost ya."

"Are you always like this?"

"Like what? Handsome? Stunning? Fun to be around? If those are the questions, my answers are yes, yes and oh yes."

"No. A smart-ass."

"Ahh, now you make me feel like we're married already. I'm ordained to be a minister, you know," he said with importance, puffing out his scrawny chest.

"I'm sure. It's easy to do anything online. Seriously, how long have you been here?"

Cutty was thoughtful as he stared out toward the Caribbean. He had lots of lines around his mouth, from smoking, drinking or laughing, or probably a mix of all three. He seemed to Abby like the kind of man who made sure he lived his days, each and every one, with a kind of gusto. Many drinks, many laughs and lots of women.

"I don't know. I think I got here in the late '80s. I can't

remember anymore, and I don't wanna. I was offered a deal to come to Ricky's and run the dive shop here, complete with a room that would be my apartment. So I took the deal. And now I'm here." He smiled and gave a curt nod to show he was done telling his side of things now.

"Okay, well, that tells me about you when you got here. I'd like to know about you in the U.S."

"What makes you think I'm from the States?" he asked as he drained the last of the beer from his Carib.

Abby wasn't sure if he was being humorous or if he was going to be that new friend whom you hang out with because they kind of annoy you, yet you go back for more because they are also so entertaining you want to unleash them on other people so that they, too, feel the wrath.

"You sound like you're from the Northeast, actually. I'm guessing Connecticut."

"Close, Alex Trebek. We'll go Rhode Island for now." He then leaned in closer and whispered to Abby, "If it's even a real state."

This was how it went. For the next hour or four, Abby sat and verbally jousted with Cutty. He was disappointed when he realized she didn't have a deck of cards with her, but he quickly perked up when Mikey came around the bar with the pack from the night before. Turned out Cutty had dreamt he set them on fire, so obviously everyone could now rest.

They were in the middle of a wicked game of rummy when Ziggy came careening down the rocky drive with a cab full of people. From the blurry looks of them, Abby thought they must be students. This was proven when they all got out of the cab, backpacks in tow, chattering about tests, small animals and other medical terms that Abby knew even if she was sober she'd never understand. So she didn't feel bad that in her drunken state she thought they were speaking in Greek.

The four kids had come together from school and swarmed a table on the patio. There was a flurry of activity as they got settled in, ordered dinner and some drinks from the bar, opened computers and began to review their studies. Watching them all hover around the table together, Abby realized how much she missed the camaraderie of knowing other people that are a part of "your world." People you can talk to, get advice from and give advice to, or, in some cases, people who are so close you finish one another's sentences.

While Cutty was chatting with Ziggy and dealing him in on a game, Abby found she was lost in thought at all she had left behind. Her home, a job that didn't want her and a relationship that set sail in the most embarrassing manner. Abby sighed as she thought about her knack at finding relationships that were doomed to fail. Whether it was a personal relationship or a professional one, she felt as if she kept getting evicted from a world that was perceived as the "norm." Where folks got married and had 9-to-5 jobs and went home to their loved ones and picket-fenced houses. Where IS the fairy tale?

"Abby, where you go?" Ziggy noticed that Abby had mentally checked out.

"She's probably wishing we would play strip poker so she could then be lucky enough to see --" Cutty stood up and began to twist back and forth at the waist -- "all this hot madness." He waggled his drunken eyebrows at Abby as she giggled at his absolute silliness.

"I was thinking of home. I know it's only been a few days, but I miss it a little."

Ziggy started dealing the cards while Cutty watched Abby intently.

"You won't miss it soon. Or you'll get so irritated here you'll have to go back sooner than you thought to get your Target or Macy's fix. I know how it is." He smiled and leaned over to pat her on the shoulder. "Retail therapy. Spend some money to have something else to whine about."

"You whine about women a lot. And other things, too. So maybe you should just shut your face-hole," Abby giggled to Cutty as she flicked him in the ear.

"Abby, we heard some shoutin' today in de house." Ziggy's face showed his concern. "I don't want to be gettin' in da middle, but I don't want it to be crazy for de two of you in de house, either."

"Ziggy, it's gonna be okay. It's gonna take time because Ben is a spoiled brat."

Cutty and Ziggy threw their hands up and both went "Whooooa!" at the same time. Both men couldn't help laughing at Abby's pissy outburst, but Abby was over it. "Thank you for the rum drinks, boys. I may tell Ben off tonight."

"Don't go and do that. What's it going to help? How much older are you than he is? Like ten years? Get over it. Maybe if you sleep with him . . . "

"Oh, Cutty, you are just up to the brim full of good ideas. No, I am not sleeping with him." Abby shook her head and scowled at the good Captain. "And so what if I am ten years older than he is? He is still an adult and needs to act like one. He is a passive-aggressive kid that needs to stop being such a turd or he'll get spanked. S-P-A-N-K-E-D." Abby was mimicking the motion of spanking an ass, hip-hop style. She had no idea she was really starting to look like a drunken idiot.

"You know what? I feel like I'm a good person. I like people and I like to be liked. There is nothing --" she was pointing at Cutty because he was beginning to open his mouth -- "wrong with that at all. Not one bit. Not at all, I say. So, put that in your peace pipe and smoke it, Cap'n."

The three of them played their card game in silence until Cutty piped up with an alternative idea.

"You could stay with me, hot stuff."

"Ew. No way!" Abby and Ziggy were both laughing at the thought. They were finishing up the game and all three found themselves in small fits of laughter as they chatted with one another, exchanging barbs. Abby really liked these guys and was happy she had met them. They made up for the fact that she was living with chip-on-his-shoulder guy.

The game ended, and Ziggy was the winner, which caused a drunk Cutty to go into a fit of aggravation that the cards had let him down yet again. Abby broke away from the loud commotion to pay her tab at the bar before she headed back to La Cantina.

One of the girls from the group of students was up there as well, getting a Diet Coke. Abby was standing next to her and watched her pull out her money to pay for her drink. Apparently the girl noticed, because she felt the need to bring it up.

"If you're thinking of grabbing my wallet, I'm going to warn you. I'm a college student, so good luck in there."

Abby would have been mortified, but she was spirited beyond much reason at this point.

"Actually, I was looking at the bills you are using. Are those EC?" Abby thought she might have been seeing monopoly money if they weren't.

The girl smiled at Abby. "Yeah, it's EC. Looks a lot like it's fake, huh?" She had a thick accent from the South, maybe Tennessee or North Carolina? Abby couldn't tell. She was a tan girl, very pretty, pearly white teeth and beautiful curly blonde hair. "I'm Tracey Lee. You're with them --" she bobbed her head at Abby's table of clowns -- "so you must be local or visiting a local?"

"My sister owns La Cantina, and I'm here doing business for her. I'm Abby George."

Tracey's face already showed some signs of recognition. "Oh, wait! You're the one that got shoved into Ben's little one-bedroom, aren't you?" Tracey started laughing. "Oh, yeah. Heard about you today. You puked last night."

Maybe Ziggy wasn't the town crier Abby had decided he was. Nope. Seemed he had some competition from the young Ben.

"Yes. That would be me. The evil girl that took over Ben's small pool house. I'm a big jerk, as you'll probably hear all about the next few weeks." Abby wanted to not be irritated and sarcastic, but there was no way to hold her emotions back now. Ben was obviously so irritated he was sharing this issue with his friends at school. Not that she could blame him, but now she was "that girl."

"Don't get mad at Ben. He happens to be my partner in one of my classes. It just came up that you're here and he's a little stressed out." After she said it, Tracey's face showed she wanted to take it back.

"I'm sorry. He just confides in me. We're friends. Please know . . . oh, crap. I'm going to stop." Tracey looked down and shook her head. "I have a knack for saying the wrong thing at the perfect time. I think it's a Southern thing." She smiled sheepishly at Abby.

"Funny, I seem to have a knack for showing up places at the right moment and creating all the wrong problems. Maybe we should be friends."

Tracey looked Abby up and down, sizing her up. "I could

hang out with you. Maybe just not tell Ben." She winked. "What's your cell so I can text you to make plans? There are some rugby matches coming up, plus we have soccer games against the medical schools here -- the human med school. And I like to hike when I can, so maybe I can show you the island." Tracey was lit up from the inside, her golden skin and blond hair seeming to glitter in the last rays of the sun's light as it fell into the balmy Kittian night.

"I'd love any of it. All of it!" Abby gushed. "I don't have my cell yet, but as soon as I do I can call you. Why don't you give me yours?"

Tracey grabbed a pen from Mikey and scratched her number on a cocktail napkin.

"Did they explain to you the ins and outs of the island mobile?"

"No, just that I needed to get one. One of the innkeepers is looking to see if there's an extra at the house for me."

Tracey's face twisted as if she was trying to place something. "I think I may have one as well. I'll look around and stop by tomorrow or the day after. I'll take you to set it up and show you how to add minutes to it. They are pay-as-you-go for the most part. Everyone texts here and doesn't try to call because it wastes minutes and money. Remember when cell phones first came out in the States?"

Abby thought beyond her iPhone, beyond her Razr phone, beyond . . . "Like the boxy Nokia ones? With old-school texting, not a 'qwerty' keyboard?"

"Yep. You just stepped slightly into the Dark Ages." Tracey winked again. "I'll show ya the lay of the land. Ben's being a jerk, but we're not all like that."

Someone from Tracey's group motioned for her to come back over. "I gotta get back to those guys. We have a surprise quiz in two days. Friend of mine's the assistant to the teacher throwing it, so we all know. Surprise!"

Abby smiled and let out a happy breath. "I'm so glad I met you. Thank you, Tracey. You really turned my day around."

"Eh, there's bigger problems out there, right? Like passing school. Talk to you soon." And with that, Tracey hurried back to her group to continue quizzing.

Abby was smiling as she returned to the table to join Ziggy and Cutty, bidding them good-bye. As she gathered her things, she noticed a man standing on the balcony of his hotel room looking down at Ricky's. Cocking her head to the side, Abby peered up, watching him watch the sun as it dipped below the Caribbean Sea for the night. She realized it was the man that had been sitting at the bar with Cutty the night before. And even from this angle she could still make out his square jaw and handsome features.

As if sensing her gaze, he was suddenly matching her stare, smiling to one side and looking at her quizzically. Abby laughed and waved, feeling embarrassed at having been caught peeping on someone in a private moment. He smiled and waved back, then disappeared from the balcony.

Taking this as her cue, Abby began her trek back to La Cantina, feeling fairly satisfied about her day.

CHAPTER 5

"Dat be needin' some patchin' for sure."

Abby stared at Buddy as he teetered on his ladder propped up against the side of the house. He had shown up a day earlier than expected, thanks to Maria's plan in which Buddy's wife, Anita, knew he needed to be somewhere. The man that arrived was definitely not someone Abby was expecting.

Buddy was a heavyset man in his late forties with some gray hairs starting to peek their way through on his hairline and out of his nostrils. He had a limp and one of his eyes didn't seem to move from side to side. Abby was pretty sure the roof was doomed.

Much to her surprise, he had deftly set up the ladder and quickly scaled it to the top, assessing the situation that needed to be fixed. He was nodding and grunting as he looked around, but overall seemed pleased with the amount of work that lay before him.

"It just needs a patch or two, but other den dat de rest of de roof is fine. Some water had pooled up from de last few storms, making it weak. I can get supplies and fix it."

Abby nodded, impressed. "Great, Buddy. Love that. How long will it take you?"

Buddy was pulling a piece of the roof off with him, to take as a sample for other tiles to match. "Hmm," he grunted. "Maybe six weeks? Seven?"

Abby was floored. "What? Six or seven weeks? You said you just needed to patch a few spots."

Buddy looked down at Abby from his perch. "I got to get de tile to match from da mainland and get it shipped over, Abby. Den I got to get de crew to do it. Plus I got other roofs to be fixing on de island. Your roof isn't de only one dat be needin' work."

Abby's first reaction was to insist he put them first, but instead she decided to think outside the box.

"I've noticed a lot of construction on the island, Buddy. Surely someone would have some tiles like these? Everyone seems to use the same kind to protect from the storms, right?"

Buddy shrugged. "I don't know, mon. I just order from de mainland but I guess it could be dat someone has de same kind here."

Abby smiled at Buddy. "Okay, so I'm thinking that before the order is placed and we are put on hold, can we try to get the tiles from one of the local construction sites? We can't need that many . . . can we?"

Buddy peered across the roof and shook his head. "I tink we can get by wit fifty tiles."

Maria had appeared next to Abby and was squinting up in the midday sun at Buddy now, too.

"We ain't got time for an order from the mainland, Buddy! I know you can make it happen . . . or do we need to talk to Anita again?"

At the mention of his wife's name, Buddy's body had

mildly shuddered. Seems we know who wears the pants in that family, Abby thought.

"Fine, Maria. Tell you what, I be trying to find dese tiles, okay? But I may need help putting dem on de roof. Deal?"

Abby jumped with joy. "Buddy, it's a deal, even if I have to climb up there and help you get those tiles in!"

Abby turned and was heading back to the pool house, but Maria stopped her.

"Girl, I got a list here for you."

Abby looked quizzically at Maria. "List?"

Maria laughed, winking at Abby. "Yes, girl. Of other repairs. Spots on the walls that need to be touched up wit paint and light-switch plates that be needing replaced. And that's just to start."

Abby looked over the list, taking mental notes on what needed to be addressed. "Great, thank you, Maria. I'll get to work on this."

"Some of the supplies you need are in the house already. Ziggy has a toolbox for you and some paint. Anything else you need you can get in town."

Buddy had loaded his ladder and was climbing in the truck. "Okay, I got to go now, but either me or Anita will call you and let you know what happens wit' de tiles." With that, he nodded at the two women and sped out of the driveway.

"I thought he was going fishing," Abby said to Maria.

Maria grunted. "If by fishing you mean fishing on the north side of the island for a bottle of rum, then yes, Buddy was going fishing." Maria grinned wide. "Anita's my cousin, so I got a little pull there."

Abby felt Maria's hand rest on her shoulder as she guided her into the main house so Abby could get down to business.

From that day onward, Abby's new pattern began to form. Most days began with the screen door to the pool house slamming in the morning. Ben was always running late, so he was usually rushed. Only once did Abby dare to bring up to him that it would be nice if he didn't slam the door closed when he was leaving. It did not go over well.

As Ben was about to leave one morning, she had tried a tactic to get his attention called "asking nicely."

"I know you're in a hurry, but since I'm not having to get up as early as you do, do you mind not slamming the door when you go?" Abby figured it was reasonable.

Ben's stony expression was hard when he replied. "That bothers you? Hm. Must be rough." He responded by slamming every door, even a majority of the kitchen cabinets, as he left for the day.

At this point, Abby would generally shuffle into the main house for some coffee with Maria and busy herself with getting organized with the work she needed to accomplish that day. The first few days she had managed to change all the light-switch plates out in the inn, as well as replace every light bulb. She had tested all the beds to make sure their posts were still secure and the mattresses were still good, only being busted leaping onto a mattress once by a visitor. Abby had been shaking the headboards and bouncing up and down, testing for squeaking sounds or loose boards when she had noticed the woman staring at her with her mouth open from the hallway. She started to explain, but realized how insane she looked. So Abby just smiled at the woman and kept bouncing, shrugging her shoulders, testing the bed frame.

One particular morning, Abby found Maria checking in a

couple, the Bellfields, who had arrived for their honeymoon. Abby was still her in pajamas and wiping sleep from her eyes as Maria introduced her.

"And speaking of the owners, this is Abby. Her sister owns the inn."

Abby smiled at the couple. "Good morning."

The two looked at Abby and smiled, but also seemed slightly appalled. The happy grins that were present a moment before had disappeared. They took the key to their room from Maria, nodded goodbye, and walked away without even a backward glance at Abby.

"What's their problem?" Abby was sincerely perplexed.

Maria turned to Abby and fully took her in. "Have you looked in the mirror?"

Abby stared at Maria for half a second before running to the mirror in the front hall.

Abby's face was covered with little black dots, smudges that, when she rubbed at them with her fingers, came off. She smelled her hands in an attempt to guess what it was.

"Smells like . . . cigarettes?"

Maria nodded. "Looks like you've been smudged, girl."

Abby ran into the washroom by the front door and splashed water on her face, cursing Ben under her breath. What is his problem? He smudged me with ashes?

Abby emerged irritated.

"Why would he do that?"

Maria laughed. "I don't think it was Ben. A few of those marks looked like paw prints."

Abby rolled her eyes. "So the cats did this to me?" She sighed. "I can't win here, Maria. No matter what I do, it seems the world is stacked against me."

"Checks and balances. Something has to even out, girl."

Maria was sympathetic, but Abby could tell she was also determined not to get in the middle of the small war that was raging in the pool house. "It takes time. Those cats probably got in one of the ashtrays and brought it in the house. Don't be so quick to blame Ben."

Abby felt slightly betrayed by her "house mother," but didn't let it show. She couldn't blame her.

Pouring herself some coffee, Abby sat at the computer to attack the new job she had created for herself while waiting for Buddy to come through: bookkeeping. Abby was enjoying the feeling of having people depend on her and felt inspired by her productive repair days, so she had taken over the computer and helped by logging the finances so Maria had one fewer item on her to-do list.

As she was sitting at her workstation balancing the books, the phone on the desk rang.

"La Cantina!" She forced herself to smile when she answered.

"Sounds like someone woke with sunshine in her heart." The Southern drawl clued Abby in that it was Tracey, calling to save her from her seclusion. Tracey was becoming a great friend to Abby. Southern mothers raised them both, so their backgrounds were similar. It made it easy for them to fall into a tight friendship. This of course led to Tracey bringing up Ben, not too often, but enough just to check in with Abby and see how she was doing with their living situation.

"Ha. Ben's cats attacked me while I was sleeping. Even the felines are rising up to take me down. How's your day?"

Tracey laughed. "Over! We have a ton of tests this week for midterms. I'm sure Ben told you."

"Tracey, do you really think he shares anything with me?" Abby asked her friend.

"True." Tracey understood. "I'm going to one of the beach bars to study. Be by in an hour to get you?"

Abby felt her heart leap in her chest. "I'd love that! I'll be ready."

They disconnected and Abby finished up her data entry. She did a quick check-in with Maria to see if she was needed for anything at the inn. Maria gave her the green light to enjoy the interlude by shooing her out the back door.

♦♦

"HE NEVER REALLY SAYS ANYTHING, SO I'VE RESPONDED IN kind, Trace." They were sitting at The Ship That Sank, one of the bars in South Friars Bay. It was a spot where a lot of the Rhodes University students liked to study, eat and take swim breaks. It was also where the monkeys lived in the trees and goats roamed on the hill behind the restaurant. You never knew if they would make a surprise appearance. Abby loved it.

"Smart thing. One day he'll have something to say, and if you want --" she reached across Abby and grabbed a fry -- "you can answer. Otherwise, he will have missed his chance to get to hang with a really cool chick." She ended her sentence with a big grin and a swig of her water.

"Thanks," Abby replied as she chewed thoughtfully on her fries and stared over the waters of the bay. "The other day we got into an argument over how to change the litter box -- the stinky litter box that his cats crap in. I bleached it and apparently that is something he didn't want to happen. Trace, it smelled so terrible and I sleep next to it, so I went out and bought new litter and then I scrubbed it out and bleached it. I didn't think I would ever argue with someone over how to change a litter box, much less get yelled at so much by one person. It just sucks. I don't think anyone has ever hated me like this, at least not anyone who isn't related to me. I mean, when you're related, you always kinda hate each other."

Tracey, ever the good friend, just listened as Abby vented.

"You know, I knew coming here would be different. It's not home. Home was familiar and this is still new. There are days where I can handle the freedom, you know? Some days I want to hear the noise of the streets or look out the window and see the Hollywood sign in the distance. I want to put on heels and go out to a fun party in my best dress." Abby looked at her friend sheepishly. "Stupid, huh?"

Tracey smiled across the table. "No, it isn't. Living on an island is different. I mean, there's a reason they tell you to go for two weeks and then come back. That way you never have time to get 'island fever,' ya know?"

"Yeah," Abby giggled. "I think the days when the power goes out because everyone on the island uses air conditioners are the best . . . I mean, try having to explain that to guests at the inn, when they are paying to stay in paradise and it's bloody, freakin' hot. And it's not like anyone is in a hurry to fix it when it goes out. Sometimes it seems to take days to get anyone to pick up a phone to repair anything here! And the days the cable goes out? The worst! They always seem to be the days I just want to lie there and soak in some bad television or see what's happening in the rest of the world."

Abby sighed heavily as if she were winding down, so Tracey began to speak. However, it seemed Abby was still not done yet.

"Did I mention, the other night I was watching NCIS on the little TV in the living room and Ben came down and kind of yelled at me, said it was 'too loud'? The thing is so tiny that even when I have it cranked up, I can't really hear it over the fans he has running to circulate air through the house!" Abby was only getting warmed up.

"And his guitar playing. Tracey, he thinks he can play the guitar. So he does and at all hours. Never mind if I'm sleeping or trying to . . . he does it because he needs to unwind, or it's a study break. Or he's drunk or his rugby team won a match. It's gotten beyond ridiculous. So much so that me, I'm tiptoeing around this guy to be a nice roommate and he has taken up a hobby of rudeness. All aimed at me. I have bought groceries, offered to help around the house, and changed the litter box for those smelly felines. I did laundry the other day, and to be nice added a few of his things that were sitting there as well. Did he say thank you? No. He saw his things folded and rolled his eyes, marched upstairs and slammed the door. That was that."

"Abby, don't push anything," Tracey warned.

"I'm not! I really am trying to stay away. If I stay any more out of the way, I'll be on the next island over. And Leigh's been no help. She's so busy; I only get emails saying she's sorry and she will make it up to me." She threw her hands up in the air. "It's too much to handle. He's a beast."

Tracey looked around to make sure no one could hear her, then she leaned in to Abby and whispered, "There's more to it than he's telling you, or anyone for that matter."

Abby leaned in as well, with a sweet smile on her face, and replied sarcastically, "Whatever."

"Abby! Look, he'd kill me if he knew I was going to tell you this, but I think you need to know in order for you to understand why he is such a basketcase this semester."

Abby started to make a snide comment when Tracey interjected, "Please, Abby. I'll tell you this and then you can make a decision on Ben from there. In fact, if he still irks you after I explain where he's coming from, cool. No more Ben talk. Deal?"

Abby pursed her lips together and slowly nodded. Ben was becoming the bane of her existence.

"When I say Ben hasn't had it easy, I don't mean because his car broke down or his checkbook won't balance. Ben is one of those guys who shouldn't be here, but is. In fact, Abby, he's a genius. Or rather an idiot savant," she giggled. "He came here on a partial scholarship from his last school, Virginia Tech. I met his mom, Carla, on orientation day. His dad passed away when he was a little boy. Anyway, he's here, and it's his last semester, right? Ben decided he needed to 'let some steam off' during finals, so he went for a run one night by the cane fields near your place. He got jumped by locals and stabbed. He showed up on my doorstep at 2 a.m. My roommate and I threw him in the car and got him to the hospital."

Abby, slack-jawed, stared at Tracey in disbelief. She felt a foreign feeling in her gut for Ben . . . sympathy.

"He recovered and was out in enough time to take his finals. Which he did, and he passed with flying colors. Then he went home for Christmas break and found out they had failed him anyway. One of the teachers couldn't believe he had managed to take off time to recover and still pass everything. So he was held back a semester."

Abby was flabbergasted. "Are you kidding me? They can't do that, can they?"

Tracey nodded her head. "They can and they did. And he had already failed out a semester in his first year, a lot of kids do. You're on an island, away from home the first time, you know." She shrugged her tan shoulders. "This is his last semester, and if he fails this, it's his three strikes. He's out."

Abby was digesting this information as Tracey continued.

"On top of it, his scholarship? It only covers the semesters he was estimated to be here. Seven semesters. Not the extra two. He and his mom aren't really rolling in the dough. The pressure he is under to pass and then figure out loans on top of everything else? Tremendous pressure. Me? I'd have thrown myself into the sea with some concrete blocks around my ankles," she said with a smirk. "Seriously, it's a lot for a twenty-seven-year-old, who now has a mystery roommate." Tracey grabbed Abby's arm tightly. "I don't think any of this is about you. Not one bit. You have to know that."

Abby couldn't process all the information. Poor Ben, she thought. That's a lot for one person to go through. Hell, it's a lot to go through if you are in the States with your family and friends around you, but to be on a remote island without close family? How has he made it this far by himself?

The water was lapping at the shore in its usual hypnotic way. Abby was zoned out watching the waves slap onto the beach and drag back sand, pulling it as if gifting it back to the Caribbean, thinking about her new roommate's plight.

Abby was sure Leigh had no idea that all of this was happening. Abby knew she needed to try to get in touch with Leigh again to get her to understand why Abby wanted out of the pool house. Not because of her own space this time, but because she wanted Ben to have his.

"Wow. I feel so selfish and immature right now. I made this whole thing about me, not even thinking of the fact that Ben was going through his own drama." She shook her head, annoyed with herself. "I owe him a huge apology."

Tracey's reaction surprised Abby. "No! Do not let him know I told you. He didn't want you to know. I think his ego is bruised from everything, and he doesn't want someone he just met to see him as a failure."

"Failure? Hardly. That's a traumatic experience to come out of, and he's still going? And pushing forward with some laser-beam focus, I might add. Granted, some of that focus is to make me crazy."

"Please, Abby, don't let him know that I told you. If he wants to tell you, let him." She was starting to gather her things and put them in her backpack so they could leave. "Hell, I failed last semester, too. Not because I was stabbed but because I failed an important test. A few of us did, actually. They call us 'Team Repeat.'"

"Team Repeat?"

"Yep. We're all busting our butts to get through this semester and get home. It's not easy down here. Well, to live here. I miss my family and my farm. I want to go to a 7-Eleven or anything but the stores here. I want winter again."

Abby was beginning to gather her things as well when Tracey stopped her.

"You know what's funny? You and Ben are a lot alike." She was laughing as she said it.

"What do you mean?" The last thing Abby wanted was to be compared to her arch-nemesis.

"I can't put my finger on it, Abby, but you're not as different as you may think. Even the way you order your food. I've never met two people that love to smother everything they eat in ketchup." Tracey was thoughtful as she added, "Not to mention, you're two of the most stubborn people I've ever met in my life!"

Abby smacked at Tracey playfully. "Whatever."

"Hey, do you want me to take you to the airport tomorrow so you can get your license?" Abby wasn't sure, but it felt like Tracey was changing the subject.

"I guess so. Will they make me take a test or anything?"

Abby had feared getting behind the wheel on the island. Everyone drove like maniacs, passing each other without abandon and driving at all speeds. She was sure there had to be a set speed limit but that no one had shared such info with anyone else.

"Oh, no! You give them some money, and you have a license. Well, show them the one you have from the U.S. That way, they know you're at least kind of competent." She grinned.

"Let's do it. Maria keeps offering for me to use her little car if I want to get around. I may as well make the most of it while I'm here." Abby was throwing the last of her things into her little pink Puma bag when she stopped. "Tracey, thank you. For everything. The tours, the background on Ben, pushing me to do things like get a license or come out and chill or get away from the other side of the island while you study. I mean it. Thank you."

Tracey shrugged her shoulders as if to get the compliments and praise off her. "You're funny. It's nothing. It's nice to have someone like an adult here to hang out with, too."

Abby cracked up. "'Like an adult.' I think that's the best compliment I have ever gotten!"

The two grabbed their things and made for Tracey's car, making plans for the next day while the monkeys threw leaves at them from their perches above the parking lot.

❦

LA CANTINA WAS LIT UP WHEN TRACEY DROPPED ABBY OFF. More guests were checking in with Maria, asking her questions about the landscape and history of the home. Abby waved at the group and started to make her way to them when she noticed Ziggy was on the roof in the same spot where Buddy had been earlier in the day. Uh-oh, she thought. That can't be good.

Abby rerouted her course and made her way around to the side of the house where Ziggy had parked his ladder. Quickly and easily she took each rung, climbing to the top. As she hit the peak of the house, she looked down and realized how high she was. Closing her eyes and willing herself to carry on, she called out to Ziggy.

"Hey, you find something interesting up here?"

Ziggy was shaking his head. "No, mon. I was in da bathroom, looking at de light fixture you said you needed replaced when I saw de spot."

"Spot?"

"Yeah, da water spot. Must have been from de last storm. So I poked it a little . . . "

Abby had a sick feeling in her stomach. She was eyeing Ziggy when she realized his hair and shirt were covered in a fine white powder. Gathering all of her courage, she went from ladder to roof and carefully crawled over to sit next to Ziggy. When she got to him, she was finally privy to the same scene he was looking down upon.

From what Abby could gather, Ziggy had decided to poke the water spot with a broom handle. He was next to her, insisting, "I didn't push it hard at all, mon. I wouldn't do no ting like dat!" Yet it appeared as if a small storm had landed in the middle of what used to be the bathroom. The hole he created was easily five feet across each way, and tile and plaster were scattered and tossed all about what was once a clean and pristine bathroom.

"Oh. My…"

As the duo was peering down into the bathroom, a familiar

face was suddenly looking back up at them. "Um . . . hi? Can you tell me what happened to our bathroom?"

"Mrs. Bellfield!" Abby was trying not to stutter. "And how is your honeymoon so far?"

＊＊

ABBY SAT AT THE ISLAND IN THE KITCHEN WITH HER HEAD IN her hands. She and Ziggy had quickly covered the hole in the roof with a tarp, managing to secure it in some crazy way between tying it to a tree, to some bricks and around the chimney. While Maria had kept some visiting prospective buyers busy showing them the opposite end of the property, Abby and Ziggy had made quick work of moving the Bellfields from the master suite to the princess suite.

Abby was in the process of discounting the room when Maria came flying in with Ziggy hot on her heels.

"Are you kidding me? You decide today of all days to poke at that water spot? Ziggy! What were you thinking?"

Abby flinched for poor Ziggy. Maria was almost like Leigh, being that she was someone she never wanted to find herself facing off against.

"I didn't tink it would blow up on me!"

Maria just shook her head. "Abby. . . "

Abby held up her hand. "I already put a call in to Anita. She's sending Buddy over first thing in the morning to see if he can patch the ceiling, although I have a feeling his version of 'first thing' is around noon. I managed to lock the doors leading into the master suite, so hopefully we can hide this mini-disaster from anyone looking at the property for just a bit until we have the room under control." Abby nodded at Ziggy. "Ziggy and I moved the Bellfields a few rooms down, and I'm going to suggest we give them half off their total bill since their dream honeymoon suite just got a surprise sunroof."

Maria nodded her head. "It kills me, but you're right." Maria cut her eyes at her husband. "You. I'll deal with you later. Help me get the laundry finished."

Knowing there wasn't anything else she could do until tomorrow, Abby made a beeline for the pool house. What she really wanted right now was a cold drink and to put her feet up.

Ben was home and actually sitting in the living room getting his rugby gear together when she entered. Instead of greeting him or making any acknowledgment of his presence, Abby came in and went into the kitchen to grab a bottle of water. When she pulled her head out of the fridge, Ben had joined her. In fact, he was blocking the doorway so she wasn't able to really get out of the kitchen.

"Can I help you?" she asked.

"I'm going to play rugby in a few minutes, and I wanted to know if --" Ben was swallowing hard here -- "well, if you wanted to come out and maybe meet some more people. See a rugby match."

Abby was surprised, and was sure it showed in her expression. She took a sip from her bottle and slowly nodded her head.

"That would be really nice, Ben. Thank you for inviting me."

"Well, I know you and Trace have been hanging out. She really likes you." He looked away, searching for some words. "I'm not an easy person to be around, Abby, especially the last few months. And that's not your fault."

Wow, Abby thought, communication from Ben. This is a monumental moment.

As if reading her mind, Ben cleared his throat and said, "This doesn't mean I'm okay with things now. It just means . . . well, it means I'm going to try."

"Fair enough." Abby put out her hand for Ben to shake. "I promise not to be pushy nor will I try to clean."

Ben took her hand. "Actually, Abby, I'd be crazy to not let you clean this place." He looked around sheepishly. "You're right."

Abby was such a sicko when it came to being orderly that her face lit up at the prospect of getting to really attack, clean and organize the pool house.

"I feel like it's my birthday," she replied dreamily while batting her lashes jokingly in his direction.

Ben laughed and pointed to the clock on the stove. "I'm out of here in the next ten minutes. Meet me by the car, and we'll head over to the field. Oh, I forgot." He pointed to a cell phone on the counter in the kitchen. "Maria dropped that here for you earlier. The number's written down on the paper beside it. She said it's filled with fifty EC for you to start."

Abby's face twisted, not understanding what he meant.

"That means a decent amount of pay-as-you-go time. But don't make calls if you can help it. Best to text here. If you want to make any local calls, use the phone in the main house. I programmed my number and a few others for you."

With that, Ben slipped out the door to stretch and run drills by the pool before they took off.

Abby couldn't believe the change of events. What had happened to make Ben be nicer to her? Maybe Tracey had said something to him? Maybe Maria and Ziggy or Cutty? Who cared, as long as there was some kind of conversation happening.

She picked up the phone. It was ancient, reminiscent of

when cell phones were getting popular a few years back in the States. Not quite the technology she was used to, but it would do for the purpose it was meant to serve. She scrolled through the names and saw Ben had added not only his and Tracey's numbers, but the numbers of Leigh, Maria, Ziggy and Cutty, too. She took the piece of paper with her new number scribbled on it and put it in her pocket. She would memorize it as soon as she could.

Abby felt a swat on her leg. Looking down, she saw that one of the two felines was giving her an unusual amount of love.

"Want something, sticky paws?" Abby narrowed her eyes and glared at the small, manipulative creature. She looked at the food dishes on the floor and realized they were empty. "Fine. Make-a-deal time, guys: I feed you, and you leave me alone. Got it?"

Abby began opening cabinets, looking for cat food. She found where Ben had stored some of his vet scrubs (In the kitchen? Really?) and also spied a portable grill that she knew they could put to good use. She rooted through more cabinets and was about to give up when she saw a bright green bag, labeled "cat food," tucked behind a box and a half-filled grocery bag.

As she reached over to grab the cat food, her arm brushed up against the grocery bag, causing it to topple over. Its contents came with it, spilling into a flustered pile on the floor in front of her. Pictures, magazines and a few books came falling out.

Abby bent down, gently pushing the kitties out of the way so she could pick up the mess. The magazines were addressed to Ben and there were some that were Leigh's as well. A few random items, like T-shirts and suntan lotion, had scattered along with the clutter. Abby shook her head as she admired her ability to make such a big mess in such a short time.

She was trying to gather all of the items as quickly as she could when she noticed a few of the pictures that had fallen out of the jumbled mess were taken of someone very familiar.

Her father.

Abby slid from a kneeling position to a cross-legged one as she began to look at the pictures that surrounded her. She couldn't help but smile, her father looked so happy in every photo. She didn't recognize any of the backgrounds, so she wasn't sure where he was or whose home he was in, nor did she recognize the people he was with. There were a few people that kept appearing in some of the same pictures, mainly a woman and a tanned blond man with the most perfect set of teeth Abby had ever seen. Abby reasoned that they were people he worked with or even old friends she had just never met, even though the blond man had an air of familiarity she couldn't put her finger on. All she knew was that her dad looked happy.

Looking at the photos, seeing him, she could almost see and hear the sounds of the hospital room on the last day of his life. There was a machine that made high-pitched beeping sounds as it struggled to keep him alive, and his labored breathing was being aided by another machine at the end of a long tube. Abby had sat there while her mother had stepped outside to talk to other family members, updating them on his condition. It had become a DNR request, or "do not resuscitate." Abby had sat next to his bed, talking to him about her schoolwork she needed to do and reminding him that she needed him for her Homecoming dance photos -- it was to be the next week and she was on the Homecoming Court that year. The fathers always brought their daughters out onto the football field at halftime for introductions, as per school traditions. Only this year, Abby didn't think she would even make it to see the Homecoming Game.

Abby had closed her eyes, just for a minute, and put her head down on her father's hand so she could sneak in a good cry that day. When she had, she felt his index finger twitch slightly. The nurses had said that when patients were in a coma, they sometimes had muscle reactions. She had gotten used to seeing his muscles jerk periodically and thought nothing of this one. Until it happened again, only this time it felt more deliberate.

Bolting into an upright position, Abby found herself looking into his father's eyes, and they were finally open. Abby's heart had leapt into the air as she thought, This is it! There he was smiling at her and moving his mouth, maybe he was trying to say something? All she knew was that he was awake. She opened her mouth to yell for the nurse when it happened . . .

The sounds of frenzied beeping and alarms echoed in her memory bank. Abby had fallen on his chest, fighting her own tears and begging him not to leave her. When she threw herself on his chest, she noticed he was desperately trying to get her to look at him. That was when she noticed he was mouthing the words, "I love you," over and over. His hand was feebly reaching up to pet her head one last time before his heart finally gave out and he took his last breath. Abby had known that day that things were not going to be the same ever again without her dad.

Summoning herself back to the present, she gathered her findings and straightened them, gently placing them all back into the bag, making a mental note to go through it all later. She knew if these were here because Leigh had brought them down with her, then Leigh would want them to be kept in the same condition. These must be keepsakes that Leigh is storing here for some reason, she thought to herself. Their father's passing had done a number on everyone -- some days Abby thought Leigh had been affected most of all -- and it took the trio their own time to recover from the blow. Leigh had faced her own demons at the time, as she was put in a position where she had to step up and become the head of the family in the aftermath of his death. Abby's mother had all but shut down and Abby was too young to understand much, leaving them reliant on Leigh.

As she placed the last photo back into the bag, Abby patted the top one fondly, closing the door again to the memories of a time when her heart had truly been shredded.

Abby then began to place the books and magazines back in the bag as well, when one of the books, The Great Gatsby, smacked down onto the floor next to her again. It had fallen open to a page where someone had made an inscription. "To my pride and joy: May the world always be your oyster. Love, Dad."

She recognized the handwriting and her heart swelled with emotion. Their dad had given both his girls special editions of The Great Gatsby as presents when they were children. It was a tradition his own father had started that he passed down when he had begun his family. Abby's copy was back home, at her apartment in Los Angeles on a bookshelf next to a framed picture of her and her dad. But why was this here, with Ben's things? Were these his things and Leigh's, too?

Even though she didn't know how this book had found its home here, one thing was for sure; Abby couldn't deny her sadness that her sister had been given twenty years more with their dad than she had. Maybe that's why Leigh keeps the things he gave her here, so I won't see them, she thought. She smiled at the thought of her sister wanting to spare her feelings.

Abby was snapped back to the present by Ben, who was calling her name from outside. She took everything -- photos, cards and books -- and quickly tossed it all back into the bag, which she then shoved into the cabinet in its original location. The cats were still eyeing her and meowing louder than ever, as if blaming her for their hunger.

"Crap . . . last thing I need is for Ben to think I was going through his things!" She stood up and grabbed the bag of cat food, realizing she was conversing out loud with the two felines. "Not that you can help me, but do you know why my sis has her things stored here at Ben's?"

The two kitties caterwauled in Abby's general direction, the volume of their cries increasing as they realized she was holding the bag and about to pour them dinner.

She added the food to their dish before she ran over to the front door to see what Ben needed. He was outside on the ground stretching his hamstrings, calling to her.

"I also wanted to tell you that some of my friends saw you with Tracey the other day in town. They think you're hot."

Even though her mind was filled with questions, Abby couldn't help but smile hearing this news.

"Is that why you want me to go to the game? If you're hoping for a virgin sacrifice, I've got news for you, Ben. That ship sailed a long time ago," she countered playfully.

Ben laughed at her answer. "No, I just thought . . . Tropical island, visitor, young college boys . . . " he was grinning ear to ear and clearly enjoyed making Abby uncomfortable.

"Ben. No. In the same way you didn't want me to clean the house before? Do. Not. Set. Me. Up. With anyone. Nobody. No friends, no hook-ups. No 'Oops, my buddy just happens to be here', okay? Look, we all have our issues. Mine happens to be having any kind of relationship -- fleeting or long-term. Got it?"

Ben threw his hands up as if she were pointing a gun at him. "Whoa, Captain Serious. I just meant that people think you're cute."

Abby realized that in her typical chick way she had just taken a simple statement and made it into a thousand other meanings. She realized that Ben did have a point. Here she was, in her mid-30s, on an island surrounded by hot, rugged young men, in their mid-to-late 20s. If they thought she was cute, then she really did need to embrace it. She had seen some cute boys herself when out with Tracey. Apparently, she still had yet to enjoy the nightlife on the island. Tracey always went out on the weekends, but Abby felt like she would be out of place, so she had never gone anywhere except Ricky's when it was dark to hang with Cutty.

"I'm sorry, Ben. I'm still smarting from the last breakup. I'm gonna grab my things. Need anything from inside before I close up?"

He shook his head and went back to concentrating on his warm-up. Abby grabbed a few extra water bottles from the fridge to throw in her bag as she headed out the door. She was actually excited to do something that involved Ben. She had a feeling they had finally turned a small curve in their relationship and was light on her feet as she made her way out to his car, with the discovery of the book forgotten for the time being.

THE RHODES BOYS WON THE RUGBY MATCH, WHICH WAS NO surprise. The boys from the medical school were known more for their ability to screw around than to be serious about anything, including sports. In celebration of the win, the team headed down to Pirate's Bay, one of the beach bars on Frigate Bay.

Abby had tried to get Ben to drop her off at La Cantina, but he insisted on dragging her with him to the after-party.

"You need to meet more people. If you meet more people, my life is easier," he stated matter-of-factly.

Abby couldn't deny his reasoning.

"I get it. You introduce me around and eventually at night you can study in complete silence?" Two could play this wicked game. Ben didn't realize Leigh had trained her in tactical verbiage.

"Exactly. If I have my way, you might be home one night a week."

Pirate's Bay was hopping when they arrived. It was a Thursday night, and apparently on Thursdays they were known for hosting the bonfire to go to on the island. The Frigate Bay area was surrounded by rental condos and hotels that allowed tourists to access the beach and island bars with ease. Palm trees flowed with the breeze, swaying back and forth in the wind, and the sound of island steel drums played on the ears.

One area of the beach had been cordoned off specifically for the celebration. As Ben and Abby walked up, a buzzed Tracey greeted them.

"Hey, you!" she yelled as she grabbed Ben into a big hug. "Congrats on the win! Not that anyone thought you guys weren't going to make it happen."

Ben was blushing as a few other ladies came over to offer congratulatory hugs and praise for a game well played. Abby watched Ben as the ladies were flirting with him. He looked uncomfortable and kept looking at her a little sheepishly. It was obvious to Abby that he was a popular guy among his fellow students.

Abby made her way to the crowded bar and ordered a drink for herself. The employees were dragging firewood out to the large fire pit in preparation for the bonfire that would start as soon as it was dark. She let out a long sigh.

As the bartender placed the drink in front of her, Abby reached for her wallet. He waved her off.

"No, mon. It's taken care of."

Abby was confused. "Huh? What do you mean?"

The bartender nodded his head toward the other side of the bar. "That guy over there. He got it for you."

Abby looked across the bar, searching for a familiar face so she could say thank you for her drink. As she was combing the crowd for someone she knew, a set of piercing blue eyes met her gaze and she knew it was him. He was smiling at her like he had from the balcony the other night at Ricky's.

Who are you? she thought to herself. He couldn't be too bad, since she had seen him around with Cutty and Ziggy. He was probably harmless, but who was he? She smiled, toasting the air as if to say thank you, and began to gather her things to go introduce herself to the handsome stranger.

As she reached the opposite side of the bar, she didn't see the man she wanted to thank. Her heart sunk just a little, when out of the corner of her eye something moving caught her attention. It was the mysterious, good-looking stranger, and it appeared he had commandeered a few chairs near the bonfire for them.

Abby slowly made her way over to him, lowering herself

into one of the empty chairs. She smiled at her new friend. "Thanks."

"You're welcome," he said in a distinctly British accent. He put his hand out. "I'm J. D."

Abby took his hand, feeling an energetic surge inside her as she touched him.

"I'm Abby."

The two strangers smiled at each other for what seemed like hours, but in real time was a matter of mere seconds. They both took swigs of their cocktails and began talking at once. Abby threw her hands up and gestured his way, saying, "No . . . you go first."

J.D. grinned at her, his blue eyes piercing into her brown ones even through the dark night.

"I tried to come say hi and introduce myself to you before. At Ricky's."

Abby cocked her head to one side. "Really? The night you were on the balcony?"

He smiled at her, his eyes slowly wandering over her body and coming to a full rest on her lips as he answered simply, "Yes."

She was mesmerized by this man, feeling an almost animalistic pull toward him, but also felt that was a ridiculous thought to have since they really didn't know each other. As she was taking another drink from her rum punch, she realized she still had her wallet in her hand from when she was at the bar. She'd never gotten around to putting it back into her bag.

As she was returning her wallet to her purse, she heard her phone ringing. And surprise of all surprises, it was Leigh. Abby silenced the call, but knew it was one she needed to deal with now. Handsome, hot, mysterious man or not. J.D. would have to wait.

Regretfully, she looked at J.D, showing him her phone.

"I'm sorry, but I have to take this. I've been waiting for this call."

"Of course." J.D. smiled at Abby, sucking her in with the sexiness of his crooked grin. "I'm staying here on the island for a bit. At the Frigate Beach Hotel, above Ricky's, actually. You?"

The phone was lighting up, signaling Leigh's presence even from miles away. Abby was feeling a bit of pressure and needed to handle this call now, but felt torn because she wanted to stay with J.D.

"I'm uh . . . at a bed-and-breakfast not too far from Ricky's." She showed him the phone in all of its lit-up glory once more. "I'm so sorry . . . Can I take a rain check?"

He nodded, smiling at her as she stood to go. As she was walking away, she felt his eyes boring into her. She turned around to smile, but he was already by her side.

"Tomorrow. Midday, lunchtime. Ricky's Café . . . will you meet me?"

Something told her she shouldn't, but she decided she would . . . and was actually thinking of saying no but realized her head had already nodded yes. As she was whispering yes slowly, he leaned in and kissed her cheek, sending a flood of warmth all through her body. She hit the talk button on the mobile just so she could break the spell.

"Hello? Leigh?"

Abby was straining to hear over the noise around her.

"Well, there's a voice I haven't heard in ages. How do you like St. Kitts?"

Abby wasn't sure if she wanted to cry, laugh or shout when she heard her sister's voice.

"Where do I start? Leigh, there is so much to talk about. You've caught me at Pirate's Bay with Ben."

Leigh hesitated slightly on the other end.

"You're out with Ben?"

"Well, yes. He's finally being nice to me. Well, as of today he is. Of course," Abby added in an attempt at being humorous, "when dealing with someone who is possibly bipolar, one must expect the days to be up and down. Honestly, Leigh, it could go one way or the other with him."

Abby heard a slow breath being let out on the other end of the line.

"I'm glad it's easier now. I figured if you knew you'd have to share a home with someone during all of this, there was no way I'd get you to go down there."

"Well, you were right." Abby sat quietly for a second, deciding that maybe now wasn't the time to launch into her sis. "It's been tough, but we'll see. Anyway, how are you? Everyone here seems happy and the repairs are flowing right along." Except for the part where one of the bathrooms now has the best view the outdoors can offer.

"Maria said you've been a great help to her. With you doing things around the inn, she is able to actually help with the sale now."

Okay, good, Abby thought. Nice call. Good discussion. Maybe I can ask her . . .

"When are we going to talk about the fact that you own a bed-and-breakfast, Leigh?"

Abby could feel a palpable tension coursing through her over the airwaves. "Eventually. I want to explain all of it to you, and I will. It just has to wait until some other cards are played out. The less you know, the better, at least for the time being. Daryl is already overly suspicious of why I have you

98

on St. Kitts. I told him you're down there acting as administrative assistant while a hybridizer gets his greenhouse set up."

Abby could hear Leigh blowing out smoke from a cigarette on the other end. Both George girls had a knack for picking up cigarettes when they were stressed.

"You're stressed. You're smoking."

"No, I'm not."

"I can hear you blowing the smoke out." I'd be stressed, too, if all I did was lie, Abby thought.

There was another exhale sound on the end of the line, but quieter.

"No, I'm not. Must be the steel drums in your ears. And you're one to talk."

"I've actually quit. Not having a job makes you rethink what you're spending." Abby wanted to steer the conversation back. "Leigh, are you sure you don't want to talk about it? And by it, I mean, why you wouldn't tell me about La Cantina being an inn?"

The quiet was deafening for Abby, even though she was in the middle of a bar with music and chatter all around her. Leigh was still holding something back, but knowing her like she did, there was no use in trying to get it out of her.

"Not yet. Just know I only do things because I have a plan."

A plan. Abby rolled her eyes at the thought.

"Okay, Leigh. Anyway, am I going to get to go back into the main house again at all? It's just really tight in the pool house, and Ben needs to pass his last semester . . . "

Leigh cut Abby off rather abruptly. "I am more than aware of Ben's needs, Abby. He emailed me that you were making the first few weeks quite difficult for him to get his studying done. What were you thinking? Turning the TV up so loud he couldn't study? Abby, you need to be the adult here."

"What are you talking about?" Abby was honestly confused.

"Abby, his hours are rough for him. He's training, well schooling, to be a vet. This costs money." More silence, then she continued, "He said you were complaining about his getting up early and rustling around?"

"Maybe he meant when he slams the doors at 6:30 a.m.?"

"Either way, it's apparent that you guys are the Odd Couple, at least from what he's been saying in his emails to me."

Unbelievable. Ben had been emailing her sister telling her it was Abby behind all of the living issues. She was watching Ben dance in the middle of a circle of ladies while Leigh went on to berate her.

"I need for you to be the adult, Abby. I want to put you back in the main house, but you need to be in the pool house for the time being. If there is a chance I can rent any rooms out, I need to take it. Ben now understands this and has agreed to be a little more . . . how do I say this? . . . forgiving of the circumstances. So, now, you need to be the one to strap on your boots and make it work."

Abby could not believe what she was hearing. This explains the change in Ben's demeanor. Leigh must have spoken to him and was probably paying him off to help "take care" of me. She wanted to scream, "You are being played!" to her sister, but refrained.

Abby felt the rage coursing through her body. She was still watching Ben as he danced around, toasting his friends from the rugby team. It was during one of these dance-toast maneuvers that he aimed his beer bottle in the air in a toast across the beach to Abby. Against her better judgment, she smiled a tight, "up yours" smile and raised her glass as well.

"Abby? Are you there?" Leigh was piping up again in her ear.

"Oh yeah," Abby retorted. "I'm here." There was no way she could let this fall to the side. Abby fired back, "You have been M.I.A., Leigh, at least to me. You have no idea what I've been dealing with down here with dear, young Ben. The fact that you would take his side without even speaking with me? It's beyond reason. He's a renter, for Pete's sake." Remembering the book she had found earlier in the day, she added for effect, "And I think he may be trying to steal from you!"

"Steal from me? Steal what, Abby?"

Abby was flustered. She honestly wasn't sure, but she was sure that she was really mad at Ben. "I found your book, the one from Dad, The Great Gatsby. Ben had it shoved in with his things. There were some pictures, too. Leigh, I really think --"

"Abby. You think Ben is stealing from me? I'm sorry, but not Ben. I've never had problems from him. Ever."

Abby couldn't believe it. Her sister didn't believe her. "Leigh, I tell you I think he's stealing from you, and I find what is evidence and . . . Fine. Where's your book, Leigh?"

Leigh was quick to stop Abby here. "I won't hear any more of this. It's petty, Abby. Be an adult. Stop behaving like a child."

"Where's your book, Leigh? And why are some of your things stored here? Did he swipe them, too?"

Silence on the other end. "Abby, I'm sure the book is here in the house, in fact I'm 100% sure that it is. I just don't know where it is among my kids' things, Daryl's, your stuff . . . "

"I know where mine is. I can tell you exactly where it is."

"Abby, enough! I'm not going to listen to any more of these accusations. Suck it up."

Abby felt like she had just been backhanded across the face. "But I'm your sister. Why are you not listening to anything I'm saying?"

Even in her pleading, Abby's argument was falling heavily on deaf ears. The fact that Leigh was not even continuing the conversation told Abby that she had made up her mind already that it was all Abby's fault. Why can't I make her see my side? she thought sadly.

"Look, Abby, I have to go. Got a meeting in an hour. Just make sure you go easy on him and stay out of the way. You are there with a specific job: to help ready the inn for sale for me. Got it?"

Abby didn't want to let it go. "But Leigh . . . "

"Abby. Stop this. Now. Do you hear me?" Leigh spat this out as if she had just eaten a raw piece of meat.

"Loud and clear," Abby spat back as Leigh disconnected the call.

Abby was still reeling from the conversation when Tracey came bopping over to her spot at the bar, the bonfire silhouetting her frame. There were people everywhere, and it was getting more crowded by the moment. Abby was feeling cornered and irked.

"Hey! Come over here and have a drink with me. I have some friends I want to introduce you to."

"Tracey, it's not a good time. In fact --" Abby was gathering her things on the bar -- "I'm going to walk to the Royal Palms Casino and get a cab. I want to go home."

Tracey stopped her from getting up. "Wait, don't go yet. It's a great night to be out. Stay and have fun. Please?"

"I can't. Just tell Ben I left and I'll see him either when he comes in and plays his guitar loudly like the drunk jerk he can be or in the morning when he slams the door and it wakes me up, okay?"

Abby grabbed her bag, threw what she thought was some EC down for the bartender and headed up the stretch of dirt road that led to the Royal Palms.

As she marched up the road, Abby was fuming. So, she thought, you emailed my sister. Saying I was causing the problems? Oh, you've got another thing coming if you think I'm going to roll over and take this one lying down, Ben!

She was so busy plotting she didn't hear his feet hitting the ground behind her as he came running up next to her on the path.

"Abby, wait!" He was out of breath when he reached her.

Abby's eyes were filled with fury as she spun on him and let him have it.

"Wait for what, Ben? For you to do something else to make me feel like crap? Or perhaps you want to email my sister again to tell on me. Does that make you feel better? I'm such an idiot to think that today you were actually being nice to me. You're an asshole!"

She was still marching up the road, except now Ben was keeping in time with her.

"What are you talking about, Abby? Emailing Leigh?"

Abby stopped and took one of the deep "in through the nose and out through the mouth" breaths that she seemed to do so much.

"Leigh just phoned. Said you had emailed her and told her I was being difficult," she said as she looked Ben in the eyes. "What I need to know is if there is any inkling of truth to that statement."

Ben looked like a kid caught with his hand in the cookie

jar. His eyes dropped to the ground, and he wasn't able to maintain eye contact with Abby.

"Abby, I . . . "

Abby held up her hand. "What is wrong with you, Ben? You email my sister with issues that are actually my issues, things I was trying to talk to you about, and say I'm the one causing all the problems? Do you realize she is my sister? The person who should be listening to me has now taken the word of a complete stranger. At least a complete stranger to me, and one --" she was wound up and going now -- "who has bipolar tendencies like I would not have ever believed."

Ben looked like he had been whipped. His face read "I'm sorry," and he had no fight in his demeanor.

"Abby, I can explain. First, you need to let me apologize. Then, I really want to explain . . . "

"No, Ben. That's okay. I don't think I want an apology or an explanation at this moment. What I want is to go back home and go to sleep on my air mattress. Hopefully, I won't have to patch another hole in it."

Ben jerked his head up, grinning. "A-hole?"

Abby saw no humor. "Not 'a-hole.' A ripped-open hole from one of the untrimmed claws of your crappy cats. I didn't mention it because I didn't want to add one more issue to the Thanksgiving-sized plate of problems we've been having. No, I fixed the stupid hole. And kept my mouth shut."

They had reached the taxi stand at the Royal Palms. Abby was reaching in her purse for her wallet.

"By the way, Ben. That's what adults do. We keep our mouths shut about the little things and broach the topics of the bigger ones. Not email our landlords to come and help us, please," she spat at him, taunting him to argue with her. Abby realized that though she was making sense, she was sounding a little childish.

"Please, don't take a cab. Let me drive you," Ben offered.

"No." Abby went up to the counter to make arrangements for her ride.

The man behind the counter eyed her up and down. He had heard Abby and Ben coming in the night before he had seen them. Their argument had been echoing, reverberating off the walls of the condos and hotels in the walkway.

"I know, girl. You want a cab. I hear ya moanin' about it from over dere," he said, rolling his eyes at her. "Where you go to?"

Abby told him La Cantina, then asked the fare so she could make sure she had enough EC to pay. One thing she had learned from Cutty and Ziggy was to always pay in EC. Paying in U.S. currency made them think you were a tourist, and some locals loved to overcharge them.

The fare was around 40 EC; Abby went in her purse to get it out and realized she only had 20. She was rustling around in there more when she realized she had overpaid her bill at Pirate's Bay with EC and U.S. dollars.

Abby turned around and saw Ben was still standing there, talking to one of the cabbies and watching her wrestle with her purse. She walked over to where Ben stood, nodded curtly at the cab driver and asked Ben, "May I borrow some money? I overpaid at the bar, and now I don't have enough to get home."

"You can go hit de ATM at de hotel." The helpful cabbie pointed toward the Royal Palms.

"No, I want to ask my friend here if he has it, but thanks." Abby realized how crappy she sounded, but she just couldn't help it. "Seems he has a few things of my families he's holding on to. Giving me cab fare shouldn't be a problem."

Ben was taken aback. "What do you mean by that, Abby?"

"I really don't want to get into it now, but I may as well tell you I found the book, Ben."

Abby had made the last statement so dramatically that when she looked up, she expected Ben to be wide-eyed and fumbling for an excuse. But when her eyes met his, they were blank.

"Book? What are you talking about?"

Abby shook her head. "My sister's book. It's from our father. I found it in the kitchen, shoved in a bag with a bunch of her things and yours. It has sentimental value, Ben!"

Ben's face was twisted with confusion. "I honestly have no idea what you're talking about. If any of your sister's things are mixed up with --"

Abby couldn't hear his excuses right now. There will be plenty of time when I get up tomorrow to figure out why he has that book, she thought. So, as maturely as she could, she covered her ears and shook her head at Ben. "Not listening anymore. Done."

"Let me drive you home, Abby. Please," Ben begged her. "I really think you may be drunker than you think you are."

Abby stared down at the sand. When she looked up at Ben again, her eyes pleaded with him. "Please, Ben. Let me go. I want to go home. Or at least go to the place I have to call home for the time being."

This time, Abby's face read of her feelings, clear enough that Ben saw it, too. The sadness, the hurt.

"Abby," he began.

The look she gave him made him stop. Instead, he reached for his wallet and pulled out 40 EC and handed it to her.

"Should be more than enough to cover it," he said as he grabbed her hand and put the money in her palm.

Abby nodded at him and whispered, "Thank you," as she made her way up to the man at the counter who was coordinating her ride.

She climbed in the first cab that pulled up, glanced back at Ben and the other cabbie, and then strapped on her seatbelt. As a silent tear rolled down her cheek, she thought about how all she wanted right now was her apartment in Los Angeles, her home, her cat and her friends. St. Kitts was feeling more like Hades tonight than paradise.

CHAPTER 6

THE KITCHEN OF LA CANTINA COULD ONLY BE COMPARED TO an orchestra performing at the Hollywood Bowl on a summer's night with Maria center stage as conductor. She was in the midst of making Eggs Benedict à la Ziggy (which meant the eggs were scrambled and not poached) and waffles with a topping of crème fraîche sprinkled with cinnamon and nutmeg served with heated maple syrup on the side.

Abby had come over for her usual morning coffee and was greeted by a stressed Maria as she entered the kitchen.

"Abby! Please, help me. Ziggy is busy trying to help some guests plan a day outing on the island and the other guests all want breakfast, right now at this very moment, and Buddy should be here soon to get started on the roof." Her face was flushed and she was breathless as she moved from counter to stove and back again, balancing all of the duties hurriedly, but with ease and precision. "I'm in a time crunch."

Abby nodded, grabbed two plates, and waited for her marching orders. Thank goodness I washed my face and pulled my hair back before I came over, she thought, as she used her butt to push open the swinging door that led from the kitchen into the dining area.

As Maria completed each order, Abby helped get the plates out to the main communal table for the early risers. Guests were seated not only in the dining area, but also in the living room, lazing around on the couches watching the news and drinking coffee.

Once everyone was fed, coffees refilled, and plans for tours and dives made, Abby, Maria and Ziggy all gathered in the kitchen to have their breakfast and coffee.

As they ate, Abby told Maria about the events of the night before: the conversation with her sister, her discovery of Ben's things mixed with Leigh's and the argument that had ended her night.

Maria chewed thoughtfully, listening to Abby and letting her vent. When Maria did open her mouth to offer insight, Abby could tell she was being particularly mindful of the words she chose.

"Ben is a special bird, Abby. Not to say he deserves special treatment or that you deserved the treatment your sister gave you. It's just that, well, there are two sides to every story. Be it an email or a stray book. Don't jump to no conclusions, girl."

Abby pondered her words, watching Ziggy as he shoveled his food into his mouth, washing it down with his mug of coffee and then getting up to refill all of their mugs. Talk about special birds, Abby thought as she grinned to herself.

"I don't think I understand, Maria. Two sides? Like his side and Leigh's?"

She shook her head. "No. Ben's side of the story and your side of the story. Ever thought that they just may be different?"

Is she smoking crack? Abby thought. Of course they are

going to be different. I'm a decent person and he's an asshole. Done and done.

"I feel like I know what you mean, but I'm pretty sure my sentiments are going to be just the opposite of what you are intending to get across to me." Abby sighed. "Just lay it on me, Maria, don't hold back. Tell me what you see."

Maria shot a look in Ziggy's direction, and in one swift motion he took his coffee and disappeared from the room as if into thin air. Abby braced herself for Maria to let her have it. Maria was taking her time, stirring her coffee and staring at the swirly look of the creamer as it integrated into the murky depths of her mug. Abby couldn't tell if she was gearing up for the kill or maybe calming herself down. After a few moments that felt like an eternity, Maria looked up at Abby and spoke.

"Sometimes, things happen for a reason, Abby. We never know what it is. It's just the way of the world. You lost your job and you weren't expecting to. Then you got the chance to come here. You come here and think you're going to be in a nice house, dealing with a few things like papers, have a vacation, relax, then get back to life in L.A. Then you don't; instead, you get --" she pointed to the pool house -- "Ben. And friends, like Cutty, Ziggy and me."

She took a sip of her coffee and looked intently at Abby.

"Has Ben told you about his problems with school?"

This surprised Abby, since Tracey had told her to keep it to herself.

"Well, he didn't, but someone else told me."

Maria nodded. "Not easy on him. Your sister knows that he has been through a lot, and she has actually helped him a lot. A lot more than even he knows. Did you know Leigh footed his bill for the hospital trip since his mom couldn't afford the whole thing?"

Abby slowly shook her head no.

"If she didn't tell you, then she doesn't want you to know, I assume. Although, I hate to assume." She winked at Abby. "It makes an ass out of you and me."

Maria was grinning, and it made Abby smile as well.

"I know you've been thrown into the lion's den or the fire or some sayin', girl. But it's time for you to adjust, just as Ben wanted to adjust, too. I knew he sent the emails to Leigh. In fact, she forwarded them all to me so I could talk to Ben and try to head off any issues here at the pass. And I thought that was what I did yesterday when I sat with him and we had a long talk about 'Abby's side of things.'"

Now it made a little more sense, Abby thought. It was like a puzzle, and Abby had just found another piece of it. "You talked to him yesterday, and that's why he was friendlier. It wasn't because Leigh told him to or he'd have to get out?"

Maria hooted with the very thought. "He's paying rent, girl! She's not letting him go anywhere as long as the roof is paid up. No, I --" she patted her chest and bobbed her head up and down -- "sat with Ben right at the pool there and we talked about being nicer to others because we don't always know the whole story. Maybe I should teach a class and make you both take it."

Abby felt less like a thirty-five-year-old and more like an eighteen-year-old who had just been scolded, but in the kindest way possible. She's right, Abby thought. You never know the whole story. I jumped to a conclusion because of my own trust issues. Now, I look at his side. I come in, I want to take over . . . The poor guy never had a chance with me being such an aggressive "friendly" gal.

Instead of responding, Abby stood up and walked around the table to hug Maria. They stood there in silence for a second, and then Maria called out to Ziggy. Seemed he had appeared at the screen door in the kitchen like a dog wanting to get back in.

"You old fool, get in here. You got people to take on tour. Get ready and go. And you --" she turned to Abby and stroked her head -- "you need to talk to Ben when he gets home from school later. Make peace."

Abby smiled at Maria and was about to say thank you when she realized what she had just said.

"Maria, did you say when Ben is home from school later?"

Maria looked at Abby quizzically.

"Yes, girl. Didn't you see his car is gone? He got up early today and went to school at 6 a.m. Like he does every day. Maybe you're still a little drunk?"

"Maybe, Maria," Abby answered. "Maybe."

Abby headed out the door to go back to the little pool house. What Maria didn't seem to understand was that Ben had left this morning at his usual time, at 6 a.m., to go to school.

And Abby never heard the screen door slam.

❦

WITH BUDDY IN PLACE ON THE ROOF, ABBY SLIPPED DOWN TO the office in the inn so she could enter a few numbers for the day's accounting. She and Maria had been co-bookkeeping in case the buyers needed answers fast, and so far they had done a great job staying on top of things daily. Maria had used to take one day a week, Sundays, to enter all of the data. With Abby there, Maria was actually able to enjoy her Sundays with a little more freedom and wasn't as tied to the inn as she had been.

As Abby was pushing away from the desk to go check on

Buddy, the phone rang. Knowing Maria was busy cleaning the rooms, she grabbed it.

"La Cantina!"

The voice that greeted Abby was laced with a clipped accent, definitely British and female.

"Hello, I'm calling on behalf of Jack Rhys. He'd like a reservation at your inn."

"Great! Let me get the book out and we can get him set up."

"He is hoping to have some time with the owners while there."

At first surprised by this request, she quickly guessed he must be interested in the inn. "Is he looking at the property, since it's for sale?"

"Yes. He's in the area presently and is planning on meeting with the real estate agent."

"Okay, I'll note the reservation and make sure the owners are aware."

Abby logged the new guest into the computer and wrote Maria a note referencing the guest's intentions as a potential buyer of the inn. As she was finalizing the reservation, she felt sad to think that this gorgeous place would be sold soon, but happy knowing it would all be taken care of for Leigh. She knew her sister wanted to sell it and move on.

Abby took a few moments to go over the comings and goings of guests and to return a few messages on the inn's voicemail before she made her way to Ricky's for her lunch date with J.D.

Abby arrived at Ricky's right at noon, and found J.D. by himself at a table, and alone on the deck except for Miss C., who was tending bar. As Abby strolled up to the table, Miss C.

began making throw-up motions from behind the bar, teasing her. J.D. caught her in mid-act.

"You two know each other well?" he asked.

Abby shook her head. "No . . . I actually got really sick here on one of my first nights out. Threw up in the Caribbean and everything."

J.D. grinned at his date. "I heard about you. Captain Cutty loves you."

She giggled. "Yes, he does. I saw you chatting with Cutty and Ziggy, too. You seem to know everyone here pretty well."

"Well, let's just say it's my job to know people." He slid a menu across the table to Abby. "Veggie burgers are okay here, but the conch fritters . . . "

"You don't have to tell me," she replied, grinning. "So, are you running for office?"

He stared at her in quizzical amusement. "Funny. But no. I'm kind of the perpetual tourist. I take a few weeks out of every summer and hit the islands to see whatever I can. I like to get to know the locals, makes life that much more interesting."

Abby wasn't sure if she should believe him or not, but really didn't care at the moment.

"Well, I'm from L.A. Transplanted here for just a bit to help my family with some business, and then I go back." She grinned at him evilly. "And my business is very hush-hush, so don't expect me to tell you anything more."

"Agreed. Let's both be mysterious, then, shall we?" His British accent dripped with a sultry edge that made her heart skip a beat.

Miss C. arrived just then with their drinks. They raised their glasses into the air and they toasted each other.

"To mysterious British men that jump islands for fun."

J.D. chuckled, retorting, "To mysterious American women that won't explain why they're transplanted."

Abby put her cocktail down after a hearty swig, and looked her lunch companion square in the eyes. "So, tell me something about you no one else knows."

J.D. put down his glass as well, contemplating his answer.

"No, don't think about what you are going to say. Just say the first thing that you think of. Go."

"Okay. Umm . . . that I give to charity every month."

"Okay . . . good one. Cute and kind."

He smirked in her direction, then pointed at Abby. "And you?"

"That I can play the drums, not very well, but I can keep a beat."

J.D.'s look was of sheer admiration. "I don't think I can even keep a beat. Two left feet, here."

Abby shrugged her shoulders. "What can I say? It's a gift."

They were about to order their food when Abby's phone rang. It was Buddy, and since she had left him on the roof, she knew she had to take it. She bit her lip and looked apologetic as she stood up. "I'm so sorry to do this again . . . "

J.D. waved her off. "Please, it's obvious you are on an important mission for the drumming alliance of America. Please, take your call," he said with a wink.

Abby barely had time to hit Talk when she heard Buddy's voice over the speaker, "Ziggy! Calm down, mon. I'm callin' Miss Abby now!"

"Buddy? What's going on?" Abby was trying with all of her might to multitask properly: focus on her lunch companion, keep her cool and also sound calm and collected as she handled a repairman on the phone. But his frantic reply knocked that house of cards over and quick.

"Abby! You got to get back here now. Quick! We need you on de roof!" And with that he hung up, leaving her staring at her phone.

It also meant that once again, Abby was going to be saying goodbye earlier than expected to J.D. Sadly she put her phone down and pushed her chair back away from the table.

"I have to go, again. I'm so sorry."

J.D. didn't seem to be someone who was easily disappointed, but the look on his face gave him away to Abby. At least he's as bummed about this as I am, she thought.

"Can I at least drive you to where you need to go?"

She started to say yes, but then realized she had driven Maria's little car. "I came prepared, actually. Rain check? Again?"

"Of course. Let me at least walk you to your car." Without waiting for an answer, he fell into step beside her, almost protectively guiding her to the parking lot of Ricky's.

As she reached the car, Abby turned to J.D. and went to say thank you, but found his lips on hers. It was breathtaking and refreshing, surprising and also monumental, since this was the first man she had wanted to kiss in a long time. His kiss was sweet and slow, as if neither of them should have a care in the world. When it was over, she slid out of his arms and into the front seat of the car.

"I hope you're serious about that rain check, Abby," he said, grinning down at her.

"I'll call you," was all she could muster as she threw the car in reverse.

"Or I'll find you," he said as he waved goodbye.

As she was tearing out of the lot at Ricky's, Abby glanced up at her rearview mirror to find J.D. standing in his spot, watching her as she drove away.

ABBY HIT THE BRAKES AND WAS ALMOST OUT OF THE CAR AS IT slowed down to a stop in the driveway at La Cantina. She had barely pulled the keys out of the ignition before she was charging up the stairs to check on Buddy.

As Abby was entering the bathroom, she could hear a symphony of voices as they cursed and hollered at one another. There was a ladder set up in the bathroom, so she was able to climb it and poke her head out of the hole to take in the scene on the roof.

At first glance, Abby couldn't tell that anything was amiss. There was tile scattered everywhere, the tarp was balled up over to one side, and things were just in a general disarray. Then she noticed the bricks from the chimney. And Ziggy sitting among the bricks from the chimney, which were suddenly not attached to the chimney stack any longer.

"Ziggy? Buddy? Does someone want to tell me why the chimney no longer looks like it's in one piece?"

"Oh mon," Ziggy began, "I tripped backwards and fell into de chimney, Abby. It just gave way! Didn't tink I hit it dat hard."

Buddy was nodding his head in agreement. "He didn't hit it hard, mon. He tripped on de tile and maybe he hit his head . . . "

Abby was on the roof now, and making her way, slowly, across the tile to Ziggy. "Are you okay? You aren't bleeding or cut, are you?"

Ziggy smiled at her. "No. I'm good." He started to stand up, but quickly sat back down. "Okay, maybe a little dizzy."

Abby nodded. As much as she was freaking out that there was more work to be done, she knew that Ziggy's health was

117

more important. And if they didn't get him off the roof in one piece, Maria might kill all three of them.

"Ziggy, tell you what, how about Buddy and I get you down so Maria can get you checked out by the doctor, okay? Please?"

Ziggy started to shake his head, then stopped, closing his eyes and holding his neck. "Okay. It does hurt." He grinned up at Abby. "Well, just a little."

"Okay. Come on. Buddy?"

Abby waved Buddy over to help her pick him up, steadying Ziggy on his feet. They worked together in silence, guiding Ziggy to the ladder and back inside the inn with little resistance and almost no balance issues.

Abby left Buddy to continue on the roof while she escorted Ziggy downstairs so they could find Maria. Thankfully, she was on the second floor putting linens down in one of the rooms.

"There you are!" Maria greeted them as they entered the room. "Ziggy, I need you to run out for me --"

Abby cut her off. "I'll let Ziggy explain how it happened, but he fell into the chimney and hit his head. He said it hurts a little, but I really think he should get it checked out, okay?"

Maria's eyes widened in fear as she flew to her husband's side.

"What were you doing up there, falling down? Are you crazy? We're lucky you didn't fall off the roof!"

Abby smiled at Ziggy and left the two of them to get organized, calling out over her shoulder, "Maria, make sure the inn is billed. Obviously we'll pay for it. Workmen's comp and all."

Maria nodded as she took Ziggy by the arm and led him to the stairs. Abby watched them go, pausing for only one second before returning to the roof to survey the amount of damage they needed to deal with now.

◆◆

THE LAST OF THE TOOLS HAD BEEN PUT AWAY FOR THE DAY AND Buddy was loading up his truck. The rest of the day had gone smoothly; Buddy was making headway with the roof despite the interlude this morning of Hurricane Ziggy. He was able to reach a few of his freelance workmen, including his brother Rush, asking for help. When the small community of St. Kitts had heard that Ziggy was hurt from trying to fix the roof, a few of the men had rallied and shown up to help. Abby was surprised and touched by the gesture, noting that the little island was much like a small town standing up to support one of their own when the going got tough.

"Dat brick be easy to fix. I get some tomorrow, Abby, and just add it to de bill, okay?"

Abby nodded. "Totally fine. Thank you, Buddy. I know this is turning out to be more than you agreed to."

Buddy shrugged his shoulders. "It is what it is. No worry." His gaze fixed across the lawn. "He be da one you need to be worrying about."

Abby followed his gaze to see Ziggy strolling across the lawn to them, his head wrapped in a bandage. Abby groaned.

"Ziggy! Please tell me you're not suffering any kind of serious injury?"

"The bandage isn't from the chimney, mon," he said with a grin. "I tripped on de way into da doctor's office and cracked my head." His lips peeled back, flaunting those yellow teeth, and he held up his hand to show three fingers. "Tree stitches."

Buddy laughed at his friend while Abby shook her head. "You're a mess, Ziggy."

"It's all good. Anyways, I be back up dere tomor--" But he never got a chance to finish.

"No way!" Abby said sternly. "Not at all. You are allowed to be in the bathroom and help with the ceiling if, and only if, Maria and the doctor agree. But not the roof. Got it?"

Ziggy nodded sheepishly while Abby shook her head. Ziggy and Buddy were already chatting quickly in the Kittian way about what else needed to be done, so she took that moment to slip away and head back to the pool house for a little quiet time and some reflection on the day's events.

The pool house was silent when Abby entered. She knew Ben wasn't there, since his car wasn't in the driveway and the telltale smattering of books and scrubs from the day weren't littered in their usual spots throughout the living room. Surveying the first floor, Abby knew there was one thing that would make her feel completely at peace right now. Cleaning.

Since they had agreed before the argument that Abby could clean a little around the house, she decided to begin her project as her "I'm sorry" to Ben. She had already planned to apologize when he returned from school, and she wanted to show her sincerity. She wasn't quite sure how to do that; all she knew how to do was clean and organize and try to make him feel a little better. And since her talk with Maria that morning, Abby knew it was time that she made more of a point with showing and not telling.

Since he had been so adamant about her not doing the cleaning at first, she decided she would focus on the kitchen area to start, since it was more general and not an invasion of personal space. That way she could also pull out the bag she found and ask him in a kinder fashion what was going on with it. No conclusion-jumping, she thought. She gathered her supplies, changed her clothes and got ready to attack the grime in the kitchen.

Luckily, the inn had a great collection of CDs that Abby was able to borrow from. She found a few different albums she loved, carted them out to the pool house and put them in the five-disc changer. She hit "Random" and began cruising around the kitchen.

Abby had always sought solace in cleaning duties, even as a child. She had vague memories of the chores that her dad always gave her. As she grew up, chores had become her escape. Quiet time to think about anything she had going on in her life and time for her to play with all the ways she could change things. Doing the dishes was one of her most favorite things to do in the whole world, and she always welcomed the role of dish washer after a big meal. It was always a good way to reflect on the night and the people who had been present.

It was with this happiness that she began cleaning out the refrigerator, washing and scrubbing the interior and exterior so it sparkled. Once she was done there, she moved on to the other major appliance, the oven/stove combo, and scrubbed it until it, too, twinkled from its cleaning.

She moved on to the same cabinets she had torn through yesterday when looking for the cat food, and found more stored items in various spots. Some of the boxes were clearly marked in what appeared to be Leigh's handwriting. Obviously, Leigh was making good use of every possible space as storage.

Abby took the bags and boxes out, placing them in random locations all over the kitchen. There were four in total, plus the bag she had found yesterday, so she decided to open them up, take stock of their contents and then seal them shut for when it came time for the big move.

Can't hurt, in case Ben's things were mixed up with Leigh's, she thought. I can separate them out, and go over it with Ben. Then later, when Ziggy wasn't busy, maybe he could help her find a better place for Leigh's things, in the main house.

Abby grabbed one of the open boxes so she could get a look at its contents. She found old clothes of Leigh's that looked like things she probably kept to use when she came down. There were shorts, tank tops and other island wear that seemed very Leigh-like. There was a bandana tucked away and a few hats -- things Leigh would use for covering up from the sun.

Abby grabbed a marker and made a note on the outside of the box and then put the box by the door. Time to open box number two.

Inside the second one, Abby found books and pictures, along with a few island knick-knacks, again similar to things Leigh would collect for herself or to give to the boys. She pulled out all of the little island collectibles and made a note to herself to grab some wrapping paper or bubble wrap so she could store them better. She then scanned the books quickly, straightening them up, and grabbed the pictures to organize, thinking it might be best to put them in an envelope so they wouldn't be harmed.

Remembering that Ben had large manila envelopes on his bookshelf, she grabbed one and reached for the pictures to get them contained before she continued further.

It was in her hurry to grab the pictures that she accidentally tossed the lot of them all over the kitchen, almost in a repeat of the day before. Abby laughed at her clumsiness and bent over to gather them up. She was surprised to see there were more pictures in this pile of her dad. And these looked like they had been taken on St. Kitts.

The first one she picked up from the pile was one of just her dad. He was standing on a beach with a drink in his hand, maybe here on Frigate Bay? His smile was large and warm like sunshine, and Abby felt tears spring into her eyes. This was the father she remembered, happy and in love with life. The next one was another shot of her dad, this time in a business suit. It looked like he was sitting in a booth of a chain restaurant, like an Applebee's or Outback. His grin was wide as he pretended to be shoveling food in his mouth. Weird pictures for Leigh to have, Abby thought. Why are all of these things here? And were these pictures taken here on the island?

It was the next one that made Abby pause. It was another one of her dad, looking happy and staring lovingly into the eyes of a woman Abby had never seen before. She was very pretty, with dark hair and a pale complexion. There was an unsettling feeling in the pit of Abby's stomach as she stared at the photograph in her hands. Maybe this was just someone Stanley had worked with or knew in another life. She took this one, put it on the counter and decided she would scan it and email it to Leigh to see who that was with their father.

The rest of the pictures were local ones, all taken in recent days. In fact, when she got to the end of the pictures, she found one of Ben standing on a dock holding a fishing pole. That was when a bit of a chill went through Abby. Her first thought was Oh no! as she realized Ben did have his things mixed in with Leigh's.

Abby felt horribly guilty as she realized she might actually be snooping through Ben's things. She decided she should just stop and wait for him to get back from school for the day so he didn't come home and find her knee-deep in his storage boxes, assuming she was rooting through them for her own amusement.

Last thing I need him to think is that I'm invading his privacy on purpose, she thought.

She was putting everything back in order when a last picture floated away from the others and landed light as a feather on the floor next to where she stood. She didn't need to bend over to see who was in the picture. Even from where she stood, she could see Ben's outline and knew it was him, but there was also another person, a woman, in this one. As she leaned down to pick it up, Abby realized it was the same woman who was in the picture with her father, only now she was much older. Instead of looking at her father with love and adoration, this time that look was reserved for Ben and Ben alone.

Abby was staring at the picture of Ben and the mystery woman when she heard the screen door open. She looked up to see Ben standing there, with a sheepish look on his face.

Abby had opened her mouth to speak, but Ben wanted to go first.

"Before you start, Abby, I need you to know that I'm sorry." He stared at his feet.

All Abby could do was nod slowly and listen.

"Please, let's just stop all of this. My best friend is coming to visit me soon and I don't want us fighting while he's here."

Abby licked her lips and wanted to answer, but all she could do was glance down at the picture she held in her hand. That was when Ben noticed it as well.

"What are you doing with that picture of me and my mum?"

Abby nodded at the cabinets.

"I . . . uh . . . I wanted to clean. That's my way of saying that I'm sorry. Since it's the kitchen, I thought it would be okay 'cause no one ever stores personal items in the kitchen. Except now I know that Leigh does it, and so do you. And since I found that book yesterday, I was trying to . . . " Abby stopped herself and stared at the ground. "I accidentally went through a few of your boxes. I thought they were Leigh's and I'm so sorry."

Ben had taken the picture from Abby's hands as she was speaking.

"Well, honestly, no harm no foul. Yes, I did store a few things under there, but I don't think Leigh did."

Again, a cold chill traveled through Abby.

"Her handwriting is on the outside of the boxes . . . "

"I know, she gave them to me to use when I first got here so I could store things. It's not like I could just go buy a box from Staples or Office Depot." He grinned. "And if you found any ladies' clothing, it's my mum's. She did leave a few of her things here as well, clothes and such for when she visited."

Abby was thoroughly confused now.

"If these are all your boxes, why do you have this picture in there?" she said as she handed him the picture of her father.

Ben looked at the picture, then back at Abby. It seemed that it was his turn to be confused now.

"Well, Abby, I don't know about you, but I like to keep pictures of my parents around to look at every now and then."

The words hit Abby like a ton of bricks. Parents. His parents. My father. Not my mother. She felt the room spin as she grabbed for the countertop.

Abby started to say something, but instead reached for the paper bag from the day before, the one that held the book she had found. She pulled it out and showed it to Ben.

"This book. This is the one I found yesterday."

Ben's face twisted with bewilderment. "Okay. It's The Great Gatsby."

"Is this yours?"

Ben stared at the book and nodded. "My dad gave me that, Abby." His face showed a glimmer of understanding. "Oh, is that why you thought I stole your sister's book? Don't think I'm well-rounded enough to --"

Abby's palms were sweating as she cut him off.

"Ben, I need to ask you something. Are you positive, absolutely 100%, that the man in that picture is your father?"

Ben looked both concerned and nervous when he nodded his head affirmatively in response to her question.

Abby took a deep breath, and with the threat of tears about to plummet to the floor from her eyes and her food about to come back up, she made her way into the bathroom to throw up. She stayed in the bathroom long enough to splash water on her face, gather her composure and brush her teeth. Once she had gathered herself back together, she returned to the living area.

Ben had been sitting on the couch holding the pictures and stood up when she came out. "You okay?"

How do I tell him this? Abby wondered. How do I tell Leigh? How do I . . . Wait. Leigh. Abby felt like the coincidences were piling up a little too high here. Slow down. Just take it a step at a time.

Abby sat down on the couch and looked into Ben's concerned face, struggling to find her own strength to try to get out the words that even she didn't want to hear.

"Ben, this man in the picture. The one that you say is your father."

Ben nodded, suddenly looking a little pale himself.

Abby's mouth was dry, and her tongue was sticking to the roof of her mouth. "I'm thrown by this, because I know him, too."

"You know my dad?" Ben's face was registering confusion. It was twisted in the way Abby's tummy was twisting up inside her right now.

Abby nodded. "I do. I know him well, or at least I used to."

Abby's head was racing as she realized the impact her words would have once they were said out loud. She had closed her eyes in an attempt to keep her tears back and quiet her thoughts. Realizing it was useless, she opened her eyes again and turned to face Ben.

"He's my dad, too," she whispered, slowly and solemnly, as if they were in church on Christmas Eve. "Ben, this is my father, Stanley George."

The quiet was thick and strong in the room. You could hear the proverbial pin drop, it was so silent. Ben was staring at Abby, and she held his gaze, feeling like they needed to feed off each other's strength, even if it was fleeting.

"Ben, the book. My dad gave the same book to me and to Leigh when we were kids. It was a tradition . . . "

" . . . in his family." Ben finished.

Abby wasn't sure if she was feeling sick again or if it was getting hot, all she could tell was that her upper lip was starting to perspire like it did when she was nervous. She looked down at Ben's hands and noticed his nervous habit was in full effect. For that matter, so was hers.

Ben was staring at his hands while Abby stood up and paced the kitchen.

Abby's thoughts were racing on top of one another. Ben. Ben's my brother. Holy crap. I have a brother?

As if realizing the same thing, Ben cast an intense look Abby's way.

"You're my sister."

Abby nodded. "Well, I think I'm your half-sister?"

Ben nodded too. "How do we . . . "

"Deal with this?" Abby finished. "I don't know. I feel like this explains a lot but like it also explains nothing. Does that make sense?"

Ben was dumbfounded. "Yeah. Except the part that we have the same dad. So Leigh? She's also my sister?"

Abby nodded. "As far as I know . . . not trying to be cryptic, but, yeah. This is kind of a big deal."

The next few minutes felt like hours as the duo sat in silence, processing their discovery. Abby could only watch the cats as they rolled on the cold tile floor of the kitchen, begging for attention or for a petting from her. It was soothing to see them wrapping up with each other and taking care of each other, much like the way she felt she and Ben needed to do now.

She cleared her throat and wiped her silent tears away from her cheeks. Abby felt the need for a change of location suddenly. It was as if the walls of the pool house were closing in on her. She needed out for some air and space, but she wanted Ben there, too. As she looked in his direction, she realized his shell-shocked reaction could only mean he needed the same thing as well.

They looked at each other, silently standing up in unison as Abby led them to the main house to search out Maria.

WHEN MARIA ROUNDED THE CORNER INTO THE KITCHEN, SHE stopped in her tracks, her face showing surprise at the sight that greeted her.

At the center island, seated next to each other, drinking beer, were Abby and Ben. And the looks on their faces suggested that something had transpired.

"I take it you two aren't here to check on Ziggy?"

The pair shook their heads in unison.

"Should I make tea or should I grab a beer as well?" she asked the twosome quizzically.

"Depends," Abby responded drily. "Did you know Ben was my half-brother?"

Maria let out a slow long breath and grabbed a stool across from them. Then, deciding otherwise, she went to the fridge and grabbed a beer for herself. She popped the cap and took a long drink, then she stiffened up and went to the stool again, sitting down.

"How did you find out?" she asked.

Ben was the first to answer. "She saw a picture -- "

"The book, actually, yesterday," Abby interrupted.

"-- of my parents," Ben interrupted right back. "Then she said that my dad was her dad, too. Do you think it's true, Maria?"

Maria seemed ready for this and answered him straight-forwardly.

"I know it is, Ben. You and Abby are brother and sister."

Armed with confirmation of what they had only thought might be true, they now both nodded, still stunned from the events.

"I think the person you need to speak with -- " Maria began but never finished.

"Let me guess," Abby responded. "Leigh." She shook her head. "I can't believe this."

It was Maria's turn to cut her off. "Abby, she knew she was taking a risk at having you two find out the truth." Maria shrugged her shoulders. "As for you having to room with Ben? A fluke. We got last-minute reservations that made it impossible for her to say no in order to bring money in."

Abby shook her head. "No, Maria. Leigh knew and that's not acceptable. My father cheated on my mother. With Ben's mom . . . "

"What are you implying?" Ben countered defiantly.

"I don't know, Ben," Abby's voice was shaking and she was trying to keep from cracking. "This is really confusing. I feel bad for you and your mom. I'm just floored." She leaned over and grabbed his hand. "You and I are kind of innocent victims in this whole thing. Unless you knew, too?"

Ben started to respond defensively, but slowed when he saw Abby's grin.

"That's a joke?" he asked.

"Well, we should try to find the funny, don't you think?" she replied.

Maria smiled at the duo. "I have no doubt you'll be fine, but the person you need to speak to in order to iron all of this out is Leigh. I would think she could help with figuring out the best plan of attack here." She looked at Ben. "I'm sure you'll want to call your mom now?"

"Yes," he replied. "I think I should. But I feel like I need to digest this a little more before I ask her any questions. I'm guessing she probably had her reasons why she decided not to share this news with me, at least not yet?"

His last statement became a question, which was directed to Abby.

"Well, I'd love to hop on the phone and rip Leigh a new one, but I think I need to calm down a little bit myself." She stared at her beer bottle, playing with its label. "She's always been secretive and very mysterious, but in the end she has always had good reason to be." She shrugged her shoulders. "I guess I need to accept that she had her reasons for doing all of this."

Abby looked around the kitchen and let the weight of her trip so far settle in.

"When I agreed to come here, I was under the impression of one thing: that I was coming to help Leigh with a few repairs on her house. Then I find out the house is an inn, and we all know the rest of the story from here." Abby was playing with her fingers nervously. "I kind of doubt the inn is even what she says it is. There are so many lies, Maria!"

Maria was thoughtful. She leaned across the table and took Abby's hand in hers.

"No matter what you may think, Leigh has her reasons. I told you, everything has a reason, and the same goes here. When you do decide to talk to her, take it easy on her. She's had to be the only one dealing with this for many years." She looked at Ben next and took his hand. "She's wanted to tell the both of you for some time, but a promise she made was to not ever let the secret out, unless it came out all by itself."

Ben and Abby both picked up their beers and took long drinks in unison. It made sense to both of them now: the bickering, the back and forth, the feeling of being around a sibling, yet not really. Abby was both excited about the fact of getting to know Ben as her brother and angry with her sister.

Abby thought back to when she had first met Ben: how his eyes had blazed a small hint of green when irritated, just like hers did. And Maria, knowing the little family saying of "I love you but sometimes I just don't like you." She knew it had to be more than just a coincidence. And there was something in Maria's actions and the way she laughed that made Abby feel like they had known each other for quite some time, or at least that she was buried somewhere in Abby's memory bank.

"Maria, I feel like I've met you before. Have I?" Abby asked.

Maria was smiling at her now, almost apologetically.

"Yes, girl. Many moons ago. I worked with your sister in the States a long time ago. When she was putting together the deal down here for the house through the real estate agent, she called me. She wanted me to come and help run the inn in her absence. Leigh placed a lot of trust in me and has always taken care of me and Ziggy. She is always trying to make decisions in everyone's best interests, but until you speak with her, I don't want to go further into detail. You need to speak to the source. I'm not sure if it'll require a phone call or something in person, but do what you need to in order to put this behind you and move on."

They all sat in silence for a good five minutes until Maria, once again, was the first to break it.

"It's not the end of the world. You've not lost anything. You've both gained. Ben, you have a family. One you didn't know about, but a new family that you get to discover. And Abby, you have a little brother, right here in front of you. And he's been through a lot the last year. Maybe it was time that you had each other so you could find strength in numbers."

Abby and Ben looked at each other, both waiting for the other one to speak.

Ben opened his mouth to speak and stopped himself. Abby noticed and put her hand on his shoulder.

"I think from here on out we can say 'open communication' and know it's true."

"Well," he began, "I was young when my dad . . . our dad passed away. I have questions about him."

Abby nodded in agreement. "Of course. I was young, too, but I can tell you what I know. That he was a kind, generous and loving man." She got this far and started to cry. "And had a secret life that he kept from his family."

"Abby, don't assume, remember? Wait until you talk to Leigh before either one of you goes placing blame on your dad, or Ben's mum, or Leigh. No one is to blame here. Sometimes," Maria continued, "circumstances arise and it's best to move forward without fully revealing the truth. Not saying it's fair, but that sometimes it has to be done that way. Now, I'm going to make a deal with you guys as the dust settles here. Okay?"

Abby and Ben waited for Maria to lay down her rules.

"One. First and foremost, you two have got to be good to each other. Okay? Two. Talk to each other about how you're feeling and ask each other questions so you can know the other person sitting here with you now. No need to gang up on Leigh. Her ways may not be the most acceptable at times, but she only did as she was told."

She makes sense, Abby thought. Until I decide to pick up the phone and confront Leigh about this, there is no need to jump to any kind of conclusions about her or my father. But I'd still like some answers.

Abby glanced over at Ben and could see he was wrestling with his own demons. He smiled at her, and for the first time since she had been there, Abby truly felt that everything was going to be all right.

"Okay, Maria, I accept your conditions," Abby said. Ben nodded his head in agreement.

"Good. Now, I'm going to start dinner for the house. Why don't you two just sit here for a minute and take a breath -- after the day's events I think we all need to. Plus, I really don't want to let you out of my sight for a little longer until I know you won't be rushing off to do anything dumb."

Abby giggled, wondering what Maria considered "dumb." Calling Leigh and giving her hell? Or maybe Ben and I just need to get completely hammered and then wake up tomorrow likes it's a do-over for our relationship? Either way, Abby had to admit it felt good to have a partner in crime right there beside her.

I have a brother, Abby thought. Wow. If Leigh can keep a promise this serious, so can I. I have a brother. If I act like things are going to be okay, maybe he will, too.

As if he could hear her internal dialogue, Ben turned to Abby with a shell-shocked expression.

"I have a sister."

"I know."

"No, I mean . . . you. You're my sister."

"Yeah. Wow." Abby's faced reflected her mixed emotions. "You've been through a lot this year already. Look, I know I'm not supposed to know all of it, but I do. You can't afford to have news like this interfere with your studies. You can't fail."

It seemed like he was already there as well. "I was thinking that, too. Wait, how do you know?"

Abby knew she needed to keep Tracey's secret. Ben needed to trust those around him right now, no matter what.

"It's not important. I just know that something like this could distract you." Maria had placed some pretzels and chips on the table in front of them to snack on with their beer. "So, what I think is that maybe we should not say anything to anyone about the fact that we know right away. I feel like if we do that, your mom or Leigh may want to fly down here and deal with things. Sometimes, family can be more hindrance than help." She chuckled as she realized her participation in the former. "And I've proven this. So, let's deal with one milestone at a time, shall we?"

Ben played with the fabric of his shorts distractedly. "You're right. My mum would come here, and she wouldn't want to leave until I had put on a brave face. It sounds like Leigh is the same, and since you want to strangle her right now, I don't think having the two of you fighting all over the property would help me study."

"Pretty much my sentiments exactly."

"Are you going to tell me who told you? About what happened before?" Ben queried.

"I could," Abby said, "but then I may have to kill you."

He laughed and toasted the air with his bottle. "Well, at least I know you can keep a secret."

"Not as good as some people we're related to," she quipped.

"If you want," Maria said as she bustled around the kitchen making dinner, "the two of you could make yourselves useful and set the table."

"Chores?" the pair said in unison.

"Yes! It's time for something normal. If that means I put you both to work, then so be it. Or, Ben, you could go study until it's time for dinner, and Abby, you can help me set the table?" she offered.

Abby looked at Ben, who was watching Maria's every move.

"I think I just want to sit here a little longer."

Abby took Ben's hand and smiled at him. "I think that's a good idea. I can help you study after dinner if you want. And I'll keep on helping you any way I can as long as I'm here, okay?"

Ben nodded and squeezed her hand back. "It's weird. I already was starting to like you, now I'm confused."

"Like maybe you should now hate me?"

"Not you. The situation. I don't think I could hate you, Abby. Believe me, I tried."

Abby stifled another laugh as she teased Ben. "I love your stale humor."

"Most people would describe it as 'dry,' not 'stale.'"

"Really? I'd go with stale. Like bread."

"You really are full of yourself, aren't you," Ben snapped jokingly.

Their back-and-forth teasing was interrupted by Ziggy, who came in through the back door of the house. He took one look around the room and realized something was afoot.

"Mon, de air is heavy in here! Is it de humidity or did I miss somethin'?"

The trio in the kitchen all looked at one another, then filled the room with laughter. Big, good, from-the-gut laughs. The kind that you relish to break up an awkward emotional moment. Even though the news was intense, something deep down told Abby it was going to be okay.

More than okay, she thought. Once we muddle through this, it's going to be awesome. I have a brother. His name is Ben. Cool.

CHAPTER 7

THE DAYS SETTLED INTO A PATTERN THAT THE DUO ADJUSTED to with ease. Abby would get up early to start breakfast for Ben and they would chat for a few minutes in the early part of the day before he made his way to school. Maria and Ziggy would watch the pair as they sat by the pool with Ben's two cats prowling around their legs. It made Maria happy to see that they were making an effort to get to know each other before informing the rest of their family about their find.

Ben and Abby became closer by the day, spending their free time quizzing each other about likes, dislikes, favorite colors, favorite movies and TV shows, and foods they both enjoyed. Ben asked Abby lots of questions about their dad and Leigh, as well as the rest of the family. She was getting confused explaining to him the connections, so one day while he was at school she made him a family tree. He was touched by the effort she was making. In fact, she even included his mom on the tree so she wasn't left out. They talked about games they played as children and compared notes on things like dental visits and ear infections. They both noted that they had had emergency appendix surgery in their early teens, both having the scars to prove it.

The repairs were coming along, with Buddy more than keeping up his end of the bargain. The chimney stack was quickly repaired, thanks to Abby jumping in and helping the Kittians when they wanted to sit and chat, and the roof and ceiling were both well on their way to finalization despite Ziggy's best efforts to thwart them. Buddy pulled Abby aside one morning, saying, "Fingers crossed, girl, and dat roof may be done in de next day or two!" He had made his point by slapping her on the back so hard it pushed her forward a good five feet.

Most evenings Ben needed to study, so he made a permanent study date with Tracey and her group. Ben was to be at Ricky's around six almost every night to meet them for a three-hour study session. Abby, not wanting to be left out, would tag along some nights to sit and play cards or a random board game with Cutty and Ziggy.

It was on one of these evenings that Cutty made a comment under his breath to Abby about her closeness with Ben.

"What did you just say?" she asked Cutty, who was standing on a chair hanging up an old license plate he'd found. He liked to add treasures he'd collected to the walls at Ricky's.

He took a long drag off the Salem 100 hanging out of his mouth and repeated, "I said, I think you and Ben make a nice little couple. Seems to me that you can't get enough of each other these days, huh?"

Abby laughed out loud, so loud she had to throw her hand over her mouth so she wouldn't disturb the other folks studying and chatting at the surrounding tables.

"A nice couple? Really, Cutty. You're assuming things."

"No, I'm not," he countered, almost defiantly.

"Really? You've seen Ben and me together all this time and now you decide we're a couple? What if I saw that Salem 100 hanging out of your mouth and went to get you a carton of those cigarettes? We both know you wouldn't be happy. You really like Camel. I would be in the wrong because I made an assumption you liked those kinds of smokes. Kind of like how you're wrong right now."

He took another drag off his cigarette and looked down at Abby, who was handing him another one of his "treasures" to add to the wall: a baseball cap.

"You make a good point. But I know what I see."

"What is that, Cutty?"

"Two people that are doing it."

Those last words made Abby literally wretch out loud.

"Cutty! We're not . . . Ugh. Get down off the chair before I pull you off. I'll tell you what's going on."

"You're gonna tell me that you're pregnant?"

Abby shook her head at the old guy. "Please, just get down. I'll get you another beer if you will listen to me."

Cutty was already smiling, even wider than he was before.

"Ziggy and Maria are as close to best friends as I'm gonna get. I know, Abby," he said quietly as he was getting off the chair.

"About Ben and me?" she whispered back to him.

"Yep. Known for a long time. That sister of yours has a big mouth once she gets about four drinks in her. Spilled it all to me one night when we were all down here having some cocktails. Never told anyone, just knew that Ziggy and Maria were on top of things, and they respected that I knew and I respected that it wasn't my business to tell."

Cutty began gathering his tools and putting chairs back where they were meant to be. He continued multitasking as he took a swig of his beer before stubbing out his cigarette. He finished getting everything in order before he joined Abby at the table.

"We've been waiting for that boy to get to know his family. It's like watching a miniseries come to life. There's suspense, treason, espionage . . . "

"You are truly insane, you know that?"

"Pretty much," he said as he leaned in closer to Abby. "It's safe here. Your secret, that is. I won't tell anyone."

Abby was listening to Cutty, but watching Ben across the patio. She felt a renewed sense of protection for her little brother. Something that had just come innately when she'd found out who he was. The same feeling was growing on a daily basis as she discovered more and more about him.

Abby acknowledged Cutty with a smile and then, as if changing her mind, got stone-faced as she turned to him.

"I know you can be perverted, but I want you to know that I'm going to hug you now."

Cutty was taken aback. "Really?"

"Yes. We need ground rules, though. No groping, no fondling, no whispering in my ear. I just want to hug you in a nice, 'Thank you for being so good to me' kind of way. Nothing more. Got it?"

Cutty was already standing with his arms wide open.

"I'm glad I took a shower today," he said almost jokingly.

Abby giggled as she stood up and embraced the weathered old coot. He kept to her ground rules, and when she sat back down she noticed his face was red.

"Are you embarrassed I hugged you?"

Cutty pinched his lips together. "No. But I don't want that J.D. to see me hugging you. May get jealous."

Abby looked at Cutty accusingly when she heard his name.

"How do you know about J.D.?" She couldn't escape the pang of guilt she felt at the fact that since their lunch she hadn't tried to reach him. With everything going on at the inn and it being the day Ziggy was hurt, she hadn't found time. But then again he hadn't tried to find her either, as he had promised.

"I know he asked me if I'd seen you and what your deal was." Cutty lit another cigarette and looked at her with such an intense stare she thought he was trying to make her catch on fire.

"And? What did you say?"

He shrugged. "Nothing. Told him you were here doing your thing and I'd tell you when I saw you that he was askin' for ya. So I did and it's done. End of story."

Abby was dumbstruck. "That's it? He didn't say anything else?"

Cutty thought for a moment before he answered, "He did say he'd be on Nevis for a few days to meet someone named Callie. But other than that . . . nope."

Abby half-laughed to herself, deciding that the mysterious playboy from London who seemed interesting and different was actually already off and running into someone else's waiting arms.

Of course, she thought. Don't they all?

"Abby, don't look so sad. You got a good heart, and you're honest. That speaks volumes. Ben's lucky he's got a sister like you."

It was Abby's turn for her face to change color.

"That was one of the nicest things anyone has ever said to me," she leaned in and said softly to Cutty. "And the fact that it came from you makes it even better."

The two shared a secret smile together before sitting back to make themselves comfortable while watching the sun set over the island of Nevis. Cutty was sharing an old story with Abby about how the ferry that used to go between Nevis and St. Kitts had sunk many years ago, while she was trying to not let her disappointment show.

"Abby, you look like someone popped your favorite balloon. Is this about that J.D. character?"

Abby was kind of embarrassed to admit even to herself that it was about him. She looked sheepishly at Cutty, shrugging her shoulders. "I guess it is."

The weather-beaten old captain shook his head. "You know, I think there's something you should know about him."

Abby snorted. "Trust me, I think I know. He's a playboy with money to burn hopping island to island. Oh well."

Cutty looked as if he wanted to say something more, but they were interrupted by Ben and Tracey.

"You two telling secrets over here?" Tracey asked in her charming Southern way.

"Nah. Abby's trying to cuddle with me."

Abby made a face at Cutty. "How's studying going?"

Ben nodded his head. "Good, actually. These cram sessions are helping to keep me focused."

"Good. Just keep it up. And any quizzing you want me to do I'll be glad to. We can do it over dinner tonight."

"Actually," Tracey interjected, "Ben and I were talking about taking you out to dinner at one of the local restaurants here. There's a nice Italian place right by the beaches, then maybe we could go screw around in the casino for a bit?"

Abby sat on the invitation for a heartbeat before responding "Yes!" to Tracey's invite. It felt like all she had done lately was eat at the house with Ben, help Maria with the inn or hang out at Ricky's so she got some human contact besides her immediate island "family." She needed a night out.

"Cutty, you can come, too, if you want," Tracey offered.

"Nah. That casino is no good for someone like me. I like to gamble too much." He lit another cigarette and jerked his head in Abby's direction. "This one needs a night out without me. I'm the only person she ever sees, besides you guys."

Abby stood up and began gathering her things together.

"If you change your mind, Cutty, text my cell. We can come get you. Otherwise, I'll see you tomorrow around the same time?"

He nodded and stood abruptly as well. He grunted good night and then began his walk back to his room. He got halfway across the patio when he turned around.

"Abby," he called out, "do me a favor?"

Abby rolled her eyes, waiting for some grotesque suggestion. "Yes?"

"Bet twenty U.S. for me. On black. Got it?"

"Twenty dollars on black?"

He nodded. "That's the roulette table."

"I get it."

Cutty rolled his eyes at her. "Making sure."

"Consider it done."

Cutty smiled, throwing his hand in the air to say good-bye one more time, disappearing around the corner into the night.

Abby turned to the other two.

"I'm heading home to freshen up. Pick me up there?" she queried.

Ben nodded as he and Tracey made their way back to the study group.

Abby couldn't help but feel giddy with excitement, her tummy filling with butterflies as she thought about going out to the casino for the night. She quickened her pace so she could get back and grab a shower before Ben arrived to pick her up.

When the horn honked in the driveway, Abby was finishing up her hair. "Finishing" meant pulling it back into a secure ponytail, since the humidity was killing her hair at the moment, making it unmanageable.

Abby emerged from the pool house looking absolutely charming, so charming that even Tracey whistled at her as she approached the car. She had thrown on a beige tank top and a flowy skirt she had picked up one day while shopping at the Port. She grabbed her flip-flops and raced barefoot to the car.

If I were home, I would never think of going out in this kind of outfit or even fathom running barefoot anywhere, Abby thought as she climbed into the backseat.

Once settled at Tiramisu Ristorante, the trio ordered a bottle of red wine, cozying in for some good food and conversation. Not to disappoint, Ben shared with the girls, over their Caesar salad and calamari appetizers, stories about his friend Andrew, who was due in a few days for a visit that week.

Andrew and Ben had met at a rugby camp in London one summer. It was during one of these trips that he and Andrew had been roommates, and not quite the kind that get along right away. In the first few days there, they both ended up falling for the same girl, who worked at a local pub where they liked to have lunch. Andrew had actually punched Ben in the nose in an argument over her. It didn't take long for them to realize that the girl was playing both of them. They decided then and there that they were supposed to be friends, making a pact to never let anyone come between them again. They were roommates every summer after that, taking turns visiting each other as they got older. Andrew was originally from Cape Town, South Africa, but had relocated in recent years to London upon completion of his degree in architecture.

As luck would have it, Andrew had actually been in the Caribbean a lot in recent months. One of his clients had hired him for a series of projects on islands such as St. Maarten, Antigua, Dominica, and even on Nevis, so he was prone to making quick visits to St. Kitts when he could sneak them in. More often than not, he combined his work trips with pleasure, this trip being no exception.

After a dinner ripe with stories that were shared over fettuccini Alfredo, pasta Bolognese and a chicken Parmesan, Tracey announced over coffee that it was "time."

"Time for what?" Abby asked, already knowing what she meant.

"To get our gamble on!" she announced to the room, as if sharing a New Year's resolution.

Ben was already in his wallet counting his cash. "I may need to stop at the ATM . . . "

He didn't get to finish that sentence, as Tracey was already getting geared up.

"Oh, boo on the ATM. My mom taught me to just play with what you got. Don't take out any extra 'cause you're gonna spend it." She peered across the table to get a good look in his wallet. "How much?"

"About eighty dollars."

Tracey nodded with authority. "Then you'll be just fine. If you lose that eighty, stop. It's just to play. It's kind of like will power," she said.

Abby was sneaking a look in her own wallet to count what she had. Forty dollars. She was thinking that maybe she should be the one to stop at the ATM when she remembered her promise to Cutty. Twenty dollars of her forty was for his bet.

No sooner did she think it then Ben was already reminding her, "Don't forget about Cutty wanting a bet placed."

"I know, I know . . . Tell you what, when we get in, let's just go straight to the roulette table. I'm going to place his bet first thing."

Tracey was already sliding back from the table. "Sounds like a plan. I like blackjack myself. Oh, Abby? I saw what you did when the waitress brought the check by."

Abby shot her a sideways smile.

"Well, big sisters have to do that for their brothers, even if they are only half." She smiled at Ben as it dawned on him she had paid for their meal.

"Abby, what did you do that for? There's no need," he started to protest, but Abby stopped him short.

"Ben, shush. Seriously, there's no need for the argument. I just wanted to pay for all of us because I could. And now that I know Tracey is in on the whole ordeal, all the better. It's nice to be feeling more settled, isn't it?"

During dinner, Ben had told Abby he had confided in Tracey since there was no one else he really thought he wanted to talk to about their new dynamic -- at least not yet. Abby knew that in time they would have to come out of their little safe haven of "us against the world -- or at least our immediate family," but until that happened, she wanted to make sure they both enjoyed their personal calm before the storm.

The Royal Palms Casino and Hotel was next door to Tiramisu, so they left their car in the parking lot and made their way down the street to the casino. Tracey was going over different rules of blackjack with Ben. Ben was nodding and acting like he was listening, but there was a look in his eyes that made Abby think that there was something else going on between them besides being study partners. Hmmm . . . Something to discuss during our poolside coffee conversation in the morning, she thought.

The hotel was absolutely breathtaking. It was one of the only resort hotels on the island, and it was set up as its own little paradise. The lobby was open-air with a large fountain set across the other side of the entrance, looking out over the lounge area and shops on the interior. The opposite end of the lobby gave one a view of the pool and beyond, out to the Atlantic side of the island. Someone was playing steel drums in the middle of the room, and there was a specialty water bar with fruits and cucumbers marinating to add a delicious flavor to the otherwise ordinary beverage. There was also a rum-tasting bar set up by the steel drums where tourists and locals were gathered trying some of the newest rums from local and faraway islands.

The casino was set off to the right of the lobby, so they headed inside. First order of business was to find the roulette table so Abby could be done with the bet she agreed to place for Cutty and then continue on with some blackjack or poker.

Ben and Tracey decided to head over to the blackjack table and get started while Abby slipped away to find the roulette table. While wandering through the main thoroughfare, she heard a cheer of excitement and figured she must be close. She was right.

As she turned a corner near the Wheel of Fortune slot machines (or Wheel of MIS-Fortune, as she liked to think of them), she saw the roulette table. It was crowded, so she snaked her way to the front to bet Cutty's (her) twenty dollars on black.

As she moved closer to the front, there was an excitement and anxiety that arose in her chest. She was feeling competitive and knew she was in it for the win now. As she got to the front, she reached into her wallet and took out the two twenty-dollar bills. One was for Cutty and the other one for herself. She had decided that she would bet as well, but wanted to watch and see what the table was like first.

There were a variety of people at the table, from different countries, and they were all different shapes and sizes. There were many different accents and languages filling the air around her, but Abby could feel the anticipation in the air as everyone was placing their bets.

Abby watched the roulette table attendees for a few rounds of the game before she finally put her money on the table to change it for chips. As they were calling for bets, she leaned over and placed one chip on black, per Cutty's instructions. She was trying to decide if she wanted to join him there when she felt the urge to put her money on seventeen since it was her birthday. No idea why, she just decided to do it. Why not? she thought.

She placed her bets and then sat back to wait for the wheel to turn. As she was saying a silent prayer to herself, Abby felt like someone was watching her. She looked up to see J.D. smiling in her direction from across the table. He, too, had placed a bet and was toasting Abby across the table. Her heart thudded in her chest but she was also a little irritated. Mostly because he was there in front of her looking handsome and oozing charm. She was about to return his smile when she realized that next to him stood a gorgeous, lithe, tan, raven-haired woman with eyes as piercing as his. She was whispering in his ear, sharing a laugh or an inside joke. Or sharing some kind of anecdote about Nevis, Abby thought. I bet that's the reason he went there . . .

All bets were in, and the croupier turned the wheel to get it going. As it was spinning, he dropped the ball in, throwing in the opposite direction of the spin. Everyone was quiet as they waited for the ball to find its home. The clunking sound as it hit different numbers and bounced around inside the wheel tormented Abby. She held her breath and waited to see where the ball would land. Then she could get out of there and go home.

Abby was so caught up in the moment that when the ball landed on number seventeen all she could register was that Cutty had won because seventeen was black. Then she slowly realized she had bet on seventeen as well.

The croupier greeted her stunned expression with a huge grin.

"Did I just win?" she asked innocently.

J.D. was suddenly standing next to her, grabbing her in a big hug, acknowledging her win.

"You just won on seventeen! You didn't even know it? Beginner's luck, I'd say," he almost whispered the last part under his breath as he focused on her, watching the croupier take his money, adding it to the bank, and seeming not to care.

"I agree," she said, smiling at this handsome man whose presence and closeness actually made her heart thud in her chest with such force she thought he might have been able to hear it as well.

J.D. was motioning to the waitress as she rounded the table that he needed a cocktail, and held out his hand to Abby as if asking if she wanted one as well.

"Oh . . . no. Thank you. You've already bought me one drink. I owe you."

"Well, lucky for you, we're in a casino. So they're free," he said with a wink.

Abby smiled shyly and laughed half to herself. "Very true. However, since I won, I'm leaving."

"Not a gambler?" His voice was husky. Abby knew if she stayed, one drink could lead to . . . What? A threesome? No. She had to go.

"Nope. Not at all. I'm a responsible lady who needs to go home," she answered as she gathered her belongings. "Thank you for the offer."

They locked eyes for a brief second before Abby began backing away to collect her winnings, in an effort to navigate away from temptation. Thinking twice, she walked back over to him.

"Nice to see you, J.D."

She wanted to ask him why he never came looking for her or to explain why she hadn't called him at the hotel, but she couldn't shake the fact that he had just up and gone off to another island with some other woman. Even if there was a good explanation, she wasn't sure she wanted to go down that road. But I'll never know unless I ask him, will I? she thought.

Abby was about to suggest they go to the bar and have a drink after all, but they were interrupted by the croupier, who was insisting he pay her for her wins. Abby took that as a sign to get out of Dodge. She gave J. D. one last lingering smile and then made her way across the casino floor.

When all was said and done, Abby was walking away with $700. Despite the fact that she was nurturing her deflated ego, ripe from her run-in with J.D., she skipped off through the casino in search of the blackjack table where Ben and Tracey had parked. She couldn't wait to share her good news with them. They were, in a backward way, her reverse good luck charm. If they had come with me to the table, she thought, I might have never placed a bet at all!

Abby was on a gambler's high as she scanned the tables looking for her companions. There weren't a lot of open seats;

many were filled with boys from a visiting rugby club, or tourists, then there were some locals and a couple who couldn't take their hands off each other. It was this particular couple that made Abby take pause.

Upon further inspection, Abby could see the couple was Ben and Tracey. She wasn't able to stop the grin blossoming on her face. Good for you, she thought. Until you wake up next to each other in the morning. Bad breath, someone used the last of the toilet paper, someone else forgot to pay a bill. Yep. That's sweet.

Abby realized that her internal monologue had gone from hopeful to downright bitter. Not everyone is going to be like Matt was, she thought.

She had a small smile playing on her lips as she watched Ben and Tracey. This was new for them, and she didn't want to be the one to poop on it like a mad seagull just because her luck with romance seemed to suck. Nor did she want to be a third wheel. She decided to grab a taxi home and let them have this night for themselves.

She waved at the duo, who had looked up after sneaking some kisses to find her smiling at them from across the casino floor. She made a motion with her hand, jerking her thumb toward the exit behind her so they understood she was leaving. The grinning pair smiled and waved back. Yeah, I like her for him, Abby thought as she winked at them both. Cool and down-to-earth. Good for you, Ben. You too, Tracey.

She cashed out her chips and headed to the taxi stand, lost in her own thoughts and a little sad that at thirty-five years old, there wasn't anyone special in her life. Wasn't she supposed to be happy that it was just her? Abby felt happy, but yet she also felt . . . alone. Really alone.

She stayed in that space for the rest of her night, the big

win now long forgotten. It was replaced by her own need to be a little depressed and to feel her own loneliness right now.

As she lay there, she was reminded that there was a point just last year when she didn't want to go to sleep. Going to bed and being in pure silence was like reliving the whole horrible mess her life had become. She would close her eyes and see the proposal, Matt's beaming face as she said yes, and the plans they made for their wedding. Then the nightmare began of him boxing his things and moving in with another woman while Abby was on the phone begging for her deposits back for a wedding reception and the honeymoon that would never come to fruition. The thud in her chest echoed in her ears as she was taken back to a time where being alone wasn't good enough and being around people just wouldn't do. No matter where she was, her heart was ripped open, torn and tossed aside as if a hurricane had come through her chest. It was a lonely feeling like no other, because no matter what she did when she closed her eyes, she would see Matt and the potential they had.

That night, she fell asleep in her cramped alcove with silent tears sliding down her cheeks.

CHAPTER 8

"ABBY! DO YOU HAVE THE KEYS TO MY CAR?"

Ben was in a whirlwind. He had gotten up a little later than planned and now was in a mad dash to get out the door so he could be at the airport as Andrew was exiting the building. In the midst of studying for midterms, he had been planning and prepping for Andrew's visit with excitement.

Abby was outside by the pool drinking coffee with Maria, discussing who they'd hire as a painter to take care of a few of the guestrooms that needed to be touched up versus having Abby and Ziggy knock it out if there was time.

Abby peered over her coffee mug at Ben, shrugging his way as he stood in the doorway, pleading with his eyes. "I used the keys yesterday when I ran to the store, but I put them back on the counter."

Ben mumbled something about "stinking cats" under his breath and disappeared. Abby smiled at Maria.

"He's really excited about Andrew. The last few days I've had small lists of favors and to-dos as well as notes with 'Please, Abby, can you go to the store and buy this for me?'

The cupboards are stocked for the first time, and the fridge is packed with food and beer." Abby shook her head good-naturedly at the thought of the two drunk young men being together. "And I think he's planning a trip over to Nevis tomorrow."

"You gonna join them?" Maria asked.

Abby thought about it for a second before she answered. "I guess it depends. I'd like to see Nevis, but if we have things that need to be done here, that's my first priority."

Abby paused, looking up at the crisp, blue, cloudless Caribbean sky. "I still have to make time to talk with Leigh about Ben," Abby said with sadness. "I guess I don't know if it's the right time to go away, Maria. I think it's time to broach some of these topics with Leigh. And I just don't want to."

Abby took a big breath and closed her eyes, aiming her face to the sun. "I wish I knew how this will all end."

Maria was drinking from her mug, watching Abby intently. "It's not up to us how anything ends. Just know it'll be what it's supposed to."

There was a slam in the house and some minor expletives were hurled around the kitchen. Abby could see the two cats lounging and sunning in the window. She would even swear later that they were smiling at each other. More than likely they knew where the keys were and just weren't sharing the info with Ben.

"I know, Maria. I just need to get this over with, talking to Leigh, that is. She needs to know that Ben and I know what's up and that we want answers. Ben has ignored emails and calls from his mom, only taking enough time to write her and tell her he's in midterms, so he isn't exactly lying. I guess we both just want to let the truth come out. See what dust gets kicked up and then bury it."

"It's a plan, Abby. I think if you're ready to talk to Leigh, then you should. If you both are worried what this could mean for the road ahead, then may I suggest something?"

"Well, you seem to know best these days," Abby replied as she threw a smile Maria's way. "And any suggestions when it comes to dealing with my sister -- our sister -- are much appreciated."

At that moment Ben came flying out of the pool house, keys in hand, racing to his car.

"See you guys in a bit. The plane is coming in now," he said as he pointed to the sky. Sure enough, the group watched Andrew's plane begin its descent to the island.

"Drive carefully, boy. Tell Andrew I made his favorite jerk chicken for dinner." Maria had known Andrew as long as she had known Ben, so he was an exciting guest for everyone to see. Almost a part of the family, Ziggy had said.

Abby watched Ben as he waved good-bye and disappeared down the driveway, kicking up clouds of dust behind him as he sped away. She then focused her attention back on Maria. "Okay, where were we before hurricane Ben came flying through?"

"I was saying I think you should go away to Nevis this weekend. The roof is almost done, the ceiling is repaired and anything else can be left a day or two." Maria was all business. "We can get back to brass tacks once you return. If I'm not mistaken we only have one person checking in here tomorrow, correct?"

Abby reflected on the appointment calendar in her mind's eye. "I believe so . . . I remember talking to his assistant. Jack Rhys. And he's looking at the property. Hmm," Abby wondered aloud, "should I be here to greet him?"

Maria shook her head. "Nah. He's just checking in. I can

show him around, then the real estate agent can do the rest." Maria smiled lovingly at Abby and reached over to pat her arm. "Go take a day or two. I wouldn't tell you to go if I didn't think it would be okay."

Abby nodded. "It's a good idea, Maria."

"I know, girl," Maria said jokingly. "Trust me, there's a bigger picture here. We only just see a corner of it. That's life. You don't want to unwrap it all at once. Enjoy the journey."

"Ya know, Maria, I think you missed your calling."

Maria smiled smugly at Abby. "Therapist?"

It was Abby's turn to smile with smugness. "No. Greeting card jingle writer."

Maria's mouth dropped, but her reaction was quickly followed by laughter. "Girl. Back to work here. Let's go over what we need to do, what we need from Leigh, and then I need to get in the house and start cleaning."

"You got it. Need any help today or can I concentrate on paint touch-ups?" Abby had found comfort in helping Maria with the house. She now knew almost every inch of it and felt attached in a small way.

"Nah. I'm just making beds and straightening. You can do some touch-ups if you want, but know it really is a good time for you to take off. You can continue with your to-do list when you get back."

"If I remember correctly, Ben mentioned that one of the plantations was running a special for the weekend. Offering discounted prices for the students. I think I saw it on a note somewhere inside." Abby was already pushing back her chair from the table. "I'm going to look it up and see if I can hold two rooms."

"That's the spirit, make it happen." Maria was gathering her things and making her way back to the main house. "And Abby?"

"Yeah?"

"No matter what, trust yourself."

Abby was halfway in the door to the pool house. "Okay, Hallmark!" Abby teasingly threw Maria a thumbs-up and went inside.

Once she was in the kitchen, Abby started looking around for Ben's note. It should still be on the counter, Abby hoped. It was a plantation on the Caribbean side. Nice restaurant, cottages with porches, hammocks under palm and coconut trees. Palm Tree Plantation? Then she saw the sticky note with Ben's scribble on it. Coconut Palm Plantation! There was a number and Abby quickly grabbed her mobile to call.

She was in luck. Abby was able to hold two cottages on Saturday night. The cottages had pull-out couches on the screened-in porches, so if Ben wanted to invite anyone else along, they could make it work. They just needed to get the ferry over in the morning. She couldn't wait to tell Ben the news.

Abby realized the boys would be getting back any minute, so she hurried to get through a shower to be fresh for meeting Ben's friend. This was the first of his good, close friends to whom she would be introduced as his sister, and she didn't want to disappoint anyone, especially someone Ben was so close to.

Abby was just about to head to the main house to start a load of laundry when Ben's car came whizzing up the driveway. There were two figures inside with Ben. It seemed Tracey had been picked up along the way to the airport as well.

The group was extracting themselves from the small car as

Abby made her way over. Tracey jumped out of the backseat first and came over to hug Abby hello.

"Hope you don't mind that Ben asked me to tag along?" Tracey asked.

"What? Never. You can come around anytime you like." Abby tilted her head in secretively to Tracey. "What's he like?"

"He's great. You're going to love him." Tracey grinned.

"Good. I'm excited to meet him." Abby had noticed her palms were a little sweaty, and it wasn't from the humidity. She was excited but oddly nervous as well.

She turned toward the car so she could greet the two boys as they got out. Ben was already at the back of the car unloading Andrew's suitcases. Andrew was just emerging from the passenger's seat. He and Ben were arguing about something news-related, politics or such. Andrew turned in Abby's direction to wave hello, and it was all she could do to keep from falling over.

It seemed that Ben had neglected to tell Abby that his friend Andrew was absolutely to-die-for gorgeous. Andrew was smiling, standing in the sunshine like a glistening Adonis or at least a cute close-up version of Brad Pitt. His body was fit, as he, like Ben, still played rugby almost every weekend. He had a ball cap on to cover his dark curly hair, and it only added to the boyish charm that oozed from his very being. He came complete with gorgeous biceps that threatened to rip open the T-shirt he wore. Abby was thrown for a loop as her eyes drifted over his rugged body. The smile he greeted Abby with melted her insides like chocolate on a sidewalk at noon.

She was quick to maintain her composure. She made her way over to the car and held out her hand to Andrew as she began to introduce herself.

Andrew turned the tables on her, though. She had no

sooner rounded the front of the car to greet to him than he grabbed her and took her into the biggest hug she had ever gotten from a stranger. Taken off guard, Abby stumbled a little backward when she was released.

"Andrew . . . uh, nice to meet you," she stammered, not knowing how to react.

"Abby, I've heard so much about you." He was smiling at her with all those perfect teeth and that beautiful smile again. Abby couldn't help but be lost in his dark brown eyes.

"I've heard a lot about you as well. And I think Ben is really looking forward to getting to spend some time with you. Seems he has a lot to talk about, huh?" Abby managed to summon a wink.

Andrew was laughing. "True." His smile was wickedly twitching on his lips as his eyes trailed over Abby's body. She could feel his gaze like a searing hook in her gut. "But first, I think I need to fill you in on some good Ben stories." Andrew threw a look Ben's way as he teasingly tossed an arm around Abby's shoulders. "You know, like -- "

Ben piped in here, cutting Andrew off, pulling Abby away from his friend. "Like the time you wanted to play cards with the locals in Phuket?" Ben turned to the girls here. "Andrew had this great idea. 'Ben, let's play cards with these guys for beer. It'll be easy.' Famous last words." Ben rolled his eyes Andrew's way.

"Like I knew they were militia and they actually understood English. Apparently, they didn't like it that I was trying to cheat them at our game."

"Andrew," Ben insisted, "tell them the card game we were teaching them."

With a straight face, Andrew replied, "Go Fish."

Abby and Tracey exchanged a glance.

"Go Fish?" Abby asked.

Andrew nodded. "Yep. And I pretended that certain cards meant that we got beer or we won." He shrugged. "I just kept making up rules."

"And the drunker he was, the sloppier the game. Eventually, one of the guys realized what we were doing since tattle-tale here," Ben jerked his thumb toward Andrew, "opened his mouth to share his excitement at winning with me. We were bounced out with a few swings taken at us --"

"But," Andrew interjected with a wink, "we made it out. We were on a flight out the next day."

Ben stared Andrew down. "We got lucky. You almost got us killed over beer."

"We're okay now, right?" Andrew was charming; Abby could see that it was going to be fun having him around to spar with Ben.

"Well, I'd like to request that nothing like that happens while you're here with us, okay? When you leave, we'll still be here and I don't want our locals ganging up on us." Abby could feel her body tingling whenever they made eye contact.

I need to get it together, she thought to herself. This is Ben's best friend. And he's at least nine years younger than I am. What am I thinking?

As if sensing the need to change the subject or at least keep things moving, Tracey began to question Andrew about his job as they headed toward the main house.

"Andrew's an architect." Ben decided to boast for Andrew, in case he wouldn't do it himself. "Gets to fly all over the place for work."

"And rack up frequent-flier miles in the process?" Abby offered.

"Indeed. Although most of my trips are business-related these days."

The group was stopped short by a high-pitched scream.

"Andrew! It's about time you came back to us!" Needless to say, Maria was thrilled to see him.

"He's here for me, Maria!" Ben chided his housemother.

It was obvious that there was a lot of love in this group for one another and that they were all happy to be together. Andrew and Ben were punching each other and laughing, sharing some stories with Maria when Ziggy came in through the hallway off the kitchen, carrying some fishing poles over his shoulder and what appeared to be a gun of some sort.

"Look 'ere! He's back from South Africa and going on a safari wit'out me," Ziggy exclaimed as he grabbed Andrew in a big bear hug.

"I'm in London now, Ziggy," Andrew chuckled as he patted Ziggy on the back. "On your way to spear-gun a few fish?"

"Yeah, mon. Going to Ricky's now and meetin' da Cap'n. We gonna catch some fish, den I was gonna make us some on de grill for dinner." He cast a quick look toward his wife. "If dat's okay wit' da meal you have planned, baby?"

"My, that man gets so sweet when he wants his way," Maria remarked as Ziggy came up behind her and gave her a big hug and a kiss on the cheek. "Yes, Ziggy. Go and get some fish. The more island food we can offer this skinny man, the better!" She began buzzing around the kitchen again, prepping some snacks for the group to munch on for the time being.

"You are the sweetest woman in the world, Maria. If you weren't already taken . . . " Andrew began, but was stopped when Ziggy pointed to the spear gun he'd placed on the kitchen table.

"You see dat? I will use it on you, Andrew, if you be puttin' dose hands on my girl," Ziggy teased.

Andrew threw his hands up in mock horror and backed up behind Abby. "If you try, I swear I'll hold her hostage."

Abby was more than aware of Andrew touching her forearms. Oh no, she thought, not my brother's best friend. This is a definite no. He's the one who will always be around, you silly girl.

Not wanting to appear rude, Abby played along with the game for another heartbeat and then found a way to slide out of Andrew's playful grasp. He looked at her funny when she pulled away. She just shrugged and threw herself into helping Maria prep the snacks.

When all was said and done, Maria and Abby had arranged several plates on the counter of fruits, cheeses with crackers of all kinds, an assortment of meats, and a little veggie tray with ranch dressing for dipping. Abby grabbed a little plate and then headed over to the center island to take one of the two seats. Andrew joined her, much to her chagrin.

"Abby, Tracey here tells me you've been down here for a while now. Is that right?" Abby had the feeling he already knew the answer but was just trying to be conversational.

"Yes, that's right . . . and I'm here for a little bit longer. Then it's back to Los Angeles for me." Abby's voice was actually a little down as she said this last part.

"I can't imagine leaving paradise after being here for so long. Although, Ben seems ready, too. He's very excited to get back to the States." Andrew was being very friendly to Abby. Was he flirting with her?

Behind them, Tracey was helping Maria get drinks together for everyone. They were stirring up some pitchers of lemonade and iced tea. Ziggy was busy cutting up fresh lemons. And here sat Abby, feeling out of place in a room she was usually so comfortable in.

"I'm a little sad to leave here, in a bittersweet kind of way," she piped up, as if she was afraid of the silence and needed to fill it. "I think it'll be really weird heading home and not knowing what I'm going to do."

Andrew's eyes were boring straight into hers. "What do you mean?"

"Not too much to tell, really. We hit the recession, I got laid off, and I came here. Now I get to go home and find a job." Andrew started to say something, but Abby stopped him. "If you're going to tell me to be more positive, I get it, but facts are facts. Things are just different for me and a lot of other people right now."

"I was going to say that I feel a lot for the Americans right now." He stopped long enough to take the glass of lemonade that Tracey was offering him. "But now that you mention it, that was very negative of you to say."

Abby looked at him and was about to go into her usual "I'm right and you're not" tirade that was reserved for when people were sassy, but the smile in his eyes told her he was joking, so she pinched her mouth closed and smiled at him.

"You're a teaser, aren't you?"

"I've been called a pisser."

Abby was reaching for her napkin as Andrew was reaching for some more food on his plate. Somehow the two of them grazed hands, and Abby could swear the electricity shot up into her shoulder. She snapped her hand back, but she did it too fast, because she saw a look of confusion register on Andrew's face.

"Uh . . . Trace. Don't make my drink, I'll come around and pour my own." Abby was already off her barstool. Anything to get away from the close proximity she was in with Andrew. "I like a certain mixture."

"Is it your Arnold Palmer?" Ben teased.

Abby laughed as she got up to make her favorite beverage.

"Yes, Ben, I'm making my golfing drink."

This made Andrew perk up. "You golf?"

"Well, I have to do something in my free time." Abby was stirring her drink and heading back to her spot next to Andrew. "Actually, free time that I used to have in my other life. I hate to admit it, but I've not played at all since I've been here. It's too hot."

"Nonsense. We need to go out one day before I leave. Maybe when Ben's back in classes you can entertain me?"

Abby was taking a drink of her concoction and had to fight to keep from spitting it out. "I'm sure we can find some time for me to 'entertain' you, Andrew."

"Good. Now," Andrew had turned his attention to Ben and Tracey, "these two mentioned going to Nevis tomorrow for a getaway at one of the hotels."

Maria scoffed at Andrew. "Maybe you should all ask Abby what she went ahead and did earlier to make life a little easier on all of you."

The group all turned, waiting for Abby to spill her news.

"Well," she began, "I called the plantation you mentioned, Ben."

"Coconut Palm Plantation?"

Abby nodded. "I held two cottages for us. They sleep up to four in each. That way, if you have friends that want to come, bring 'em. I just want my own bed in one of the cottages, okay?"

Ben was shocked but happily so. "Abby, thank you. I kept meaning to do that all week, and I kept forgetting . . . all week." He had his arm around Tracey's waist. She had a grin plastered on her face as well.

"This has been such a rough semester! I'm ready to go and just relax and enjoy some sunshine."

"Hiking. We should totally go hiking," Ben said.

Abby and Andrew both snorted at the thought. The timing was so perfect it made the whole lot laugh.

"I guess I know which two will be on the beach most of the time," Maria said.

Abby was nodding her head in happiness. "Indeed." She looked Ben's way. "I think when we get back from Nevis, we should talk to Leigh and get this over with."

Ben looked a little pale at the thought. Abby totally understood. "I know you're worried because of how rough school's been for you, but I think if we can get this out now, while you have a few days off to deal with it . . . well, I think it's better in the long run. You need a clear head. We both do."

Ben stared at the floor, soaking in Abby's suggestion. After a few quiet moments lost in his thoughts, he looked at Abby and nodded.

"You're right. When we get back Monday, let's call Leigh." He pulled Tracey in a little tighter to his body. "That way I can talk to my mum, too."

Abby smiled at Ben. It was so cool that she had a brother. She had always felt very protective of family members, even if they did drive her nuts, and with Ben it was the same. She wanted to protect him from any falling-out this phone call with Leigh could have, knowing that it could impact the world they were creating for themselves down here.

"Okay, kids. I'm done with all of ya. You too, Ziggy," Maria said as she began to shoo everyone out the door. "Take some drinks and food for the road. But I don't want to see any of ya until it's time for dinner. Got it?"

Everyone began to trail out the door. Ziggy was packing his gear in his cab, while Ben and Andrew were getting Andrew's luggage and taking it into the pool house, leaving Abby and Tracey together.

The girls made their way to the pool, each knowing the other wanted to sit. They let their feet dangle in the cool water as they sipped their beverages in silence and enjoyed being still.

It was Tracey who broke the peace finally. "Andrew's cute, huh?"

Abby rolled her eyes at Tracey. "Well, yes, he is very cute for a guy who is the same age as my little brother. Next question?"

Tracey laughed at Abby. "You're funny, Abby. He's cute. There are a lot of boys here who are cute. And," she added as she let her feet turn swirly circles in the pool, "I think you'd make a great cougar."

Abby's jaw dropped at that last comment. She looked at Tracey, only to find she was biting her lip to keep from laughing.

"Are people really and truly okay with cougars? Why can't an older woman interested in a younger man be a grown-up cat with an attitude? 'Cougar' sounds so, oh, I don't know, so . . . lecherous." Abby's reasoning made Tracey bite her lip more in her outstanding effort at stopping her laughter.

"So many of the guys down here have hooked up with older women, not that you're old," Tracey was quick to ad-lib. "What I mean is that with tourists, teachers, and the occasional horny mom who shows up, well . . . the boys here are pretty hot on it, too."

Mumbling an "eh" under her breath, Abby rolled on her side to face Tracey. She had grass stuck in her hair that she was pulling out as she pointedly changed the subject.

"So, Coconut Palm Plantation on Nevis. I'm so excited. Do you know the ferry run times?"

"We can look it up online, subject changer. Runs like every thirty minutes."

Abby absentmindedly nodded. She was playing with one of the sticks she had found in her hair and was drawing pictures in some sand.

"Abby, I'm not trying to push you on anyone or to do something stupid. I just want to see you happy. I see how hard you work to make the people around you happy. The hours you've spent assisting Maria around the inn so she doesn't have to work so hard to clean the rooms, or the detail you've put into repairs that go above and beyond what your sister was asking of you. You've been working nonstop. From what you've told me about your life back in the States, you always seem to work in jobs tailored around other people's happiness." Abby felt Tracey's eyes watching her as she added, "Don't you think it's time you got some of that happiness as well?"

You have a point, Abby thought. But to think I might find something that magical here, wouldn't that just be wishful thinking?

Tracey was watching Abby with such hopeful eyes. Abby smiled at Tracey and finally told her what she wanted to hear.

"Yes, Trace, I do. I think it's high time I was happy, whatever that definition may be. Happiness is an air mattress these days. I'm not really looking for anything romantic, but if it comes along while I'm here, then so be it."

As she finished this last sentence, Abby could see Andrew through the kitchen window. He was smiling at her as she walked up to the house. J.D. can suck it, she thought. He missed the boat.

She felt her heart flip as she smiled back at Andrew, knowing that the fact that they were about to share a small space for the next week could complicate this situation that much more.

CHAPTER 9

IT WAS AN EASY PACKING JOB -- BATHING SUIT, COVER-UP, some shorts and T-shirts, a couple of sundresses, and a pair of jeans. Abby started to pack a sweatshirt, then laughed at the thought of even needing it on the island, tossing it back into its cubby.

When everyone had disbanded after the meal, Abby had decided she wanted to pack for the trip. She tackled her clothes first. Then, thinking she was alone in the pool house, she looked for her toiletries so she could get them organized when Andrew appeared in front of her wrapped in a towel. Abby's thoughts could only remind her she was in a no-touch situation.

His South African accent seemed a little thicker when he spoke. Or maybe Abby was just hearing everything in slow motion.

"Are you okay, Abby?"

Abby realized she was hard-core staring at his abs. Wow, she thought. Never thought I was an ab girl, but wow . . .

"Umm . . . " she cleared her throat, which sparked a coughing fit. Andrew watched her with amusement.

"What I meant was, yes, I'm fine. I was just wondering if the towel you had on . . . if that was mine and then I kinda zoned out. You know, wondering why I'd pack it when we're going to a hotel."

The smile that played on Andrew's beautiful full lips was torturing Abby for some reason. She wasn't sure if he was truly humored by her or was fighting the urge to make fun of her. And the electric current that was generating between them was not helping matters one bit.

"The towel? Ben said I could use it. If it's yours, my apologies. Want it back?" He was grabbing at the edge, teasingly, as if he was about to take it off and hand it over.

Abby shook her head and laughed nervously. "That's okay. Keep it on, there, sailor." She took a hot second to recover. "I just like to pack for any situation. Makes me a little neurotic, I guess."

Andrew nodded his head, turning around to head up the steps to Ben's room so he could change. "Neurotic. Yes, just what I was thinking as well."

Abby snapped her attention his way to make sure he was teasing. From the smile that had enveloped his face, she could see he was.

"Yeah . . . Well, back to packing." Abby found herself awkwardly playing with the rings on her fingers yet again.

Andrew opened his mouth to say something when Ben walked in.

"Hey! You done? I need to shower, then we should go grab a beer, right?"

Andrew turned his gaze away from Abby, focusing on Ben. "Sounds good. Give me five."

"Ben, leave out what you want to take tomorrow and I'll pack it for you. That way you guys can get out of here. Cool?" Abby was desperate for anything to keep her mind and hands busy.

Ben and Andrew both let out a whoop of excitement. "Told ya, Andrew. Abby's the best. I got lucky." Then Ben bolted up the stairs to get ready to go out.

Andrew turned around, trailing Ben up the steps to his room. "Yes, you did say that, Ben." Andrew then turned back to look at Abby again. "You did get lucky." He then shot her one last wicked grin and disappeared into Ben's room.

Abby felt her body shudder just a bit. I'll find something annoying about him in no time, she decided. Then I can move on.

◦◦

MORNING CAME QUICKLY. ABBY HAD PLANNED AN EARLY RISE so she could have her coffee, waking up properly by sipping peacefully on her caffeine by the pool. She was so busy daydreaming that she didn't see the gigantic centipede that had begun making its way across the terrace toward her bare foot. It was a big one, measuring about ten inches. And its little legs were swiftly bringing it closer to Abby's unsuspecting feet.

Snapping out of her dreamy state to see the pincered insect approaching quickly, Abby made a split-second decision.

In her mind, she pictured herself jumping in a fluid motion from sitting position to standing on the chair, or maybe using the chair as a launching pad, like Jennifer Garner would in Alias, or Angelina Jolie in one of the Tomb Raider movies, so she could jump over to the pool house, landing by the door, and get one of Ben's boots, twirl around and pummel the rippling caterpillar-like demon to a bloody and deliberate death.

Unfortunately, Abby wasn't quite so graceful. When she saw the centipede, she let out such frightened, guttural sounds that one might be forgiven for thinking she was fleeing from a mass murderer. Meanwhile, she was trying to hoist herself on top of the chair to remove her feet and legs from harm's way. But as luck would have it, her flip-flop caught one of the plastic chair rungs, making it wobble just long enough to make her lose her balance and descend into a slow-motion free fall.

It was only fitting that at this precise moment Andrew emerged from the pool house to check on the commotion. As Andrew's foot touched terra firma outside the front door, Abby was slowly falling backward, toward the pool. At the same time, while it was sinking in that she was about to fall into cold water at 7 a.m. for her own horrific wake-up call, her robe was beginning to slide off her body. Arms flailing as she tried to hold on to the small bit of fabric covering her bra and panties, Abby still had her eyes on the centipede and was barking at Andrew to "KILL IT!!!" She hit the water, chair still caught in her flip-flop -- her robe on the ground next to where she'd stood.

Andrew was already using Ben's boot to crush the centipede. As Abby raised her head out of the water, she watched as the creature lifted his body one last time toward Andrew before he delivered the crushing fatal blow.

Abby bobbed in the water, breathing heavily, not sure what to do. Andrew turned, pointing at the centipede. "Got it," he said, and grinned.

"Great. That's just great." She was unhooking her shoe from the chair and putting them up on the side of the pool. "I'm glad."

Andrew was trying not to laugh as he surveyed the scene: Abby's coffee had toppled over, her robe was on the ground, and she was in the pool half-naked, hoisting out a dripping deck chair. His attempt to suppress his amusement was unsuccessful.

Abby rolled her eyes and looked at him with indignation. "Okay, I get it. Ha ha. Abby, you're a mess. Ben, did you see Abby run from the centipede 'cause she's a sissy? Tee hee hee . . . Let's Facebook this with a status update. Oh, no, wait! I'm gonna tweet it. Bwah ha ha."

Abby's attempt at sarcasm only made Andrew laugh harder. She was a pitiful sight, dripping wet and looking forlorn, but as she looked around at the yard and how it must have looked from Andrew's point of view, she started to giggle as well. As they were laughing, Andrew picked up Abby's robe, bringing it over to her by the poolside.

"Here, Abby. I would not be a decent man if I left you in the pool half-naked after running from such a mean, evil, large, gigantic --"

"I get it, Andrew! Look. Those things are evil and that one was gigantic. I've heard stories down here about their stingers." Abby motioned for him to turn around so she could climb out of the pool and put her robe back on. "People go to the hospital because of those things!"

"Well," Andrew began, with his back turned away, "you handled it with such graceful, catlike reflexes." His lips were turned up in an evil grin.

Abby was leaning her head over the pool now, wringing out her long brown hair. "I know sarcasm, Andrew. I can be pretty sarcastic myself. You are not as subtle as you think."

He turned around and took a step closer to her, bringing them almost nose to nose. "Maybe I'm not trying to be subtle,

Abby. Subtlety is not an attribute I'm usually known for." Then with a flash of his perfect wicked smile, he disappeared back into the house.

Abby was still reeling from Andrew's closeness to her space, appalled at her lack of smoothness in reacting to the situation, as she cleaned up her mess. Ben soon came charging out on his way to pick up Tracey. He barked at Abby to make sure she was ready so they could make the ferry. Abby looked down at her condition and couldn't believe Ben had just flown past her, like some male Wicked Witch, shouting orders like a drill sergeant. He hadn't even noticed she was soaking wet, nor did he realize he had stepped over the bloody mess of a centipede.

As she was about to go inside, Andrew came racing out fast on Ben's heels. He stopped long enough to address Abby before he jumped in the car.

"By the way, your bum?"

Abby's mouth dropped open as she turned to face him. "What about my . . . bum?"

Andrew smiled that perfect and wicked smile one more time. "It's quite lovely." He then jumped in the car and the boys were off on their mission.

Abby shook her head, mortified that Andrew had seen her act so ridiculously. She didn't have time to think about it long, though, because she needed to get ready. They had a ferry to catch if they were going to get to Nevis, and she was determined to be ready on time.

❦

Unspoiled paradise. That was the one descriptive phrase that popped into Abby's head as they drove from the ferry landing on Nevis to the Coconut Palm Plantation. Abby marveled at the lush tropical foliage as the car made its way around smooth elegant turns on an untouched parcel of land. Monkey Crossing signs appeared every few miles, as did produce and fruit stands with locals selling their wares. It was as if this beautiful island had been plucked right from a story and dropped down for them to discover, with houses, resorts and a few restaurants speckled amid the landscape. Where St. Kitts was clearly more geared toward the tourists that headed to escape to the Caribbean constantly, year-round, Nevis was its unshaken twin. Serene, peaceful and nurturing.

Abby was in heaven. She was so wrapped up in the visual stimulation of the island that she almost forgot about the equally stimulating Andrew. He had been smashed in next to her in the backseat for the whole trip, except for the forty-five minutes they were on the ferry and could get out of the car. While on the ferry trip, Abby had jumped out of the car as soon as they were allowed, saying she needed to stretch.

Abby spent the rest of the ferry ride talking about anything she could think of with Tracey so as not to get caught in a conversation with Andrew. Especially when she had nowhere to escape to because they were on a boat. Abby even waited until the last possible minute to get in the car so they would not be touching skin on skin for as long. She was begging silently to the universe to get her to her room so she could get her head together.

They were all not fully prepared for the beauty that was Coconut Palm Plantation. As they pulled in, the side parking lot kept the view of the hotel grounds partially hidden. There was a rundown sugar mill that had been preserved and still stood stoically at the entrance of the hotel. The main home itself resembled a Southern plantation. The house was from the

18th century and had a sprawling porch all around the second floor. The view from the porch overlooked the "Avenue of Palms," a stretch of land that flowed from the main house down to the beach. It was there along the avenue that the cottages were situated, just a brief walk from the beach, pool and lounge areas. It was breathtaking.

As they were all finding their way to their cottages, Ben and Tracey found they knew quite a few people who were in the other cottages as well. Almost every small group they passed called out hello or asked where they were staying. It seemed this was the place to come for a study break, and Abby had a feeling it was going to be more of a party weekend for these guys than a "back-to-nature" getaway.

Ben's cabin came first, and the trio went inside to get settled and changed. Abby skipped off to her cottage, excited at her chance to just lie out and relax.

Abby's cottage was adorable. She had her own little porch, complete with a pull-out couch and a kitchen table. There was a coffeemaker, tea bags, scones and a fruit basket all sitting on the table welcoming her. Tucked in the basket was also a small bottle of rum, with a few bottles of fruit juice. A perfect welcome to the island hideaway!

Her bedroom was right beyond the sitting/porch area. There was a king-size bed, mosquito netting draped all around, and a fan spinning above the bed that looked like something straight out of Raiders of the Lost Ark. Its blades were made with palm fronds, and it spun slowly and rhythmically in the cool, quiet space. Abby was ecstatic. And what she was paying for both cottages for the night was such a dream compared to prices she would be paying if she were in the States. It was a win-win, like the fact she was able to pay for it with her casino winnings.

As she was getting changed, there was a knock at Abby's door. Abby threw her sundress on over her suit, calling out "Come in" to her visitor. When she came out to the porch area, Ben was sitting at the table with a big grin spread over his face.

"I trust by that big ole smile that you are pleased with our accommodations?" Abby put on her best fake British accent to amuse her brother.

"Dude! It's like this honeymoon suite over there." Ben was shaking his head in disbelief. "I mean, I've heard about this place, but I had no idea it would be so incredible."

Abby peered on the other side of the bedroom door and smiled. "Yeah, I've got a nice little spot in there for when I lay my head down tonight. I have to say, I feel a touch guilty having all this space to myself."

Ben nodded in agreement. "Which is why I thought I'd ask you a favor . . . "

Abby groaned. She could see where this was going already. "I know I said I felt guilty, but I was really saying it only for effect."

"I know. And I would not ask this if it wasn't important to me. But Tracey and I really would like to have one night while we're here to ourselves. Do you know what I mean?"

Yeah, I do, Abby thought. "Go on."

"Will you please let Andrew sleep on your pull-out couch? Just one night?"

Tracey appeared as if by magic at the screen door. "Abs, please know that we wouldn't ask this, but . . . "

Abby started to open her mouth, but Ben stopped her. "But I have a surprise roommate, and Tracey has two roommates. It would be cool to have some alone time."

Abby couldn't find an argument, nor did she feel like it.

"Just so you know," Abby looked at both of them seriously, "if he snores at all and it wakes me up, I will smother him."

Ben and Tracey grabbed Abby in a big hug before rushing out the door to go inform Andrew of the change in plans. Abby was not surprised at all when a few minutes later there was another knock at her door.

"I'd ask who it was, but I'm pretty sure it's the guy who was just tossed out on his bum," she threw at Andrew playfully.

"I haven't seen the guy in ages and I get tossed to the side like a springbok on safari. Not that a springbok would ever get tossed, but you know what I mean." He put down his bag and jerked his head toward the couch. "I take it that's my spot?"

Abby nodded. "Yep. Bathroom is off the main bedroom. Please just don't wake me up if you can help it. Snoring, door slamming, talking in your sleep . . . it's all off-limits."

Suppressing a smile, Andrew nodded his head and threw his bag on his new bed. "Well, that's all settled. Ben said they'd be over to get us in a few minutes and then we could hit the beach."

"Sounds good. I'm gonna go put a few more things away. Then, um, maybe they'll be here." Abby was already backing into her bedroom, more aware than ever of his commanding presence.

"Can I help?"

You bet you can, Abby caught herself thinking.

"No, that's okay. I've got it," she said as she closed the door behind her. She really didn't have anything to put away, but she needed time now to gather her wits.

Abby began rearranging the few items she had already unpacked, taking them out of the drawers she had placed them in and refolding them while finding new homes for everything. Once that was done, she went into the bathroom and began organizing her toiletries so they were in order of use. Anything to keep from having time alone with . . .

"What are you doing?" The sound of his voice was not calming since he had just scared the absolute life out of her. She jumped, screaming involuntarily at the same time.

"Andrew! Do you understand people have heart attacks from fear?"

His wicked smile was back, playing on his lips. "Didn't think you were that old, but okay, grandma, I apologize."

Abby blew out a big huff of breath and stared him in the eyes. "What do you need?"

"Well, Ben said he'd be right back about fifteen to twenty minutes ago."

Abby looked around the room for a clock, but in paradise there was no such thing as time. "Okay. And?"

"And . . . well, let's see. If we were to add this up. They asked me to stay on your couch and not theirs. That's one." He held up his left-hand pointer finger for added effect. "Ben isn't back, and it's been quite awhile. That's another one." Now he used his right-hand pointer finger to show another "one." "One plus one equals -- well, I'll leave that up to your imagination." Andrew tacked a smug smile onto the end of the sentence while wiggling his two fingers in the air at Abby.

Abby made a face. "That's gross. I don't want a visual of what may be happening in their room." She groaned for emphasis. "Let's just go to the beach. I'm sure they'll find us."

"When they come up for air they might. Until then, we can humor ourselves, right?"

"I guess we have to." Abby walked over to the desk and grabbed a piece of paper and a pen, writing out a note for Ben.

"Are you going to slide that under their door? Don't you

know one should never go a-knockin' when the cottage is a-rockin'?"

Abby closed her eyes in mock horror. "Please. Stop. I really don't need to even begin to think about . . . "

He wiggled his eyebrows at her. "Your friend or your family? Which is worse to have a 'visual' of, as you say?"

Abby let out a half-scream, half-laugh. "Okay, Andrew. Time to keep you occupied. Grab a towel, let's go." She then flipped her hands in his direction to shoo him out the door.

As they headed down the path to the beach, Abby could not help but sneak glances at Andrew. Between his biceps and strong jawline she was mesmerized, but trying to keep her cool. Andrew looked like he was carved out of stone, and his features -- so smooth and perfect. She shuddered a little in an attempt to shake it off.

And he was staying in her cottage.

CHAPTER 10

"YOU NEED MORE SUNSCREEN."

Abby woke up from her nap on the beach with Andrew's body blocking her sunshine. Normally, Abby was the girl who liked to hide under the umbrella, not letting her skin see the light of day. Yet instead of fighting the bronzing that was just meant to happen when you lived in the Caribbean, she'd decided to embrace it. It was her last hurrah before permanently resorting to spray tans only.

Abby squinted her eyes against the glare of the sunlight and peeked out from behind her hand at Andrew. "Why do you think I need more sunscreen? Am I blistering?"

"Well, no, but I -- "

"I know how to apply sunscreen and when to reapply it, Andrew. But thank you."

Andrew was nodding in agreement. "Well, judging by the tan line that's happening on your shoulders, next to the red skin, I would think more sunscreen would work." He again shook the sunscreen lotion bottle at Abby.

Abby was already sitting up and looking around for the

bathrooms. They had made their way out to the private beach area the resort had blocked off for guests of the plantation only. Luckily, they also had their pool, pool bar and bathrooms all in the same spot. Abby was up and heading to the bathroom to see her tan line in the mirror.

When she finally got there, she discovered that Andrew was right. She was working on a sunburn now. Not even more sunscreen lotion was going to help. She sighed to herself and headed back outside to join Andrew.

Andrew was talking to a young man in shorts and a polo shirt that was embroidered with the Coconut Palm Plantation logo. As Abby walked up, the employee was off and running to make good on whatever request Andrew had made.

"If you're ordering drinks, I hope you thought to get me one as well," Abby teased.

"Actually, I asked for an umbrella for you. That way you don't have to leave just yet." Andrew then looked over at Abby and brought out his perfect, crooked smile again.

"Thank you. That's sweet." Abby smiled shyly at Andrew. She felt her stomach do a tiny turn when he met her gaze.

The employee came running back over with the umbrella, staking it in the ground for Abby and Andrew. In no time, they were settled in underneath the shade, safe from the rays of the Caribbean sun. Abby had curled up on her lounge chair, ordering a rum punch "with extra ice, please," and was flipping through a magazine. Andrew had buried himself back into his book, or so she thought.

"Is that Austen you're reading or Shakespeare?"

"Wow." Abby put down her People magazine. "I'll have you know that this magazine is at least five months old. I found it at Ricky's. It's just for me to look at the pictures."

Andrew laughed. "I'm sure there's more to you than that."

He had bookmarked his page and turned his full attention to Abby.

Abby nodded, rolling on her side to give Andrew her full attention as well.

"You're right." She leaned in, and gestured for him to lean in as well. "Some people watch CNN for news. I watch E! Entertainment or read Perez Hilton."

Andrew chuckled. "Very deep."

Abby laughed out loud. "I try." She toasted him with her drink.

"You're going to take over my job. I'm comic relief. Or at least that's what I want to be for Ben while I'm here." Andrew's face became serious suddenly. "He's been good to me, he and his mom. They always cheered me on through school. My own mom passed away when I was young."

Abby was floored at this sudden open book she had in front of her. Dammit all to hell. Being sensitive only made him hotter.

"My dad -- our dad -- passed away when I was young as well." Abby let out a heavy sigh, turning over onto her back. "I wish he had been honest about what he was doing. I feel like Ben was always supposed to be around. Like we wasted so much time not knowing him."

Andrew was spinning the cup that housed his rum punch, watching the ice cubes clink up against one another. His expression was intent as he stared into the cup, as if he were looking for the bottom of a well.

"You looking for answers?" Abby inquired.

"No. Counting my blessings. I guess that's what you'd call it in the States." He winked.

"Yes," Abby giggled, "we are known to count our blessings." She surveyed the patch of beach they were sitting on. "If

I was to count any blessings, one would be sitting here on this beach right now. Once in a lifetime," she dreamily said.

"I agree." Andrew was looking around as well, still spinning the cup. Abby was focused on the water and the breeze, so she didn't notice he was watching her. "I've found that when once in a lifetime comes along, you have to jump on it. Do you agree?"

Abby thought about it for only a second before responding. "Of course! I think that if you don't take chances or go for things that are put in front of you, then you could miss out on something fantastic." She was quiet, then decided to make it relate to herself. "Like me living here, for instance. I was laid off, and I could have been sad about it and tried to find work in a country that has the highest unemployment rate in years. Did I? Nope. This opportunity came along. Now I'm here." Abby was smiling to herself.

Abby turned her head to find Andrew looking at her in that way she had seen Ben looking at Tracey. His gaze was strong yet layered with sweetness, and it made her feel a little awkward, but also very tingly and excited.

"You're pretty interesting, Abby."

Andrew's eyes were boring into hers, as if reading her mind. Or at least attempting to guess at what was happening in there. His beautiful dark eyes. Abby could not help but feel mesmerized by them. Her tummy was doing more somersaults than ever before. So many that they were literally taking her breath away.

Abby was about to say something to break the thick energy that had settled in a little cloud around them when she heard her name being called from behind her. She rolled over to see Ben and Tracey making their way across the sand to their little piece of the beach.

"Well, about time you guys made it." "We figured you'd be out by dinnertime at least." Andrew and Abby were talking over each other, sitting up to tease the couple as well as to break their own spell.

Ben smiled at his sister. "Took some time to walk the grounds." He looked around, soaking in the scene. "Pretty nice."

Abby, seeing her chance to flee from her libido, jumped up.

"Now that you guys are here to keep an eye on Prince Charming," she jerked her head in Andrew's direction, "I'm off. See you guys later."

Abby was moving so fast, she was kicking up sand in her flight. She did manage one final shy smile in Andrew's direction, then headed back to her cottage so she could calm her raging hormones down.

❦

ABBY NEVER GOT A CHANCE TO REST UNTIL WELL AFTER dinner. When she had gotten back to her room, the maids were there turning down her bed. One had seen how sunburned Abby was and had gone to get some vinegar for her from the kitchen. She had returned with a cupful, instructing Abby to lay in a bath in order to help turn the sunburn into a tan.

So, she had done just that. Filling the tub about halfway with cool water, Abby added the vinegar and slid in to soak. The smell was terrible, but she managed to stay in the tub for the thirty minutes they had recommended. She emptied the tub, got out and stood in the shower to rinse off. When she was done, she noticed the smell was lingering. Abby got back in and rinsed off for a bit longer, this time making sure to get her back good and soapy, even thought it hurt terribly when she was rubbing her skin.

The smell was still lingering. "Pickly. Ew." Abby decided to try one more time. She got in, lathered up with soap, shampoo and shaving cream, all in an attempt to kill the smell. Again, the result was that Abby smelled like a bottle of vinegar. She was mortified.

Abby was lathering on some coconut lotion she had with her when she heard the front door open. Followed by, "What is that smell?" Abby realized Andrew must have been hit straight in the face with the odor that was her new nightmare. She wrapped up in the hotel robe and came out to face the music.

"It's me. I smell like pickles."

Abby had no sooner spoken than the door flew open. Ben walked in, covering his mouth and nose with his hand. "What is that?"

Abby rolled her eyes. "It's me! I took a bath in vinegar -- the maids told me it would help my sunburn. It took the sting away, but now I smell. And I smell really bad."

"At least you're aware of the scent you have around you, Pigpen," Ben said. Abby took a playful swat at him.

"Shut up. I can't go to dinner with you guys like this. Every table will smell me."

"I don't think I could even enjoy a meal with the smell of cleaning products so close to me," Andrew said, speaking as if to Ben but sending the zinger to Abby.

"Great." She sighed and sat down on the bed. "I'll stay here while you guys go to dinner. There's no point in me going anywhere."

Ben and Andrew both pooh-poohed the idea. "No way," Ben said. "This place is known for their food. They are offering a special dinner menu with low prices for students as well." He puffed his chest out like a chicken and did a happy dance for their enjoyment.

"He's right, you know. Let's all do dinner together," Andrew said, laughing at his friend. "We can go early, then you can come back here, and we'll hose you down or something. I'm sure if we throw some chlorine on you from the pool . . . "

Abby shook her head, acting as if she was disgusted. "Chlorine. Whatever." She looked at the back of the door where she had hung the dress she was wearing to dinner. "Okay, fine. I'll do dinner. One condition."

The guys both nodded.

"If I still smell bad after dinner, I'm coming back to the room to just go to sleep. Okay?"

"Trust me, Abby," Ben said, "if you still smell after dinner, I will find a way to lose you."

"Ha!" Abby retorted. She grabbed the dress off the door and headed into the bathroom. "When's dinner?"

The boys looked at their watches. "Meet in the dining room at six?"

Abby nodded and headed back in the bathroom. She was about to close the door when she realized Andrew was there and he wanted to get ready. I'm so selfish, she thought, chastising herself.

As she went back out to the porch, she could hear Ben talking to Andrew, now in planner mode. "Grab your things, and we'll go back to my room so you can get ready, cool?"

Abby didn't hear Andrew's reply, so she popped her head around the door so she could assess the situation. "Hey, Andrew, did you need -- "

"I'm a day ahead of ya, Abs. I got him from here. Don't want him in your hair more than he already is."

Abby took a quick peek out of the corner of her eye only to see that Andrew was staring at her, waiting for her to react somehow. Not sure why, Abby decided to play it cool. Cooler than she had been.

"No, we don't. Thanks, Ben." She then stood there, awkwardly. "Okay, then. See you two at dinner." And with that she closed the door to the bedroom and went back about her business.

But not before registering the way Andrew's face had fallen, not much, but enough.

*

THE RESTAURANT WAS BUZZING EVEN AS EARLY AS SIX IN THE evening, when they had arrived. Since the majority of the property was rented out to students for the semester break, it seemed only fitting that the five-star restaurant was overtaken by nothing but vet students. All of them were out having fun, and some were already a little drunk.

All during dinner, people kept stopping by the table to say hello to Ben or Tracey. A few of them knew Andrew from all of his visits out to see Ben. Abby held her own for a few conversations, but inevitably, the other people would get a whiff of her new vinegar perfume and would end up excusing themselves to go back to their table or to the bathroom. They usually never returned.

One of the visits was from a girl in Ben's class named Adrienne. It didn't take long to guess that she was very popular with the boys at the school. Tracey leaned over to tell Abby that she rose in popularity because she was a "total ho. Slept with a professor and at least ten students I can think of off the top of my head," Tracey explained. Abby feigned some disbelief, but the short-shorts and tank top that barely covered the girl's chest clued her in that Adrienne was looking for more than a restful weekend.

To the chagrin of the table, Adrienne pulled a chair right up next to Andrew, starting a conversation with him. Andrew, who had been in the sun all day and was a few whiskey drinks in with Ben, was loving the attention. She smiled, touching his arm and using her fingers to suggestively touch her décolletage as she laughed at everything he said. Including "Pass the pepper." Abby was disgusted. Not just for the girl, but with Andrew as well.

Abby stayed long enough to watch them flirt, to the point that she was absolutely grossed out. When the check arrived, she threw her money down and stood up so abruptly it jarred everyone sitting at the table.

"I'm heading back to my room. Have fun, good night." She started to leave, then as an afterthought she added, "Oh, Andrew? Huge favor. Please just be quiet when you come in, okay?" She then threw a tight smile his way and turned to leave.

"Abby, I thought you were going to hang out with us tonight?" Tracey asked, sounding genuinely sad by the fact that she was leaving them so soon.

"I'm going to head back and relax. Maybe get this smell off of me. Thank you, though." She then blew Tracey a kiss and hurried back to her cottage.

As soon as she opened the door, the tears flooded. Where is this coming from? She thought as she leaned against the door. Just because some hot girl in her twenties was flirting with the guy I secretly have a crush on? Like I care about that. Him or her. Oh, who am I kidding? I'd be pissed no matter what her age was. UGH!!!

It had to be something else. Maybe it was PMS. Abby honestly wasn't sure where it was coming from, all she knew was that she didn't like the feeling she had. She was sifting through her tears when her cell phone rang.

She hadn't even said hello when the familiar voice started in. "I'm in Miami. Should be to you guys by tomorrow afternoon. How's everything there?"

Abby sighed to herself when she heard Leigh's voice and subconsciously sat up a little straighter.

"Um, hi, Leigh? What do you mean you're on your way down?"

Leigh was quiet on the other end of the phone. "My, someone is in a somber mood tonight. What's your problem?"

Abby took a minute before replying to her sister. She could hear that she was agitated. Leigh's voice would shake slightly when she was looking for an argument, and she could hear a low rumble tonight.

"Well, Leigh, I was actually going to call you tomorrow or Monday. There are a few things going on down here that I need to clear the air with you about."

"I'm going to be there in less than twenty-four hours. The real estate agent sent me an email saying someone was there that would be making an offer and Maria has been reporting that the repairs are going well. Is that true?"

Abby was stunned at the news. "Well, I know there have been potential buyers in and out, but when I left this morning - - " Abby didn't get a chance to finish, because Leigh cut her off.

"What do you mean, when you left? Where are you? I thought your sole purpose for being on St. Kitts was to help me, Abby."

But I have been! Abby fought the urge to scream.

"I decided to take a little break for a night with Ben and a few of his friends. We're on Nevis. Now, like I was telling you about -- "

"You're on Nevis? With Ben? Abby! I get word that someone is almost ready to make an offer and you're not even there? What about all of the repairs, Abby? How are you being so irresponsible right now? I asked you to help with one thing and you take off?"

Abby was starting to feel her patience with Leigh break.

"Maria told me just yesterday that it was more than fine for me to take a few days. I think we both know I'm not going to leave her in the lurch!" Abby was pissed. "As for the repairs, everything has been flowing along quite smoothly; in fact, I'd venture to say I'm ahead of schedule. The inn might even be in better shape than when you first purchased it." The last part Abby threw in more for effect, but she was truly proud of how much attention she was paying to all the small details around the inn. She had hoped Leigh would be happy as well, but wasn't sure any longer in light of the current conversation.

The other end of the line was silent. Dead silent. When Leigh did speak, Abby could tell she was putting on a show to choose her words carefully.

"Abby, I sent you down there to help me get this house taken care of. How can you do anything I need you to do if you're off screwing around on an island with the tenant and his buddies, while Maria and Ziggy are doing all the work?" Leigh sighed heavily. "This truly feels quite typical of you, Abby. I ask for help, you blow it off. Have you really done anything to the inn or am I facing a huge mess?"

Oh, no she didn't.

"How can I screw around, Leigh? Did you seriously just ask how I could be so bold as to screw around when my dear sister so desperately needed me to do something for her? I ask myself the same thing every day. Especially when she neglects to give me all the information necessary."

Abby waited with bated breath for Leigh to pipe up. But she didn't.

"Leigh. I know." Abby made this statement slow and cryptic on purpose, almost through gritted teeth. She wanted Leigh to feel the impact.

She knew Leigh was still on the other end, but there was no sound, no movement. Nothing. "Leigh, we need to talk about this. About all of it."

After what seemed like an eternity, but was actually about ten seconds, Leigh spoke curtly. "You know about the inn. We discussed that, Abby."

Abby was going to blow a gasket. "No, Leigh! I found a picture. Of our father with Ben's mother and they were together. I know that Ben is our half-brother. And the book . . . he has the same book Dad gave us when we were little." Abby was upset again. "Dammit, Leigh. I need you to tell me the truth. How long have you known about Ben?"

Abby regretted the way this was going. It was all pouring out over a bad connection. Not ideal, but finally out in the open.

Leigh took a big deep breath in. Abby thought she might have put the phone down because this time the silence went on for what felt like a minute. Abby didn't want to rush her. If there was one thing she knew about her sister, it was that she did always have a reason for the way she did things. This would be no exception.

"I've known about Ben since you were fifteen years old."

The weight of the statement punched Abby in the heart like a ton of bricks. "Since I was fifteen?" Abby was calculating how long ago that was. "So, for a little over twenty years you've known about Ben?!"

Abby could feel the weight of Leigh's load over the line. It was heavy and sad. "Yes. I've known since Dad told me." Leigh's voice was quivering. "He told me when he was dying, Abby. Dad told me about his other life when he was dying."

Abby felt her world start to spin. She wanted to throw up, go to sleep and scream like the lead actress in a horror movie, all at the same time. "Ben would have been seven."

"Yes."

"So, Dad kept him hidden . . . "

Leigh finished Abby's sentence. "For seven years. Abby, it doesn't make him a bad man . . . "

Abby held up her hand to stop Leigh from speaking, even though she wasn't in the room with her. "No. You don't get to defend him to me right now. In fact, you, of all people, don't get to defend anyone. Dad may have hidden him for seven years, but you and Ben's mom or mum or whatever she's called, you both kept this from everyone else for the last twenty years? Are all of you insane?"

The normally collected Leigh was finally snapping on her end as well. "No, Abby, I'm not insane! I just wanted to keep the peace. Hell, Mom didn't need to know her dead husband had cheated on her. And Ben's mother? She didn't care as long as Ben was taken care of. She loves him enough for all of us, Abby. And she wanted to keep it that way. But then this situation came up. I never thought it would come out like this. I wanted to be able to tell you, to tell him. It just never felt like the time was right."

Abby felt nauseated. *Leigh could have told us all a long time ago and we could have moved on. Did she have her* reasons? What would I have done if I were in her place? Her thoughts were tripping over one another in succession.

"In Maria's email she said a lot had been going on, but that you and Ben were close. Is that true?" Leigh's voice was hopeful, looking for clues from Abby.

"Well, yeah. I mean, not at first. But finding out you have the same dad kinda makes you war buddies by default." Abby paused before adding, "I really like Ben, Leigh."

"Dad made me swear, Abby. He didn't want anyone to know. In his will, he left me extra money and asked me to invest in this inn. It was something he was already researching and planning on buying for 'the family.' I had to honor his wishes and I knew it had a chance to at least turn a profit, helping both you and Ben out in the future." Abby heard the familiar click of a lighter from Leigh's end. "I couldn't lecture him as he was dying that he needed to come clean. He knew Mom wouldn't understand and that he would be leaving her with so many unanswered questions." She inhaled deeply.

"So the inn is not just yours?"

"No, Abby," Leigh answered quietly. "It's ours."

Abby was stunned. "I guess I'm just not understanding, Leigh."

"You don't have to." She took another drag off her cigarette, so loudly Abby felt like she was smoking it, too. "Dad left me in charge of it, but La Cantina belongs to all three of us. Carla even pushed Ben to apply to Rhodes knowing I could help take care of him as long as he was on the island. For the last few years, the inn has been packing in the tourists and making good money. I always knew as soon as Ben was done with school, or shortly thereafter, I would sell it, dividing the profit for all of us. I just didn't plan on it being so soon."

Abby couldn't believe her ears. "So the house wasn't given to you from Ken in your first marriage?"

"No."

"Why St. Kitts, Leigh? Why here?"

Her sister was silent on the other end of the line. "I honestly can't tell you the answer to that one, Abby. I wish I had the answer myself. It was what Dad wanted."

"Why don't you -- ?"

"Abby." Leigh's voice was terse. "I have enough on my plate."

Hearing the tone in her sister's voice inspired Abby to change the subject. "Does Daryl know?"

Leigh's voice remained terse. "He knows now. I had a feeling that you knew, just from the way Maria's email read. So I told him."

"And?"

"He's taking a few days off to re-evaluate our marriage." Leigh dissolved into tears.

Abby was glad she was sitting down. Her knees felt weak even though she wasn't using them. "I'm so sorry, Leigh."

They sat in silence for a long time, Leigh sobbing and Abby just listening.

"So," Leigh finally cleared her throat, back to business as usual, "you can understand why I'm in Miami. I'm on a plane tomorrow morning that will get me into St. Kitts by the afternoon. I think it's more than obvious now that I need to come there."

Abby was nodding on her end.

"Abby, you there?"

"I was sitting here nodding my head."

Back to her game face, Abby could feel Leigh shaking her head at her from Miami. "I've already talked to Ziggy. He's picking me up when I get in. I'll be there to help push the sale ahead. It served its purpose." She let out a long sigh. "That real estate agent there is making me nervous and I just don't trust him." She gave another burdened sigh. "At least a lot of this other crap is out in the open now."

Abby wanted to brace her sister for Ben and all of his questions. "I think Ben is the main person you have to explain things to."

"I had a feeling. It's time we dealt with what Dad didn't. Or time I dealt with what he didn't." Leigh was solemn.

Abby felt a small pang of sympathy for Leigh. "If I had had to carry a secret like this for the last twenty years, I have no idea how I would have handled it." Abby was thoughtful. "I love you, Leigh. Doesn't mean I agree, but I do love you."

Leigh was appeased. "I love you, too."

With that, she hung up, leaving Abby in her romantic cottage alone to sift through the pieces of their conversation. Things were about to come out in the open, and she was glad they'd be able to close the book on this one. Permanently.

CHAPTER 11

EVEN THOUGH ABBY WANTED TO CURL UP IN BED AND SLEEP her way through the night, she opted instead to make herself a rum drink and head down to one of the hammocks the hotel had strung up on the beach.

As she was swaying back and forth between two palm trees underneath the stars, she let herself be lost in thought, drifting through the events of the last few weeks. So much information gathered in such a small amount of time. Her head was spinning.

And now she needed to pack up tomorrow and head back to La Cantina to ready herself for Leigh. On one hand, Abby was grateful for this. On the other, she was happy here on Nevis lying out and relaxing. And of course, there was Andrew. Who was probably off in some cottage getting to know Adrienne a little better. And then there was J.D. They were two vastly different men, who both brought out something in Abby that she couldn't put her finger on, not quite yet. She rolled her eyes at the ridiculousness of her whole situation and took a swig of her rum punch.

There were a few scattered groups along the shoreline, all hanging out and partying together under the stars. No cares right now, she thought as she watched them. These kids are so happy. No clue that the world out there can be so twisted. Things can change at the drop of a hat, and we have to bend with them or be broken in the process . . .

Abby found herself wistful at the thought and a little jealous. She wanted to be one of them, without a care in the world. Instead she felt like she had the weight of it on her shoulders.

She was so wrapped up in thought that she didn't hear Andrew as he sauntered up behind her.

"I've been looking for you."

The sound of his voice made her jump, knocking her off balance in the hammock. "You should warn a girl when you're sneaking up on her."

"Wouldn't have had the same effect, now would it?" he asked, flashing those dark, handsome eyes her way yet again.

"You've got a point." Abby took a drink of her rum concoction. "Where's your friend?"

"Ben? Or Tracey?"

"Don't be coy with me, Andrew. I meant the girl." Her two drinks at dinner and the one she was working on now were taking their toll. She was feeling sassy. "Adrienne."

"That tart who wanted to get in my pants?" He was grinning at Abby. "How should I know? I left to find you, see if you got back to the room in one piece."

"You did?" Abby sat up and stared at him in disbelief. "Then why are you here on the beach?"

Andrew laughed at her. "Didn't take a private investigator." He looked around. "Beach, resort, gorgeous night . . . you do the math."

"You've got a point, detective." She wavered for a moment,

wondering how much information she should share with Andrew. "My sister called. She's in Miami and on her way to the island. She'll be here tomorrow."

Andrew pulled up a beach chair next to the hammock. "Really? That's intense." He watched Abby as she swayed back and forth in the hammock some more. "What happens now?"

"I guess we'll see." She smiled shyly at him.

The pair sat in silence for little longer until Andrew spoke up.

"If you want to talk about it, I'm here." He was leaning forward in his beach chair as he spoke. "I need to be perfectly honest about why I was looking for you tonight."

Abby cocked her head in his direction. "Why's that?"

Andrew looked down at his hands, then back at Abby. "Abby, I'd be a liar if I said I came to find you because I wanted to make sure you got back safely. I mean, I did. But, what I really wanted was to find you so I . . . well, so we could hang out some more."

This perked Abby up. She tried to sit up again but the hammock was giving her grief. She decided to lie still and try to be cool.

"Oh? Really?" Her attempt at sounding coy was coming across more flippant.

Andrew had stood up and was now standing over the hammock, looking down at Abby. Was that expectation dancing in his eyes?

"Yes, but I want to get to know you." He stopped and cleared his throat. His silhouette was glowing because of the moon behind him.

Andrew was moving closer to her now and she could feel that energy, like a bolt of lightning shooting out and hitting her full on. Only she wasn't sure what she wanted. She had met J.D., and as much as she hated to admit it, her thoughts flowed there more often than not.

But he's not here right now, she thought. He could have been. And I promised myself I'd stay open. This is being open, right?

Andrew leaned into her, closer to her than they had been yet. She could taste his breath as he spoke to her.

"This whole day I wanted to kiss you . . . I mean, as soon as I got here, there you were and you immediately did something to me."

Abby could feel her tummy doing those upside-down flips all over again. She found her eyes kept lingering on his perfect rosy lips.

She started to get up, but he stopped her. "No," he murmured heavily, "that's not the way I want this to go."

His right hand was softly stroking her face, as if detailing every inch for his memory bank. He then took her drink out of her hand, placing it on the ground, and picked her up, standing her on her feet in front of him. For someone nine years her junior, he was making up for his age in expertise.

They stood in front of each other, almost nose to nose, as close as they could be without completely touching. His hands were caressing her back, and he began running his fingers through her hair. Abby could only stand there and stare into his eyes, almost scared to touch him back.

When she finally did, she let her hands gravitate toward his arms, and she began to touch him. His breathing was speeding up, and he was almost digging his fingers into her back as he rubbed it. She slowly trailed her eyes up his chest, along his collarbone, meeting his gaze again.

It was at this moment that Andrew leaned in. His lips

closed in on hers, so soft and sweet. She could taste the salt air on them as she pressed her body closer to his, letting herself enjoy the moment.

As they pulled away from each other, Andrew smiled sweetly at Abby.

"I've wanted to do that since I got here."

"You just got here a few days ago, silly."

His eyes were smiling as he looked down at her. "As soon as I saw you, I was smitten. Your smile, your laugh, and the way you move. I hate to sound corny, Abby, but you're very easy on the eyes."

Abby could feel the heat rising to her face. Andrew kissed both cheeks.

"You're blushing."

Abby shrugged her shoulders. "It's what I do." She looked deeply in his eyes, grinning from ear to ear. "That and I just made out with my brother's best friend."

Andrew's face turned serious. "Does that bother you?"

"No, well, actually I can't really say. This is a first for me. I feel like the lecherous aunt who preys on her nephew's friends."

"Except you're more like a lecherous big sister," he teased.

Abby swatted Andrew. "You're terrible."

He pursed his lips together and kissed her gently on her forehead. "Yes, according to you."

Abby felt his hands coming up over her shoulders and stroking her collarbone. She closed her eyes, enjoying his soft touch, wishing in some part of her that she felt strong enough to let it go further. She was about to halt their activity when his finger lifted her chin and their lips met again.

This time the kiss was different. It was a feverish rush, looking for answers to quiet questions that hadn't been asked.

Abby could feel her face flushing with more energy and warmth, the electric tingles of her body emitting more heat than she thought was possible. Andrew was clearly feeling the same intensity as he grabbed her waist and pulled her in closer to him.

It was Abby, of course, who pulled away first. Andrew was surprised, but he took her hand in his and smiled at her.

"Now we get to spend the night together in that romantic little room," he said, wiggling his eyebrows at her.

Abby laughed. "Don't get any ideas, mister."

Andrew's face said everything she needed. He kissed her one more time and then led her by the hand back to their room.

Abby knew if she didn't get any sleep that night, she'd be fine. After all, she could sleep when she was dead.

❦

THE MORNING SUNSHINE FILTERED INTO THE ROOM TOO EARLY for Abby. She lay there for a moment, wiping her tired eyes. Her tired, swollen eyes, that is. Crap! She thought. That's what you get from sitting up all night long.

When they had gotten back to the room, the pair curled up on the bed together, talking -- asking questions about each other and playing "get to know you." Andrew was more than respectful. Granted, there were a few times when they were making out that he pushed for more, but Abby was firm in holding her ground. As much as she had wanted to tear his clothes off, something made her hold back.

She rolled over to see if Andrew was still asleep only to find him gone. As she sat up, she heard the door to the cottage open. Andrew came into the main bedroom, grinning and holding a couple of to-go cups.

"Coffee?" He posed this as a question, but he had already put it by her bed.

She took the cup, enjoying the bedside service, and looked around for creamer.

"You looking for milk?"

Abby nodded. "Well, creamer."

"You said last night you like creamer, no sugar."

"I did." She nodded her head and smiled coyly at him.

Andrew walked back around the bed to Abby's side. "I was listening, you know." He nodded at her cup. "Your milk is in there already." He sat down next to her, scooting her over a bit so he could sit closer to her.

Abby took a long swig of her coffee. As soon as she had pulled the cup from her lips, Andrew's lips were on hers.

"What's that for?" Abby asked when they had parted.

"Because I can," he teased. "You have a problem with it?"

"Not at all," she replied as she stretched her body, lounging even deeper into the pillows that surrounded her like a cloud. "In fact, I could get used to this whole thing: coffee before I even get out of bed, being served to me by some hot waiter with an even sexier accent."

Andrew laughed out loud. "You're funny." He kissed her forehead and then settled in next to her on the pillows. "Crabby Abby."

Abby hid her face in her hands. "You caught me at a weak moment. You got a lot out of me last night."

Andrew leaned over, looking in her eyes and wrapping his long soft fingers around hers in order to pry her hands off her face. "I liked it."

"Well . . . good. I'm glad I didn't bore you to death." She winked at him, adding, "You're only here for a few more days anyway, so . . . "

There was a flash of sadness in Andrew's eyes as he stopped her from finishing her sentence. The smile that was on his face had disappeared. "Let's not talk about how long I'm here, okay?"

Abby sat up and kissed him solidly. "You're right. And, I need to head back over to St. Kitts now. Leigh will be in this evening, and I want to make sure we're ready for her arrival. She's got answers, and I've got questions."

Abby jumped out of bed and threw on her beach cover-up. Reaching for her phone, she realized it was dead after the marathon conversation with her sister the night before and quickly plugged it in to give it the juice it desperately needed for the day ahead. She grabbed her coffee -- and Andrew -- and they headed over to Ben's room. She wanted to make sure Ben had fair warning of what was about to land back at home.

The door to Ben's cottage was wide open. On his pull-out sofa were a few bodies, carnage from the events of the night before. There were beer and rum bottles placed haphazardly or knocked on their sides in all parts of the room. Abby was shocked, not surprised. Just shocked.

"I forgot to tell you, Ben mentioned if we wanted to stop by last night to have a drink, we should."

Abby found her mouth was stuck in the open position. "A drink or a keg? Wow!" They both stifled their laughter as they crept into the main bedroom.

Entering the main bedroom was like walking into another universe. It had remained untouched, most likely due to Tracey, Abby decided. It was always the girl that stayed on top of things, wasn't it? And boys were pretty dirty, so Ben was probably drunk and letting everyone do what they wanted.

Yet there was only one body in the bed, and it was Tracey. She was passed out and snoring. Abby swore that she even snored with a Southern accent. Her blond hair was matted on her face as if she had been up running just before they walked in. While they were surveying the scene, the bathroom door opened and a refreshed and clean Ben stepped out.

"Well, good morning. Didn't expect to see you two when I came out. You're lucky I got dressed first."

Abby pointed to the front room. "What, pray tell, blew up in there?"

"Ah." Ben nodded. "Tracey." He looked down at the snoring girl snuggled deep in the bed. "I think half the beer bottles that are out there are hers."

Abby and Andrew both cringed. "She's going to be feeling it. Make sure you get her some water and food for her to have when she wakes up," Andrew suggested, slyly pinching Abby's butt as he said it.

"Good call." Ben sat down. "I was actually on my way over to get you -- Maria called. Seems the air conditioning blew last night."

Abby's stomach turned. "No, no, no . . . are you kidding me? Where's the phone?"

"She said she'd call Buddy and see if he and his brother Rush could come take a look at it. A couple of the guests were complaining, but it's not terrible yet." Ben returned to prepping for the day. "So, what do you guys want to do today?"

"I was already planning on heading back early, but now I really have to go." Abby took in a big breath. "Can you take me to the ferry?"

Ben looked at Abby and then to Andrew, waiting for someone to tell him why.

"Did you do something to piss her off?" he finally asked Andrew.

"No, you ass."

Ben looked back to Abby, still waiting.

"It's Leigh. She's flying in today so I'm heading back over to meet her -- now I need to get there to make sure the air conditioning is handled or I look irresponsible. " Abby turned to Ben. "I don't expect you to cut your trip short, but I thought if you wanted to be there when she arrived, well, then you have the option."

"She's coming today?" Ben was clearly surprised.

Abby nodded. "Yep." She was lost in thought. Suddenly, like a slap in the face, the true purpose of her trip dawned on her. "Ben, I think she wanted me to come here so I would find out about all of this. Leigh was sick of keeping the secret for Dad. She wanted us to meet and figure this out so it would all come out."

Ben was confused. "What makes you think this now?"

"Listen." Abby was in her serious Nancy Drew mode and speaking a mile a minute. "I wondered why she wanted me to come down here and help with the house, well what I thought was a house. But really, who turns down a chance to go to the Caribbean? I mean, she mentioned something about it being international and people here were on island time, so I figured it was more of her being a control freak. Then I get here, and I find out it's a business, so I'm thinking if this is a business, why should I be here? Knowing Leigh, I figured she had some grand scheme for me and that I just needed to go along and not kick up my heels for once. Then we find out we're related. Maria gives me a little lecture about how people do things sometimes so they will be found out." Abby was actually impressed with Leigh at this moment. "It was never about the sale of the inn. That was the excuse . . . Leigh saw the chance to get me here so I'd 'discover' her secret." Abby was nodding, understanding Leigh's motive to get her down to the Caribbean now. "Good show, Leigh. Good show."

Ben was soaking it all in. "She sent you here on purpose?"

Abby clapped her hands together. "Exactly! She made it so I had to meet you."

Andrew piped in. "Let me get this straight. Your sister kind of spearheaded this crazy plan to get you here so that all of the truth would come out? That's what you think?"

Abby was nodding excitedly. "It makes sense." She turned to Ben so she could address him directly. "Daryl left her, when she told him everything, to think about their marriage. She's coming here to clean up our dad's mess. Ben," Abby went over to her brother and took his hand, "you get to be a part of a real-life, completely dysfunctional yet still operating family right now. I was going to say you should stay here, but I think you guys should pack it up and come back, too. Not right away, but think about it."

Ben wasn't able to meet Abby's gaze. From behind him, they heard a moan and the rustling of sheets as Tracey drunkenly rolled over.

When Ben did look up, he was smiling and it looked like he was fighting back tears. Abby's instinct was to tease him, but she pretended not to see them. "I'll come back later, after Tracey gets up." He grabbed Abby and hugged her, tightly. "You're right. This is family. I like having a crazy family. It's so weird."

She gave him a last squeeze. "Perfect. I'm going to go check out and grab my things. If you don't mind, can you drive me to the ferry?"

"And me. I should go back now, too." Andrew had spoken up suddenly, causing Ben to look at him with interest.

"You want to go back now, too? I thought you wanted to go get pictures of Princess Di's vacation home for your mum?"

Andrew cleared his throat. "Another time. I actually have a message from work to get a hold of my boss." Andrew reached out to squeeze Abby's hand. "And, Abby may need moral support."

Ben wasn't buying it. "I'd believe your work phone call a bit more if I hadn't seen two people making out on the beach by the hammock last night. You wouldn't know who that was, would you?" He looked, with playful accusation, at both Abby and Andrew.

"I know who it was. It was Abby and Andy. Ha ha HA! Andy. Not Andrew. Andy. I like that. I'm still funny." Tracey had spoken, but it was drunken sleepy mumble. No sooner had she said it then she was passed out again.

Abby feigned a surprised look and pointed at Ben. "We'll deal with all of this later, okay? Right now I'm getting ready to go. If there are any South Africans in the room who want to come with me, then please do." She turned to Andrew. "The more the merrier." With that, she slapped his bum and skipped out the door, and all the way back to the cottage.

🌺

THE RIDE BACK ON THE FERRY WAS PROVING TO BE DIFFERENT than the ride over to Nevis. Abby was pressed against the rail, watching the island fade away as the boat sliced through the crystal blue waters of the Caribbean. Andrew was behind her, with his arms wrapped around her waist, kissing her neck and enjoying the view. He was trying to sneak his hands up the front of her shirt when Abby's body shook with excitement.

"I need my cell phone!" Abby was patting her pockets and looking in her bag to see if she had thrown it in her purse.

Andrew, amused at her sudden shift of attention, tried to help. "Weren't you texting with it in the car?"

"I was..." Abby dropped to her knees and began tearing all of the items out of her purse, shoving them into Andrew's vacant arms to hold. "Why do I carry a bag this big when I don't need anything in it but my phone, some money and sunblock?"

Andrew was still grinning as he watched Abby check all of her pockets one more time, then she dove back to the purse one more time. It was on the second inspection of her purse that she realized the fabric in her bag was torn, so the phone had slid behind the lining and was trapped between the purse and it's liner. Abby pumped a fist in the air, while the other hand was busy with fingers reaching and searching for their prey. As she firmly grasped the cellphone in her grip, she knew there was one more thing she needed to do in order to help make things right in her family's world.

Andrew sat down next to her, and wrapped his arm around he as she was dialing the digits. She could feel her energy growing more and more nervous, almost agitated. She wasn't sure how this call would go over. She did know, as she reached out for Andrew's hand, that she was glad he was there with her as she did this.

On the other end of the line, there was a click and a familiar voice said, "Hello." It was a masculine and deep voice, and like a breath of sane, fresh air.

Abby smiled, not only for Andrew, but also for the voice on the other end.

"Hello, Daryl? It's Abby. We need to talk . . . "

CHAPTER 12

"Ziggy, have you seen Captain Cutty lately?"

Ziggy was prompt in picking up Abby and Andrew at the port to hustle them back to La Cantina. Abby was perched in the front seat of Ziggy's cab with her hair flying wildly since the windows were down. She knew she looked a mess, but didn't care. She'd made out with a hot boy and was on her way to get ready for Leigh, thus finally getting some answers. She felt things were right in the world.

Andrew hooted from the back seat. "How is that old dog?"

"Cap'n Joe be askin' bout you, Andrew. You go see him or he may kick dat ass." Ziggy wagged his finger at Andrew in the rearview mirror.

"Zig, why don't you take Andrew to say hi, but drop me at the house. I need to confer with Maria and figure out the air conditioning situation before Leigh gets in."

Andrew's head tilted quizzically.

"You sure?"

Abby turned and smiled at the handsome man in the back-seat. "Yes. Go have fun."

Abby leaned into the back to kiss Andrew, then turned her attention back to Ziggy.

"Ziggy, you gave Cutty his winnings, right? From the casino?"

Ziggy's head bobbed up and down. "Yeah, mon. He spent it already."

Abby shook her head. "Of course he did."

"Who won money at the casino?" Andrew piped up.

Ziggy was beaming with pride. "Abby won money for her and Cutty. She took $700!" He looked sideways at Abby. "What you spend it on, girl?"

Abby returned the sideways look. "The hotel on Nevis and a few of Ben's bills." She was blushing. Not just for her good deed but also from the faded memory of J.D. and their shared flirtations that had led up to the night at the casino. It seemed the memory of their shared steamy kiss was once again finding its way into her daydreams. As if reading her thoughts, Andrew began to stroke Abby's hair and massage her shoulders from the backseat, bringing her almost guiltily back to the present.

"You good girl, raised right." Ziggy's head bobbed up and down with happy approval. His eyes were smiling as he looked in the rearview at Andrew. "She already know how to take care of her brother."

They came to a sliding stop at the end of the driveway leading to La Cantina.

"Have fun, guys." Abby smiled at them both, knowing they would. "See you soon?" Abby tried to casually toss the last part to Andrew, in a devil-may-care fashion, but the tone of her voice gave her away.

"Sooner than you think," he replied as he jumped out of the car, stealing a kiss as he stole her seat.

The cab pulled out in a haze of dust and sand as Abby made her way to the main house. She bolted inside, finding Maria in the front room struggling with a not-so-understanding guest.

"Seriously, the heat is, like, 200 degrees in our room! This is ridiculous, come to the Caribbean and not have any air conditioning. How can you run an establishment that -- "

"Hello! Hi there, maybe I can help?" Abby came to a halt in front of an exasperated Maria and the angry guest. "I'm Abby, my family owns this establishment. First of all, thank you for joining us here -- " she motioned to herself and Maria -- "but please understand that we are not 'limin',' just trying to get some workers out here to help us help you have a great vacation."

This seemed to momentarily appease the guest, so Abby went on.

"I tell you what, while we are getting repairmen here to alleviate this issue, how about I call the Royal Palms Casino and arrange for a lovely lunch, poolside, for you and . . . ?"

"Her husband, Brett. This is Mrs. Liz Docksteader," Maria helped, smiling now and nodding her head with Abby.

" . . . for you and Brett. Would that be all right?" Abby smiled widely at this woman, willing her to give them another chance.

And it worked. "Okay." Liz smiled back at Abby. "It's just so hot . . . "

"I know, trust me. When I first got here I had my adjustments to make as well." Abby grabbed the phone off the main desk. "Tell you what, go get your husband, we'll arrange a way over and I'm going to call them right now and set it all up, okay?"

Maria escorted a grateful Liz back out to the main foyer as Abby disappeared into the kitchen.

*

IN RECORD TIME, ABBY HAD GOTTEN BUDDY AND HIS BROTHER Rush out to the inn to work on the air conditioning unit. Promising to pay them a bonus if they could get it going before Leigh landed, Abby had stood on the ladder watching them work, intermittently handing them tools or grabbing needed items from the truck for the two men as they toiled away at the old unit on the roof.

"I've seen more of this roof since I've been here than I ever thought I would. Ever. I see why people don't want to run things like bed-and-breakfasts. Or be a landlord."

"Girl, it's just a broken air conditioner. And lucky for you, it's just a dirty coil. Rush already got it almost cleaned up -- then we go."

Abby breathed out a heavy sigh of relief and lowered her forehead to the top rung of the ladder. "If I had known saying yes to coming here would mean all of this . . . "

"What, responsibility?" Maria's head had popped up from the newly inlaid skylight in the master bathroom. "Look at this, Abby! We have a skylight and the ceiling work in here is better than it's looked in ages."

Abby giggled. "Who knew Ziggy poking a hole through the roof would mean a new skylight? And at a fraction of the cost of replacing this part of the roof." She leaned over to pat Buddy's back. "Thank you again for making all of these repairs so darned quick!"

Maria had disappeared back into the house, but her head reappeared. "Looks good, girl. Although after seeing where you did all of the touch-ups through the house, I really think the whole second floor could use a fresh coat of paint."

Abby smiled at her friend. "You're right. I'll get some samples for Leigh to see. Maybe I'll have time to paint a few of the guest rooms before the sale goes through."

Maria was peering intently at Abby. "Or maybe there could just not be a sale." She nodded in Buddy's direction. "You know, that man has never come out here so fast as he did for you today. His wife even said it."

Buddy was grinning at Abby. "I like you. You work with us, not like some of the folks that have places here."

Abby smiled sadly at the sweet older man. "I think your handyman skills are the best, Buddy. I'm glad Maria knew you. You've saved my butt on not one but three occasions with this place."

"You know, the guy Jack that checked in here?" Maria's eyes were dark. "He's the man from London that wants to make the offer and he told Rush the other night he might tear it down to make condos here."

"What?" Abby was stunned. "No."

"It's true." Rush was bobbing his head at Abby. "Dis guy be at de bar talkin' da other night. Said he was here because he heard de inn was for sale. He wants to buy it and tear it down. He just bought Ricky's, too. Not sure what he gon' do wit' it."

"Ricky's? I didn't even know it was for sale." Abby felt as if her heart had been punched. "No. That can't happen. He can't tear down La Cantina."

"It's for sale, Abby. What can you do about it?" Abby could tell by Maria's inflection that she was trying to disguise her own sadness.

"I don't get it. Tearing it down seems so . . . irrational."

Abby turned her attention back to Rush. "So this man, this Jack, what do you know about him?"

Rush shrugged his shoulders. "He been here touring St. Kitts and looking at Nevis. Stayin' at de Royal Palms, Ricky's. He buys property on islands and makes it ready for tourists."

Abby knew it was logical -- the inn was up for sale, so therefore it would be sold. But now that she had a personal stake here, she wasn't so sure it should be demolished. It's like my own romantic notion that if this place disappears, so does what little memory I have left of my father, she thought sadly. And what about Maria and Ziggy? Where would they go?

Abby's heart was heavy. Now that she knew she had one-third of the say in the property, she felt that she owed a little more respect to La Cantina than serving it up as a sacrificial offering to the property gods. She opened her mouth to speak, but Buddy beat her to it.

"Well, ladies. Our job here be done. Go turn de air on inside and see for yourself." He nodded Abby's way. "If dey don't tear de place down, it be needin' a new unit sooner rather den later."

Abby nodded, watching the men gather their tools. She and Maria shared a quiet, secret smile across the roof with each other. "Okay, Buddy. . . . Thanks, guys."

She slowly made her way back down the ladder. She felt woozy and overwhelmed from this newest development and wanted to get her shaken body back onto terra firma.

❦

THE SUN WAS STILL HIGH IN THE CLOUDLESS CARIBBEAN SKY when Ziggy's cab pulled into the driveway at the inn. Leigh's flight had landed, and she was exiting the vehicle in her usual sweeping fashion, on her iPhone giving instructions to whomever the poor schmuck was on the other end. Abby was at the front door to greet her and could tell that Leigh was already agitated by the brusque tone of her voice.

"Well, I made it, and the inn is still standing. Thank goodness for small miracles," Leigh announced tersely as she was hanging up her call.

"I wouldn't think you'd have sent me here unless you wanted the place to be intact." Abby's reply was more deflective than defensive.

Leigh's face was tired, and her eyes had dark circles under them.

"Let's get you inside so you can relax." Abby wanted to get her comfortable so they could get into details about Ben, their dad and other various items of discussion. She also knew that with Leigh, you had to play your cards right. Don't push nor pressure. Guide her into revealing her information so she feels like she has power. It was a game they played.

"You always know just what I need. Always the assistant, aren't you?" Leigh smiled at her sister as she was surveying the property, but Abby felt like she had just swatted her in the face. It was a familiar feeling, like thousands of bees stinging her at once all over her body. "Let's get in so I can say my hellos."

Abby stood to the side, feeling like a small child, allowing Leigh to enter first. Leigh was making a beeline to the kitchen so she could see Maria. What Leigh didn't expect was to see the group that had gathered in there waiting for her to arrive.

Maria was, as usual, bustling around, barking orders. Ben and Andrew had been given duties by Maria, and they were already prepping items she needed. Leigh stood for a minute, taken off guard, but quickly composed herself.

"I see everyone has a job in here. Maybe someone could tell me what I need to do?"

Maria turned to greet her longtime friend and employer. "There's my girl. Come give me some love!"

The two women embraced, hugging and laughing. When Leigh pulled away, the tears were quietly pouring down her tired cheeks. Andrew noticed and made a sign to Abby that he was going to go to the pool house, giving the group their privacy. He managed to sneak out, undetected by the distracted Leigh.

"Why are you crying, girl? Everything is good."

Leigh wiped away her tears with a paper towel Abby handed her. "Thank you, Maria. I know. It's just -- " she turned and looked at Ben -- "oh, Ben. I'm so sorry. I should have told you about this a long time ago. And I didn't. I wanted to do the right thing."

Ben put down the knife he had been holding to chop vegetables and walked over to Leigh. "I'm not angry. Confused, but not angry."

Leigh turned and looked at Abby. "You didn't talk to him after our phone call?"

Abby shook her head. "No. That's for you to talk to him about."

Leigh nodded, then motioned to Ben to sit down. As she repeated the story about their father's dying wishes to Ben, Maria gathered drinks for everyone, whispering to Abby that "this could be a four-bottle night" as she opened the first bottle of wine.

When Leigh was done, Ben sat still. He didn't move.

Leigh was holding her breath, looking at Abby for moral support. Abby just looked at her sister blankly. After a few minutes of silence, Ben finally spoke.

"Thank you." It was simple. It was kind. It was grateful. "You were asked to do something, and you obliged. I don't know how I would have handled the situation had it been me. You did what you thought was best. Thank you. You made sure I had a home here and school funding."

It was Leigh's turn for gratitude. "I should be thanking you, Ben. This has been the heaviest burden to carry. Hell, I've told so many white lies over the years, I forget what's true and what isn't."

"Did you send me here on purpose, Leigh?" Abby wanted to appease her own need to know. "I think you hoped Ben and I would somehow figure out that we were related. Am I crazy? Is that why you set this up?"

Leigh looked at her little sis with admiration. "Busted. I told Dad I wouldn't tell, but we never talked about what would happen if the truth 'accidentally' came out." She sighed heavily. "Now, my marriage is in trouble, all because I withheld the truth from my husband. The one person I should have kept in the loop and didn't." She looked at Abby and Ben, adding, "Not that you didn't need to be in the loop, but he's my husband. I have to face it. I kinda screwed this one up."

Abby watched Leigh take a long drink of her wine. It turned into a gulp as she tried to numb her issues. "Ben's mother doesn't know yet."

"What she means is that my mum doesn't know that I know the truth," Ben interjected. "I wanted to wait to tell her after we spoke."

Leigh understood. "Of course." She gestured toward the office door. "If you want to use the main line here to call her at home, you can. I think she may be as relieved as I am now that it's all out."

Ben nodded, still a little shell-shocked, and headed out the door of the kitchen to use the phone. He quickly changed his mind and walked back over to Leigh.

"I know this may be odd, but . . . " And with that, Ben hugged his newfound sister. Leigh was ecstatic.

"I'm sorry, Ben. I really am."

"Don't be. You had to do it." He cleared his throat and looked around the kitchen. "I'm going to go call her." He smiled at Leigh. "Then we can all move on."

Leigh watched as Ben left the room, then she turned to Abby. "I wanted to tell you so many times. I was honestly following what Dad wanted, but I also never thought you were mature enough to handle it."

Her words sliced through Abby like a hot knife.

"I'm sorry, Abby . . . I just . . . "

Abby sat at the stool that Ben had just vacated. "It's fine." She threw a sideways glance at her sister. "It's what you do."

"Abby . . . " was all Leigh could muster.

"No, Leigh, I'm serious." Abby knew that if she didn't address this now, it would fall to the side. "I love you, but I'm done. Maybe it's me, but sometimes I feel that your words are supportive and kind, then there are the times that they are biting and condescending." Abby looked down at her hands. Once again she was playing nervously with her rings. "No more, Leigh. I'm an adult. Some days I feel like you still don't see me as one."

Leigh's face was twisting slowly. Abby thought she was getting ready to blow her top. She wanted to close her eyes and brace for the wrath. The silence between them felt like an eternity.

"You're right. I do see you sometimes as my immature and irresponsible little sister." Her tone was stern and matter-of-fact, but a bit softer. "I guess I need to stop doing that, huh?"

Abby fought her inner surge of sisterly irritation, choosing instead to whisper, "Thanks." She was staring out the window watching some monkeys run through the backyard. "Did Mom know?"

"No. Mom thought Dad was faithful all of the years he was on the road for business. This was a one-time slip. He thought he was in love. He led a double life with Carla."

Hearing the name was jogging a faded memory, one that Abby must have put aside a long time ago. "Carla." She was slowly nodding her head. "Wait . . . Of course! I can't believe I didn't think of it before . . . "

Abby had retreated into her thoughts, combing through a memory from years ago. "I think I met her, Leigh. I met someone named Carla one day when I was with Dad. Running errands."

It was a vivid memory for Abby. She had been shopping with her father. He had dragged her with him to their local Home Depot to get some supplies for the house. Abby's mom couldn't come; she was grocery shopping, maybe? Either way, Abby was looking for cleaning supplies, then had gone to look for her father. She had found him in a heated argument with a strange woman in the gardening section.

"They were arguing, or 'talking loudly,' to use the phrase Dad used to. He introduced us. I was nervous or maybe I was scared, I think?" This was more of a question than a statement. "Her name was Carla."

Abby had been so sure that all the facts were out, but now she felt that there was more that Leigh wasn't telling her. It was only a second before Leigh confirmed that thought.

"Abby. There is so much more I need to tell you, but I can't."

Abby glanced in the direction where Maria had been standing, searching for support, but she had disappeared from the room as well. This is too weird, she thought, feeling her blood pressure rise and trying not to shake. Who is my father and what did he do?

"Leigh, I need you to tell me. Please," she was begging.

Leigh shook her head. "I can only dredge up the past one giant step at a time, Abby." She sighed heavily again. "Let's just get this cleaned up here and then we can move forward."

"No, Leigh. You always keep me in the dark. I need answers. Now. None of this 'when the time is right' you're giving me. I deserve more."

"You do. I just can't tell you the whole story about Dad and Carla."

Abby was floored. "And why not?"

Leigh grabbed Abby's arms and looked her dead in the eyes. "Because it's not mine to tell."

Abby fell quiet. She was now angry and irritated with her sister.

"He's my dad, too. And Ben's. We kind of have a right to know."

"I don't agree." Leigh reached in her purse and took out her cigarettes. "If you want to know, you're going to have to talk to the other person involved here."

"Ben?"

"No, ding-dong." Leigh shook her head at her sister. "Carla. Ben's mother."

"Well, how do I do that when I don't know her?"

Leigh shrugged. "I can't help you from here. Carla's the only one who can fill in the gaps for you and Ben."

Abby was flabbergasted. She wanted to argue further but knew Leigh well enough to know that she wasn't going to budge. Abby knew this was one conversation she couldn't let go of, but vowed to walk away for the time being. "Let's change the subject, then, so I don't get more irritated. What's up with Daryl?"

Leigh shrugged her shoulders as she walked over to the kitchen window and lit her smoke. "He's mad that I lied. He's furious that I kept a secret from him and hurt that you knew before he did. He's just not happy . . . with me."

"I get it. I mean, I was mad, actually more shocked. I wanted to be really pissed." Abby looked at her sister leaning against the windowpane, almost as if it were a life raft. "I just knew I couldn't be. And really, even though it's all kinda screwed up, it's kinda cool. We got a brother."

Leigh smiled. "And I helped to keep that relationship a secret from all of you for years." She was shaking her head in disbelief. "I'm disgusted with myself."

Abby stood up and closed the gap that had been between her and her sister. "No. You aren't allowed that emotion right now. Okay?"

A sound in the other room brought them back to attention. Ben was done talking to his mother and was coming back.

"Well?" Abby asked.

Ben was smiling. "She's happy that I know. She cried, and she feels bad. For me, for you," he motioned at Abby, "and for you. She said that the day Leigh called her to tell her the story your dad had relayed was the day she knew our lives had gotten more complicated."

Leigh smiled at Ben. "Are you okay? With all of this?"

Ben grinned at his two sisters. "So, tell me about my nephews."

Leigh almost sank to the ground. "How do I have so many good people around me?"

"You're just lucky." Abby's tone was teasing. "All right,

Ben, start asking this woman questions. I think she's ready to answer," Abby added, winking at her sister.

But I haven't forgotten, Leigh, Abby mulled. We still need to talk about Carla.

●●

ABBY WANTED TO GIVE BEN AND LEIGH SOME PRIVACY, NOT TO mention take a moment for herself, so she found her way to the front porch. Lowering herself into a chair, she laid her back against the cold wood and closed her eyes.

Listening to the quiet sounds of the palm fronds swaying in the wind and rocking methodically in her chair, she was lulling herself into a state of self-hypnosis. As she felt her mind begin to drift toward total peace, she heard the familiar noise of someone clearing their throat for attention. Abby shielded her eyes from the sun and slowly opened them to greet her company.

"You look relaxed." It was a man's voice, but the sun was behind him and she couldn't make out his face, though his voice and accent rang familiar. Abby smiled, tilting her head to get a better look.

When she had adjusted her angle, Abby was surprised to find J.D. standing in front of her.

"I . . . I am actually," she replied. Abby found herself very happy to see him, which made her feel a bit guilty as well. "It's a good porch to rest on."

The handsome stranger motioned to the chair next to Abby, asking permission to join her. She smiled and nodded as he lowered himself into the matching chair. The two sat silently rocking together.

"So," she said, breaking the quiet. "Are you staying here at the inn?"

"I am, in fact I just checked in and was walking around exploring the property." He had turned in his chair to face her.

Abby nodded, taking a moment to glance sideways and take in his handsome profile. And the rugged features that made her heart race. She guessed he was in his late thirties or early forties. His grin was slightly off balance and his skin had a nice glow to it, obviously from being in the Caribbean sun for a few weeks now.

She pulled her hair up into a loose bun, securing it on her head, and leaned forward slightly, adjusting her flip-flops. "I take it you like St. Kitts?"

She looked back at him only to find him grinning at her almost mockingly. "Like St. Kitts? I could live here. I've thought about it for years."

"Really?"

He nodded his head. Abby felt his eyes on her as she sat back into the chair again, stretching out her body in an attempt to find a more comfortable position.

"My family came here for vacations when I was growing up." He leaned forward, scooting his chair closer to Abby's. "Why do I feel like you don't want to see me?"

Abby squinted her eyes at J.D., taking in his rugged features. Her eyes scanned his features as she went over the pros and cons of this island-hopping playboy in her mind.

"It's not that I don't want to see you. I do . . . or I did." She sighed, sitting up and pulling herself to the edge of her seat, facing J.D. "I have a lot going on and really don't need things to be complicated right now."

"Complicated?"

She nodded. "Yep. And you," she said pointedly, "you seem like the kind of guy that can cause complications."

J.D. feigned mild horror at the accusation. "Me? Complicated? You're the one who never called."

It was Abby's turn for faux horror. "You're the man, allegedly," she teased. "I figured if you wanted to see me bad enough you'd figure it out. Plus, you seemed pretty occupied yourself the other night with that beautiful woman by your side."

J.D.'s smile was broad and enticing as he leaned closer to her. "Why do you think I'm here, Abby?"

As she was opening her mouth to answer, the front door opened and Ben stepped out onto the porch.

"Hey, Leigh wants you in the kitchen," he said, eyeing J.D. with interest.

"Okay," Abby answered as nonchalantly as she could. "Be right in."

Abby turned away from Ben, trying once again to answer J.D.'s question, but Ben interrupted.

"Ummm . . . Abs? I think she meant now."

Abby turned and gave him a look of "got it!" and smiled tightly.

"Okay, Ben. I'll be right there."

The two stopped for a moment, watching each other almost comically, with Ben looking at Abby and then looking at J. D., and Abby making motions with her eyes for Ben to go back inside. Ben finally retreated into the inn, leaving the pair alone on the front porch.

"Let me guess." J.D. eyed her up and down, stroking her body with his eyes. "Rain check."

Abby stood, steeling herself to go inside, but J.D. stood

with her, stepping closer to her and leaning in so his gaze matched hers. She could feel his breath on her lips as he spoke.

"I don't know why, but I just don't think we're done here, Abby. You owe me a dinner. Or at least -- " he brushed away the hair that had fallen in front of her eyes -- "one more kiss."

Abby's gut lurched as J.D. wrapped his arm around her waist, pulling her body closer to his. Her mind was screaming for her to stop, that Andrew was a mere property line away, but her body was insisting she keep her close proximity since it wouldn't move. Her breath was heavy and hot, and she was struggling to keep her eyes focused on J.D.'s and to not let them be drawn to his lips. She wasn't sure why, but she couldn't turn off the pull she felt to this man. And right now, she didn't want to.

J.D.'s hand was under her shirt, massaging her back, his other hand stroking her hair. Abby closed her eyes in an effort to gather the courage and the strength to pull away, but it was just enough time for J.D. He leaned in, kissing the tip of her nose and then making his way down to her lips, pressing himself closer and kissing her so tenderly and sweetly but with such heat that it was all she could do to stop him.

Abby pulled away, extricating herself from his tight grip. "I can't do this right now. I'm sorry." Abby's guilt for what she felt and for feeling as if she had betrayed Andrew weighed on her insides.

"And . . . Well, obviously I need to go. Duty calls." She awkwardly stepped back. "I hope you enjoy your stay here at the inn."

"Why, thank you." He grinned playfully at Abby. "And we're still not quite done."

Matching his gaze, she lifted her head as regally as she

could, mustering her confidence. "Well, we are finished for now."

"Really? Because?"

Abby scoffed. "Because I said so." She was almost defiant as she pulled her posture up just a touch, making herself more poised. "It's not like we really know each other very well, now is it?"

"Well, maybe if you gave me a chance to explain what I was doing on Nevis and why I didn't come find you sooner, we could get to know each other a lot better. But I get the feeling you want to debate this issue a little more. Am I right?"

Abby felt an irritation in her gut that she couldn't squelch. It was a familiar feeling from relationships past and not one she felt she needed to revisit. Not today.

"You can keep your explanations and your reasons why you were galavanting around St. Kitts and Nevis with some girl." She nodded curtly and folded her arms to indicate that she was serious. Although Abby wasn't sure whom she needed to convince more, J.D. or herself.

It was apparent, however, that J.D. was more than amused. His lips were twitching as she was stepping back farther from him. "Well, okay then. Your word is golden. I guess I'll see you around the inn?"

"Actually, yes . . . My family owns La Cantina, so you'll see me around." She looked up and could have sworn she saw shock in his face that quickly melted into a smile as he took a small bow. She almost asked what was wrong, but the sound of her name being yelled from the back of the inn stopped her.

"'Bye, J.D. Enjoy your day." She threw one last glance his way as she quickly retreated into the inn.

CHAPTER 13

ABBY WOKE UP ON HER AIR MATTRESS FEELING A LITTLE cramped. Not until she attempted to roll over did she remember that Andrew had curled up with her to sleep for the night. In her guilt from her lapse with J.D. the day before, Abby had all but burrowed her body into his all night long. Abby lay there for a few extra minutes, relishing the fact that she was encompassed in his strong arms. Another wonderful night with a wonderful guy. A sweet and wonderful man who was here right now with her, not jetting off somewhere to be with someone else, like J.D. had done.

Abby lay there silently wondering why she would even be remotely attracted to someone of J.D.'s character, especially when she had Andrew.

Andrew has all the golden qualities a woman looks for, she thought. He's open and kind, honest and loving. Everyone gets along with him and he really makes it a point to make me feel comfortable. Most of all, he seems to genuinely care about me. About "us."

Then there was the mysterious J.D., who had appeared on

her first day at Ricky's and kept popping up. He was rugged and handsome and when she thought of him she couldn't deny the wave of excitement that spread through her body. It was different than what she felt with Andrew, and she wasn't sure why.

Lost in her train of thought, all Abby could think of was that Andrew felt safe. Like coming home. Like there was love to be found here and maybe . . . just maybe . . . a real future. And there was truth and honesty. But would that be enough?

To top it off, Abby had to face the fact that Andrew was leaving for London in a few days. They had talked after dinner the night before about his work schedule, and he was due to go to L.A. for a few meetings a year, so they had agreed it was something to look forward to.

Abby was careful to roll out of the bed slowly so she wouldn't disturb Andrew. As much as she wanted to snuggle up to him more, or wake him to join her, she needed some alone time to sort through all of the information buzzing around in her head.

She brewed some coffee and went to her usual spot out by the pool. For a minute, she thought she was about to have an anxiety attack. Who wouldn't with all of this news? she thought as she sat quietly for a minute then began her own internal download of all the events thus far.

So I need to talk to Carla. Abby's thoughts were as disgruntled as she felt. Makes sense, and I want to do it in person. Abby felt a twitching in her gut when she thought of being face-to-face with the woman who had stolen her father's heart. While she knew a simple call would do, there was something inside of her telling her she needed to be in front of Carla to talk about the past and get some clarification. Abby knew for her own sanity, she needed to have this talk live and in the flesh. And I have to think of her as Ben's mom, not just as my dad's mistress. Kinda helps take the sting out . . .

There's so much more to this, Abby thought. Dammit, Dad, I should be so mad at you, but I can't be. You're not even here to give me the answers yourself! Feels so selfish of you to go to your grave with so much deceit. How can one person make a decision that affects so many lives yet never reveal it? So all of this means getting to London. Okay, I'll figure that one out, too. And now J.D.'s here? Staying at the inn?

She was staring into space, processing her thoughts, when Ben approached the table. "You okay?"

Abby was surprised to see him. "You're up early." She nodded as she registered that he wasn't just getting up, but rather he was just getting home. "Ah, I see. It took a little longer than you thought to drive Tracey home, huh?"

"Yeah." Ben answered, then thrust his head toward the pool house. "Is Andrew in there or your new friend?"

Abby stuck her tongue out at Ben. "Shush. J.D. is a guest here and we've run into each other a few times over the last few weeks." She was struggling to act nonchalant, but felt her cheeks flush. "He seems nice enough."

"Whatever."

Abby swatted Ben playfully. "Whatever? Really? I didn't do anything wrong."

Ben's grin was wicked as he answered, "Yet."

"Anyway . . . " Abby wanted to change the subject. "I was sitting here thinking about your mom and the fact that we need to talk to her to understand more."

Ben's tone was hushed. "I feel like there's more to the story, don't you?"

Abby put her head in her hands. "Ben, when you called your mum yesterday, I was talking to Leigh, asking her questions about everything." She hesitated, knowing that she didn't want to burden Ben with this but also knowing she had to. "She told me if I wanted to know the whole story, it wasn't hers to tell. That I had to talk to Carla."

Ben was surprised. "Talk to my mum? Why's that?"

Abby shrugged her tired shoulders -- tired from carrying too much covert information. "I don't know. She said Carla could answer my questions." She was quiet for a second, wondering if she should tell Ben about meeting Carla. She decided it was for the best.

"Ben, I've met your mother. Once, a long time ago when I was little. I was with my dad and she was at a Home Depot."

Ben's reply was sarcastic, not that Abby could blame him.. "You met my mum at a Home Depot? Of course you would, because whenever she needed anything she just flew to Maryland to get it at the rockin' Home Depot they have there."

"I'm not saying it makes any sense, Ben. All I know is that you and I have more in common than a dad. We've been kept in the dark about a lot of things. This is just another freaking hurdle for us to jump." Abby's demeanor turned serious. "Don't tell Leigh I told you."

"What? Why?"

Abby shook her head, almost violently. "No. Just don't." She reached across the table to where Ben was sitting and took his hand. "Do you trust me?"

Ben stared at her, as if she were a unicorn.

"Ben. I'm being serious. Do you trust me?"

"Of course." He looked sheepishly at his sister. "I just want to graduate."

"I get it." There was movement from the main house, indicating that Maria was up and getting breakfast ready, which meant Leigh would be up as well. "Okay. We tell no one that we suspect there's more. No one. Not Tracey. Not Andrew. Not your mum. Agreed?"

Ben smiled at Abby. "Agreed."

He got up and started to head into the pool house. As he opened the door, he turned to his big sis. "This is what it's like, huh?"

"What, having a screwed-up family that likes to hide the truth?" She grinned.

"No. Having a sister who you know will do anything for you."

Abby was touched. She swallowed the tears that sprang to her eyes. "I have to say, Ben, you're the best surprise I ever could have gotten. I'm glad I found you."

"Me, too, Abby. Me, too."

And he disappeared inside the pool house, leaving Abby to her thoughts, which she needed to sort through. Like how she was going to get to London.

She was brought out of her thoughts when her mobile chimed, alerting her to a new text message. Abby looked down at her phone, read the text and smiled, loving the fact that her plan was coming together, and faster than she had thought.

※

"WELL, GOOD MORNING, SUNSHINE. HOW DID YOU SLEEP?"

Leigh was in the kitchen pouring coffee into her "I'm The Boss!" mug. Abby crossed her path while getting a plate of food for her and Andrew.

Abby put on her best smile and answered her sister. "Good, thanks. Going to have some breakfast and then head out to sightsee with Andrew for a bit."

Leigh nodded, eyebrows raised. "Well, well. I kind of

sensed there might be a little more to you and Andrew. Am I right?"

"Yes, well, no . . . I mean, I guess, yes. Let's just say we're having fun while he's here and leave it at that, okay?"

"Fine by me. Consider the topic dropped." Leigh had already shifted her focus. "Hey, Maria, I'm meeting with the buyer here tonight so we can hammer out all of the final details. I have to say it looks good. La Cantina should be a done deal by the end of the week."

Maria, busting into the kitchen with an armload of dirty linens, dropped her wares and put an arm around Leigh. "You okay with that?"

Leigh laughed. "Am I okay with it? Don't worry about me, Maria, I'm fine." There she goes, Abby thought, acting like it's all hunky-dory. "The real question is, are you and Ziggy okay with staying on as property managers for these guys?" She beamed at her friend.

Maria clapped her hands together. "Of course! Oh, Leigh, thank you! I knew you'd make sure to take care of us." Maria then literally leapt into Leigh's arms.

Abby felt a tug at her heart. Leigh didn't know.

And she'd have to tell her.

"Leigh," Abby kept her voice level and spoke slowly, "rumor has it that the man buying La Cantina is going to tear it down. For condos."

A look of sheer grief slowly fell onto Leigh's face as she looked at Abby, then back to Maria, taking in the notion that this could be true.

"Where did you hear this?"

"Rush, one of the repairmen, he overheard this man Jack talking at the bar the other night. Said he was going to buy La Cantina and knock it down." Maria shrugged her shoulders and leaned in to hug both girls, one under each arm. "Nothing you can do."

Leigh slowly lowered herself into the chair again, holding the edge of the table. "This place is too wonderful to be torn down. It really is magical here. Maria, you've done so much with it and cared for it with so much love over the years. What will you do?"

Of course her sister would look out for Maria. As much as it pained her, she had to acknowledge that Leigh was fair and would aim to make the transition smooth for those involved. Her methods might not always have been carried out in the nicest and most sincere fashion, but she always attempted to do the best thing. And this time it seemed as if her plan suddenly had a hole in it.

"Don't worry about us. We'll be fine. Worry about you." Maria smiled at the George girls. "Your dad would have been proud of you, Leigh; you held up your end of the bargain as long as you could, following his wishes. La Cantina had a good run and served its purpose."

"But it can still do more." Abby was flabbergasted that both women seemed so forgiving of the fact that in a few days' time the inn would be sold and there was a huge possibility that preparations would begin for tearing La Cantina down. "With a few more repairs and revising the marketing outreach, maybe a few room giveaways to some VIPs back in L.A. or even some outreach to politicians in D.C. or charities doing benefits, this place would get a nice little surge in the numbers."

Abby was delighted that Leigh was smiling at her, but realized it was a patronizing one as soon as she went to speak. "Oh, Abby, you just don't know, do you? It costs money to do those things."

"Leigh, you just don't get it, do you? I understand that, but there are ways to make things happen that don't involve -- "

Leigh threw up her hand in her signature "stop talking" move that she always used on Abby. "It doesn't matter. The place is going to be sold. End of story."

Leigh was on her way out of the kitchen when she turned back to Maria. "Did Daryl call?"

Maria's face was placid as she shook her head no. Leigh turned and hurried out of the kitchen. Abby felt defeated from their exchange and wanted nothing more than to just get off the property for a bit. Vowing to shake it off, she thanked Maria as she gathered the plates that were overflowing with enough food for eight people and made her way back to the pool house to deliver the food for the guys and wake Andrew.

To her surprise, he was up and showered, sitting at the kitchen table chatting with Ben.

"Good morning, you look refreshed," he said as he pulled her onto his lap.

"What can I say? It's a gift. Here," she placed the dishes on the table for the boys. "Compliments of the chef. I just wanted fruit. The rest is all you."

The two boys dug into the plates with reckless abandon. Abby went to change and found their plates cleared when she came back to the kitchen.

"Well, that was no joke," she teased.

Ben was already up and heading out the door. "I'm off, guys. Need to go check my animals at school then hit the books. Andrew, you sure you're okay hanging out with this one today?"

Andrew acted put out. "Well, I was hoping to hang with you today. But you won't make out with me, so yes."

Abby rolled her eyes. "Whatever!" she teased right back.

After Ben was gone, Abby straddled Andrew as he sat on the chair. "So, what do you say we go to Brimstone Fortress?"

Andrew kissed her square on the mouth. "I think as long as you're there, I don't care where we go."

"Good. Get your shoes on. I'm driving." Abby grinned wickedly and held up the keys to Ziggy's cab.

"Ziggy's letting you drive?"

"No, Maria is. Her car needs to stay here in case Leigh needs it, and since Ziggy's asleep still . . ." Abby smiled conspiratorially in Andrew's direction. "So I want to get the taxi back before he needs it." Bless Maria and her good ideas, Abby thought. She had asked Abby her plans for the day and when she found out Abby wanted to drive across the island, had offered Ziggy's keys to her without hesitation.

Andrew was impressed. "A taxi ride for free? Let's do this."

❦

THEY MANAGED TO ARRIVE AT BRIMSTONE IN ONE PIECE. ABBY realized when she was driving over why she didn't want to drive at all -- the Kittians loved to drive like madmen. They sped and zoomed all over, making it hard for her to relax since she was used to a more structured environment behind the wheel. After a few near collisions and some angry words from another driver, they arrived, laughing and intact.

They climbed the hill to the Brimstone Fortress, a gorgeous architectural masterpiece that had been constructed by African slaves starting in 1690 through 1790. It commanded a complete tactical view of the Caribbean, designed to protect the island if and when the French were to invade.

Being an architect, and surprised he had not explored this

before, Andrew was in heaven. He talked to Abby about the mortar that was used, as well as the volcanic rock from which it was constructed. He was so enthralled he danced up most of the steep hiking spots all day. She was happy to see him so elated. And so sad to know it would end in just a few days.

They were at the top, sitting next to an old cannon and looking over the Caribbean, when Andrew brought up the subject of his imminent departure.

"I know. And you were right when you said we should just enjoy this. So, let's do that, okay?" She was almost pleading with him to stop talking about it.

"Abby -- " he was blushing -- "I never thought I could meet someone like you. You're strong, you're beautiful, you're sexy, you're smart and capable of just about anything." He took her hand in his, stroking it slowly with his forefinger. "I know it's only been a few days, but I don't like thinking that this time next week I won't be waking up next to you."

Abby swallowed, hard, to fight the tears that were threatening to spring up. "Well, it's not next week. So let's just enjoy this, okay?"

Andrew wasn't satisfied. "Abby, I'm crazy about you." He took her face gently in his hands. "I don't fall like this. And I don't like thinking it's just for a week."

Andrew pulled her closer to him, so they were almost touching, as if to kiss. "I'm thinking you could be that once-in-a-lifetime chance, so I want to give it a shot."

Before she knew it, Andrew was kissing her passionately. She, in turn, was melting into his arms, her mind spinning, not sure if she should trust this man or run screaming. She wasn't off and running yet, but she still felt like something was holding her back.

Abby pulled away. "Andrew, I can't give you an answer.

I'm literally at a crossroads in my life. At a time when I should know what I'm doing, or at least at an age when the world thinks I should be settled and making money and getting married . . . I just have baggage right now." She took his hand. "I'm not saying no, I'm saying I don't know. Can that be good enough for right now? Please?"

Andrew looked crestfallen. "Because I'm younger?"

"No, of course not." She was shaking her head from side to side. "It's me. Me and right now."

"Is this a case of 'It's not you, it's me'?" Andrew was watching her thoughtfully. "You don't lie as well as the rest of your family, Abby. I'm okay with you being older, how come you're freaked out that I'm younger?"

Abby was getting a little anxious. Why are we talking about this right now? "Andrew, please, let's just enjoy today and not go there anymore right now. Okay?" She was officially pleading.

Andrew shook his head. "Abby, I'm leaving soon." He took her hand again. "I'll drop it, but I need you to know, I'm willing if you are."

Abby laughed. "Andrew, this is fun, and it's a whirlwind, and you're so ridiculously sexy and amazing. I just can't say what we do next, at least not right now. Besides, I couldn't ask you to commit to a long-distance relationship so soon. That's crazy."

Andrew snatched his hand away from Abby's grasp just as his phone signaled an incoming text. "Saved by the bell."

She watched him as he scanned his phone, reading the incoming text, making a face when he was done with it. "Well, that's that. My boss wants to meet tomorrow so he can show me a property he's purchased. Then he needs me to head back to London to get a jump-start on this particular project."

Abby nodded thoughtfully. "Okay."

"But this conversation isn't over."

Abby nodded. "Fair enough." She leaned down and kissed his forehead. "You're getting red from the sun and I'm sure Ziggy will be looking for his car soon, anyway. Ready?"

It was with an air of sadness that the new couple walked down the hill from the fortress, hand in hand.

●●

ABBY HAD PULLED IN AT JUST THE RIGHT MOMENT. MARIA WAS sending Ziggy out on errands. "Mon, I need to go! Let me in dat car, girl." Ziggy was mumbling something about a menu change and needing to pick up some of the guests at Port Zante.

Abby and Andrew walked into the sitting room and found Leigh in there on her computer.

"How was Brimstone?" Leigh asked, more distractedly than really caring.

"Good. Why's Ziggy muttering something about another menu?"

"Oh, well, the dinner tonight has now become just apps and cocktails tomorrow night for Jack, one of his guys and me. All the details will be finalized then so they can start moving the money." Leigh was excited. In fact, she was close to jubilant.

"Congrats!" Andrew exclaimed.

"Thank you! It is good news. Once the sale is finalized, I can put more money in Ben's account, and he can pay off some more on his loans."

Abby had a nagging question that she needed to ask. "Leigh, why can't we keep the inn?"

Leigh looked over her glasses at Abby. "Why would you ask that?"

"Why wouldn't I? Seems logical."

Andrew, in his practiced art of exiting a room quickly, found a way to slip out and disappeared.

Leigh took her glasses off and motioned for Abby to sit down.

"Leigh, I know this place inside and out now. I know what other repairs need to happen, and I also know I can personally tend to ninety percent of them with Ziggy or Buddy's help. We implement some marketing and promotions and I bet we will be turning folks away!" She smiled at Leigh. "Seriously, I can do this."

"Really, Abby? Do you think that you of all people could handle this responsibility? It seems to me that you can barely take care of yourself. No savings, no job, no -- "

"I can't help that I was laid off, Leigh. As for not being able to take care of myself, let's look at the fact that I can and have for a long time, you just don't notice. Mom knew I could, that's why she let me go to Europe before college."

"And then you dropped out."

Abby threw up her hands in mock surrender. "You got me. I took a job and shirked off school. But it was my choice, Leigh. I can't live the life you want me to have, I have to live my own." Abby's eyes were pleading. "You even said yourself you needed to grow up more, not see me as your immature, irresponsible little sister."

Leigh shook her head and pursed her lips ruefully. "Abby, you told me yourself that you have not saved anything since -- "

"Since what, Leigh? Since Matt left me for another woman, thus leaving me holding the bag for the whole wedding and the reception?" She threw up her hands in mock surrender. "You're right. It's time I got over that part of my life and moved on. Hell, at least let me get some distance from it!"

Abby looked pleadingly into her sister's eyes. "Leigh, I love this place and I love it here. I love these people. I have nothing else to go home to. I'm a third of this inn and I feel like I should get a shot at making a go of it."

Leigh sat for a half-second before giving her clipped answer. "No."

Abby shook her head. "I don't understand, Leigh. Why not?"

"Because I don't think you can do it."

Abby stared at the table, the words still echoing in her head as Leigh went on. "You need to go back, Abby. Get to work, rebuild. Finish school. Do something. I don't know . . . maybe contribute to society?"

"Wow. That's harsh and uncalled for."

"Really? You don't think you taking over an inn is just a little bit crazy? Do you really think you could run a business like this? All by yourself? You're the perpetual assistant, Abby!" Leigh's voice had reached an octave of impatience never heard before by humans. "Get it? Now just drop it, quit with the questions and let me work." As soon as she had vented, she regretted it.

Abby was stunned and had to bite her tongue. She kind of heard, as if in a dream, Leigh's apology. "Leigh, it's fine. I know you're under a lot of pressure. I just wish you could see five feet in front of you and know I'm not out to get you. I'm here to assist you."

Leigh stood up, closing her laptop. Her face was a canvas for apology. "I'm sorry. You of all people did not deserve that. I owe you more than that."

Abby's feelings were hurt. She nodded curtly at her sister, excusing herself to go lie down. After that discussion, hot on the heels of her tense afternoon discussion with Andrew, all she could see in her immediate future was a good, long nap.

She entered the pool house, in tears. She looked around to see if Andrew was there to see her so vulnerable. Since she didn't see him, she sat down on her air mattress and let it all loose. She began to tick down her internal list of loss.

I lost my job, I left my home, now my dad and this Carla woman? Abby's thoughts were like a NASCAR race. Then I find out about Ben, I meet Andrew, and Leigh can only scream at me when she feels like she needs to let off steam that is normally reserved for someone else. I need to take control of this. Of all of this.

It was all piling up on Abby. She had opened her floodgates, and they didn't want to be closed. All she knew was that if she didn't stand up for herself in life, then who would?

She was crying so hard it didn't register at first that someone was there, holding her hand and petting her head. Andrew had quietly joined her, not saying a word but just sitting with her. Eventually she had fallen into his lap, crying harder, yet letting him take care of her. It was then she realized this man who was holding her didn't need to be here and yet here he was. Telling her she was going to be okay and telling her how great she was, and good for being so strong for her family and those around her. It was as if he could see things others didn't. Or wouldn't.

Abby sat up suddenly and looked at Andrew. She wasn't sure what came over her, but she grabbed his face and kissed him. It was harder than she had ever kissed anyone. It was reaching, searching. Like she wanted him to answer her kiss and tell her she was going to be all right as long as they found a way to be together. Abby really wasn't sure what she wanted for her future, but she knew that right now, she wanted Andrew.

Andrew could tell that she was pushing for more than their usual make-out session. He pulled back, holding her face in his hands. "Abby, are you sure you want to . . . ?"

She answered his question by taking off her shirt.

Andrew nodded. "Okay, then. I guess you do."

And he answered her right back by walking over to the door to the pool house and locking and bolting it shut to ensure their privacy.

∞

FRESHLY SHOWERED AND STILL SIPPING THEIR MORNING coffee, Andrew and Abby sat with their feet in the pool when Leigh emerged from the main house dressed like a local in her long skirt and tank top. "Andrew, may I have a moment with my sister?"

Nodding, he stood and kissed Abby's head. "Sure thing."

Not wanting to cast Andrew aside, nor be left alone with her sister yet, Abby tugged on his arm. "Are you sure?"

"I need to prepare for my meeting." He leaned down into Abby's ear, whispering "Good luck," then headed back inside.

Abby sat swirling her feet in the pool water, waiting for Leigh to speak. Leigh in turn sat down next to her sister, slowly lowering her feet in next to hers, and took up mimicking how Abby was moving her feet, creating a small current.

Abby heard Leigh take a big breath. "Do you know I'm jealous of you sometimes, Abby?"

Not what I was expecting to hear. Not at all. "No, I actually would never have thought that at all."

"Well, I can be. I'm sorry for all the terrible things I said in there. That was not about you. That was me being crazy."

Abby kept her feet moving, willing Leigh to keep talking. Abby was worried that if she opened her mouth she might cry.

"It's stupid, but I am," Leigh went on. "Not all the time, like when Matt left you . . . " Abby swatted her sister on the arm. "But seriously. I called you a perpetual assistant and I didn't mean it. You had the balls to leave school and do something different. Something I would never do, and instead of supporting you . . . well. I've always tried to tear you down somehow or build you up. Character-building to make sure you knew 'your place.' So stupid and so immature. And I'm supposed to be the older sister."

"Leigh, it's fine." Abby began to let it go, then thought twice. "Actually, it isn't fine, but it's not like I'm an angel, either. I have done some stupid things and I've made bad decisions, but I feel like I learn from all of them." Abby was swallowing her tears now. "I really want a chance to take care of the inn, to be an owner. I want to make us money -- or maybe I'll fail miserably. I'll never know unless I try. I just need a chance."

Leigh was looking at Abby with what could have been pride in her eyes, but Abby wasn't quite sure.

"Tell you what, Abs. Let me think about it, okay? I'm not going to say no yet, but I need to really take a moment to think about this. I'm supposed to be signing it over to someone else tomorrow night."

"I know." Abby was polite but firm. "But meetings can be canceled. Offers can be pulled off the table."

Leigh started to rise from her spot poolside. Abby stood with her.

"I get jealous of you, too, you know. You have it all, Leigh.

Husband that loves you, kids that are amazing, good job." Sniffing back her tears, Abby reached out and grabbed her sister, pulling her into a big hug. "You took care of me when Mom couldn't do it and Dad was gone. Then you continued with Ben. People say I'm strong, smart, capable . . . all of these wonderful compliments. Some of that's because you helped raise me."

Leigh stepped back, eyeing her little sister adoringly. "Abby . . . stop . . . "

Abby held her hand up, copying Leigh's signature move. "Mm-mm." She shook her head. "I get to say thank you and I love you."

Abby helped Leigh brush away her tears and soaked in the smile that her sister gave her. For the first time in a long time, Abby felt the one thing she had needed all these years.

Acceptance.

CHAPTER 14

THE LOBBY OF THE ROYAL PALMS WAS BUSTLING WITH activity. It was filled with tourists checking in and out, casino-goers, locals and some students sneaking in to go to the pool to study. And Abby.

Abby spotted her morning meeting sitting at the bar, shoulders slumped as if beaten, and wearing an old T-shirt (which was not his style). She got up and made her way over.

Abby took the barstool next to the handsome man. "I've always wanted to say, 'Fancy meeting you here,'" she said. "But since you texted me that you made it without any issues . . ."

Daryl turned to Abby, his face lighting up, grabbing her in a big hug. "Abby!"

"How are you?" She laughed in his ear as she hugged her brother-in-law.

His face was sheepish. "I guess we'll see. How are you doing with everything?"

Abby shot him a look. "Which part? The part about my hidden brother or the part where Leigh owns an inn?"

Daryl smiled, just a tiny bit. "A little hard to swallow, huh?"

Abby just shrugged. "If I got mad at her every time she left out important information, I would be mad a lot. Like ninety percent of the time. I think I just gave up or just decided to finally play by my rules."

"You didn't tell her I was coming, right?"

Abby shook her head. "No. This just needs to happen."

Daryl stared at his beer. "Do you think she's ready for me?"

"Of course she's ready for you. The question is, are you ready for her?" Abby stood up, motioning to Daryl to follow her. "Come on, let's go."

Daryl looked at Abby, who was oozing a confidence and purpose like she had never shown before. "Okay, but only because this whole 'Zen-like Abby' is kind of freaking me out right now."

Abby winked at him, then made her way through the lobby to the concierge. Before they knew it, they were cruising over the island roads at lightning speed to La Cantina.

Abby was the first to walk through the kitchen door, finding Leigh at the table, working silently at her computer. She looked up as Abby entered the room.

"You were up early this morning. Where'd you go?"

"Errands. Nothing exciting." Abby watched as he sister tapped away on her keyboard.

Leigh was also watching Abby out of the corner of her eye. She stopped typing and blew out an irritated huff of air when she noticed a figure outside the screen door behind Abby. "You bring home a stray?"

Instead of answering, Abby opened the door so that Daryl could walk in. Leigh's face froze, sending a plethora of mixed emotions screaming across it. She stood up, silently walked up to her husband and stood before him.

"I can't apologize . . . " she began.

"I don't want any more apologies, Leigh. I want you." Leigh threw herself into Daryl's arms. As they were holding on tightly to each other, Abby slowly backed out of the kitchen and headed to the pool house.

Andrew was in a heated conversation on his mobile when she entered. He did find a moment to give her a look that asked how things went. She gave him a thumbs-up and headed up to Ben's room to see if he was there.

To her surprise, he and Tracey were both there. Ben was packing his things, and Tracey was quizzing him for the midterms. Abby went and curled up on the bed next to Tracey, watching Ben sort through items that might be worth keeping and set aside the ones he really wanted. She waited until they came to a break in the quizzing before she filled him in on her conversation with Leigh from the day before, regarding her wanting to keep the inn.

When she was all done, Ben paced the room. "It's brilliant, Abs. Like you were meant to stay here. I think you should run the inn."

"I know, right?" She grinned at her brother, pleased, but then her expression returned to somber once more. "Don't you find it odd that all of those pictures of your parents -- of my dad -- seem to have been taken here? On St. Kitts?"

Ben stared into the box in front of him, mulling over Abby's question. "I mean, I never really thought about it. But yeah, it does seem a little weird."

Abby's wheels were turning. "I know I'm supposed to go to Carla, Ben, and I will. I promise you. My gut tells me that there is so much more to this: to our parents, to La Cantina, to those photos you have." She shook her head as she stared into space. "I can't put my finger on it, but something is still off."

Ben smiled and leaned over to lovingly slug his sister in her arm. "Take a break and relax for a second. Hell, you're about to become a business owner."

Abby was absentmindedly playing with a string that was loose on her T-shirt. "At least I have your vote of confidence. I'm hoping I get Leigh's as well."

"Well, we are the two-thirds majority vote," Ben reminded her.

Abby nodded in agreement. "True, but I need to do this with all of us on the same page. It's the only way."

"She's got a point," Tracey chimed in. "Best to be all for one and one for all right now."

"And if she doesn't say yes?" Ben asked.

Abby stared at the wall. "I can't think about that. All I know is that the first step for all of us is to be in agreement."

"And the second step?" Ben wondered.

Abby shrugged her shoulders. "As soon as I figure that out, I'll let you know."

"Make it quick, okay?" Ben was tossing a pillow in his hands.

"Or what? You'll bully me with your down pillow?" Abby's reply was dry, as was the smile that played on her lips. Ben threw the pillow at her as Andrew was walking into the room.

"Picking on a girl?" he shot at Ben, as he grabbed Abby and pulled her onto his lap.

"Better than starting a fight with her stupid boyfriend," Ben retorted.

"He's not my boyfriend," Abby quickly interjected.

The room was quiet. Abby looked from face to face. "What?"

Andrew was staring at the floor as Ben and Tracey made up an excuse to go downstairs. As the door closed behind them, Andrew stood up, causing Abby to fall backward off his lap and onto the bed.

"What just happened?"

Andrew's eyes flashed with irritation as he turned to her. "Abby, I just spent the last half-hour trying to rearrange my trip so I could stay a few extra days. Why? So I could be with you. But don't worry. I couldn't make it happen. I'm on a flight out tonight to go home to London." He shook his head. "You don't think I'm serious, do you?"

Abby sat up, playing with the rings on her hands. She had lain in bed the night before, holding him and fighting back her own tears. Abby couldn't figure out why the gods had smiled on her in such a screwed-up way. She had always thought that this type of thing only happened in the movies. Could she really fall this hard for someone in just a few days? At what point is the risk truly for passion and love, not just for the adrenaline rush?

"Andrew, I don't want to move forward on any of this if my heart's not in it." She stared at the floor. "In a short amount of time, my whole world has flipped upside down. Losing my job, coming here, Ben, you? Can you see why I need a moment to breathe?" She looked up at him, meeting his gaze. "Do I feel something for you? Yes! Every part of me has tingled since the day I met you. I never thought that having these feelings could be so instantaneous. And free-ing. I honestly had kind of given up. Then you show up." Standing, she walked over to position herself in front of him. "You sweep in here, with your smile and humor, making everyone happy. And your kisses. Those sweet, soft lips that I love pressing mine against." She leaned into him, kissing his lips slowly, letting hers linger on top of his for a moment.

"Then stop pushing me away." He was breathing heavily into her ear.

Abby couldn't argue with that. "I need you to understand where I am right now, at this point." Taking a step back, she let out some air. "When I commit to anything, Andrew, it's one-hundred-and-ten percent. Which is why I'm so hesitant. I know how determined I get and how I can give up myself a lot of times, when I should have something in reserve." She let out a small sigh. "For the first time ever, I'm one-hundred-and-fifty percent for myself. It's someplace I don't think I've been before. And one thing I've learned about myself is that if I'm not happy with me, I'm not going to be good to anyone."

Andrew nodded curtly. "Abby, fine. You go and take some deep breaths or whatever it is you think needs to happen. I'm leaving on the 7 p.m. flight out. Tonight. Maybe by then you'll have an idea of what you want." He turned on his heels and quickly exited the room, leaving her alone.

Right where she feared she'd always be.

♥♥

ABBY MUST HAVE DOZED OFF FOR A FEW MINUTES. SHE HADN'T heard Ben come in. She opened her eyes to find him staring down at her.

"Andrew's outside," he said as he sat down next to her.

Abby closed her eyes to shut the world out again. "Shhhh."

"He's crazy about you."

Abby moaned. "I know."

Ben looked at his sister, lying half on the bed, with her feet still firmly planted on the floor. "Why do I feel like your position on the bed says a lot about how you approach life and men?"

Abby's eyes flew open. "What do you mean?"

"Well, half in and half out. It's like you didn't firmly commit to the bed, the way you're lying there."

"You can't say that just because of how I'm lying here," she snapped.

"Bollocks. I'm just simply trying to point out that maybe you aren't being completely honest with yourself right now." Ben poked her in her ribs. "What's the harm of just trying?"

Abby sat up, poking him back. "Well, you put time into something and maybe it goes nowhere. Or he might meet someone else. Maybe I do. I just think it's a big decision to have to make in the middle of everything else I have going on right now."

"Relax." There was a smile playing on Ben's lips. "Look at Tracey and me. Three years of being friends and suddenly we're more. Do we know what's going to happen?" He shook his head.

"Oh, stop making sense." Abby smiled at Ben. "You give good brotherly advice."

"I'm trying."

They sat in silence for a few minutes longer, Abby listening to the sounds of movement coming from downstairs, the signs of Tracey still being in the house. Ben was up and packing a few more boxes.

"Daryl's here. He and Leigh are inside talking."

Ben's eyes lit up. "He's here? How?"

Abby shot him a sly smile. "I called him and told him to get his butt down here. Those two are married and they are incredible together. He needed to be here, too. For Leigh, if nothing else."

Ben was nodding his approval. "Impressive."

"Yeah," she giggled. "Now you get to meet more family."

Ben stopped what he was doing and faced Abby. "Cool. The ones I know now are pretty awesome."

"Yeah," Abby said, flashing a big grin Ben's way. "We are pretty awesome, huh? Now your sisters just need to figure out their love lives."

"Abs, you can't just have a Hollywood ending."

She groaned again, staring at her feet. "I know, Ben, what girl wouldn't want that?" Abby smiled at her brother. "Let's go inside."

Andrew was nowhere to be seen as they headed to the main house. Tracey thought she had seen him walking down the driveway and Ben guessed he wanted to cool off a little so he probably went for a walk.

Abby had no time to process any thoughts at all. Once they entered the main house, Leigh's laugh and Daryl's voice took over her train of thought. They were standing in the dining room hugging and laughing.

"Well, I see things are better in here," she said to the duo.

Leigh was beaming, her face lit up and glowing. "I picked the right man, Abby. Lucky for me he's not only forgiving, but understanding as well."

"And lucky for both of us you have a sister that wanted to see you happy," Daryl added as he kissed the top of his wife's head.

Ben and Tracey walked through the door right behind her. It was Daryl who held his hand out and approached the pair. "Ben? I'm Daryl."

They shook hands, which made Leigh and Abby both fight tears, seeing the two worlds beginning to merge. With all of the madness that the last few weeks had been, Abby was ready for them all to be in a good place again as one family unit.

"Well, I think we may need to celebrate a little tonight," Leigh said, winking at Daryl.

"Andrew has to be at the airport by six for his flight," Ben said.

Leigh shot a look at her sister. "He's leaving tonight?" she asked in her "I'm judging you" voice.

Abby shrugged sadly. "Work calls."

"Ben and I are studying and packing his things, so we'll be here if you need any help," Tracey offered.

Daryl took Leigh's hand, beaming at his wife. "I'll do whatever my wife needs. I just can't believe the burden you held for so long."

Abby rolled her eyes. "Daryl. Don't let her think it's okay for her to be a martyr. You'll have a raging lunatic on your hands in no time."

The group let out another burst of shared laughter. As the ruckus died down, Ben asked Daryl if he'd like to see the pool house he had rented for so long, and they disappeared outside with Tracey to take a quick tour of the grounds. This left Leigh and Abby alone in the dining room.

Leigh sat down at the head of the dining room table, quietly surveying the room around her. "I picked all of this out. Piece by piece. Brought Maria and Ziggy in to work here. Kept an eye on everything, just like Dad asked." She sounded sad, but her face read of relief.

Abby took a deep breath and sat next to her sister. She was prepared to go for it with one last speech. "Leigh, it's okay. If you need to sell the inn . . . "

Leigh was smiling wickedly now. "I'm not going to sell it, Abby."

Abby's jaw dropped with a tiny grin of disbelief beginning to play at the corners of her mouth. "Are you serious?"

"I am. You're right. You are a third of this inn and I think you will do a marvelous job at keeping it going." Leigh patted the dining room table, smiling at her sister. "Maria and I both agree Ziggy should be kept away from the roof. And don't let him ever try to resurface this table."

Abby jumped for joy and grabbed her sis in a big hug.

"I'm going to do amazing things with La Cantina, Leigh. I promise!"

"I have no doubts, Abby. None at all." She looked at her watch. "Well, Jack will be ready to meet soon. Let's tell him together when everyone gets here, shall we?"

Abby's grin was ear-to-ear. Getting to tell someone that La Cantina was not for sale would be the best line she got to deliver to anyone ever.

Leigh pulled back and looked adoringly at her little sister. "Dad'd be so proud of you, Abby. So would Mom." She kissed Abby on her forehead. "I wish I had the balls to do this full-time."

Abby smiled. "Now I can take the torch and pick up where you left off."

"Yeah . . . well, fly, little birdie." Leigh pulled back and made a kicking motion at Abby with her right foot. "See? I'm kicking you from the nest."

Abby rolled her eyes. "Please, I jumped."

Leigh nodded. "And Andrew?"

"That's still a work in progress." She narrowed her eyes and wagged a finger at her sister. "And when I say I'm declaring independence, it's in all things. So don't you dare go butting your nose in there, either. Got it?"

Leigh held her hands up in surrender. "Hey, I'm obviously

not the one to give advice. I almost ruined my marriage. Lesson learned."

It was Abby's turn to kiss Leigh's forehead. "Good." She headed out the front door, turning as she reached it. "Just wish me luck?"

Leigh smiled, standing in the light of the dining room window looking ten years younger than she had the night before. "Luck, Abby. Nothing but luck to you."

Abby flashed a big grin, crossed her fingers and headed out the door.

CHAPTER 15

ABBY'S GAIT SHOWED SHE WAS AS DEFLATED AS SHE FELT inside. She had spent the last hour and a half walking the property and the neighborhood trying to find Andrew, with no luck.

Trudging up to the front porch, she sat down in one of the lounge chairs. She surmised that if she were to stake out the front yard, eventually he'd show up. Not that I'm even sure what to say anymore, she thought sadly to herself.

A noise at the other end of the porch startled Abby out of her daydream about "things to say to Andrew to make it all better." The front door had been opened a slight crack. It was Maria checking on her.

"Saw you come walking up the drive, girl. Looks like you're dragging a little." She stepped out onto the porch to join Abby. "You okay?"

Abby shrugged, trying to disguise her crestfallen face, but not able to. "Eh. I can't find Andrew." She looked up at Maria sadly. "I wanted to . . . well, make things right. As right as I can, anyway. I'm not sure what that means yet, I just know I need to see him."

Abby was using the tips of her sneakers to trace a heart in the sand on the porch floor. "Maria, how do you know? How do you know it's okay to take a chance? You know . . . with love or whatever it may be that seems like it's love."

Maria threw her head back and laughed at Abby. "You and your sister with your overanalyzing." She breathed out a heavy sigh and sat down next to Abby on the lounger. "You never know if it's a good idea to take a chance. That's why you take them. Chances, risks, leaps of faith." She put her arm around Abby, squeezing her close. "You're gonna find out that's all you do in life. No one ever knows. Like with you taking over the inn."

Abby sat there for a few minutes in comfortable silence before she smiled at Maria and stood up.

"Thank you, Maria." She looked at her watch. "Almost time for Leigh and me to meet Jack and give him our apologies that we are pulling the offer."

Maria nodded. "First you should go and check in the pool house one more time, Abby."

Abby eyed the woman suspiciously. "For what, exactly?"

"Just go. And remember, Abby. You don't find love. It finds you."

☙

ABBY BURST THROUGH THE DOOR OF THE POOL HOUSE, expecting to find Andrew sitting there waiting. However, she instead found it was neater than it had been earlier. Upon further inspection, Abby realized Andrew wasn't the only thing missing from the pool house. His bags were, too.

Taking a big breath, she walked outside, prepared to go across the lawn and into the meeting with Leigh. As she was walking across the yard, a familiar figure was heading her way, holding up his hands as if he were under arrest.

"Truce?" Andrew asked sweetly.

Abby gasped, and stifled the yelp that was threatening to escape her lips as she dashed into his arms. He held her close as she gripped his body close to hers.

"I thought you left!"

Andrew pulled away so he could see her face fully, kissing her forehead and stroking her hair. "I told you, I had to meet my boss today. I packed my things and put them in Ziggy's cab to save a step later."

Abby felt her insides shaking. She realized at this moment that the thought of losing Andrew had been a little more than she could bear right now. That has to mean something!

"You already met with your boss?" She was holding his face in her hands, and smiling at him. It was setting in that she was truly happy in his arms and couldn't imagine this feeling going away anytime soon.

He nodded. "I did. We met at Ricky's."

"Ricky's? Well, that was convenient."

"Actually, we met there more out of need. The family I work for, the Rhyses, are buying Ricky's."

The words had more of an impact on Abby than either one of them could have expected.

"The Rhys family? You work for them?"

Andrew's answer was slow and premeditated. "Well . . . yes. They buy property all over the Caribbean and rebuild or revamp it for turnaround or to keep. Depends on their mood, really." Abby noticed Andrew's eyes darken ever so slightly. "Well, depends on the mood of the sister, Colleen. She and her mother, Brittany, have interesting tactics when it comes to business. Not the nicest, those two."

Abby felt ill. "What about the men? The father?"

Andrew's face was questioning. "Their father is a decent man, I guess. Jack has always been good to me. For that matter, so has Jack Jr." He caressed her shoulders as if trying to get the genie out of Aladdin's lantern. "The fellows are good, honest men. Why, Abby?"

Abby, in her shock, was still trying to comprehend everything. "Andrew, your boss is staying here at La Cantina. Did you know that?"

Andrew shook his head. "No. He never mentioned it. But he asked if I'd sit in on a meeting here with someone he is thinking of buying out." He shrugged his shoulders. "I honestly figured it was a neutral territory for some local selling off one of the old sugar mills or for a real estate agent to conduct his business."

"Andrew, I hope you don't get in trouble for all of this, but . . . Jack Rhys is here to buy La Cantina. He's planning on making an offer to Leigh today."

Andrew's face twisted in confusion. "Really? Are you sure?"

"Yes, I'm sure! I took the reservation myself. He's here. And he's not going to be happy . . . " Abby took a second to pause for dramatic effect . . . "because we're not selling it, Andrew."

Andrew stood expectantly in front of Abby, waiting for her to continue.

"We're not selling it because I'm staying here. I'm going to run it."

Abby didn't have to wait long for Andrew's reaction. As soon as she uttered "I'm going to run it," he swept her into his arms and twirled her around the yard, quite similar to the way Ziggy had twirled Maria one afternoon many moons ago when

Abby had first arrived on the island. Giggling and kissing and spinning, Abby knew she could live happily if she was killed by a bolt of lightning knowing this was her last moment on earth.

"I'm so happy for you! Brilliant, Abby! Absolutely flipping brilliant!" His gaze was filled with prideful admiration. "So, you're not going back to Los Angeles?"

"No. Well, eventually I'll need to go pack things up or sort them out, but I'm going to stay here for a bit. We have some of our own rebuilding and revamping to do."

"And you're okay with this?" Andrew's signature sweet gaze was in full throttle and Abby couldn't break free from him.

"I am more than okay with it. It was my idea!" she answered, giggling. "I'm thrilled. And I'm thrilled you like the idea, too."

He grabbed her in another big hug, setting her down gently on the ground after one last spin. "Well, this makes it easier to come back here now as we work on Ricky's. Jack wants us both to be very hands-on with this project. Seems this island is pretty special to him and his family." He winked at her. "And, now, you'll be here."

Abby felt that warm heat surge through her body as she realized this wouldn't have to be a long-distance relationship, at least not for a while. It's almost like we'll be taking our time to get to know each other, she thought. It's the best of both worlds.

"That makes me happy, too. Especially since I'm not sure how long it will be until I can afford to get to London to see you. Plus with the inn and the repairs . . . "

Abby didn't get any further. Andrew was pulling an envelope out of his pocket.

"Here." He thrust the envelope into her hands.

"What is this?" Abby asked as she inspected the small, somewhat bulky package.

Andrew rolled his eyes. "Well, go on and open it. I can't tell you what it is. Technically a present should be a surprise."

The corners of Abby's mouth were already curling up into a wide grin that was threatening to encompass the lower half of her face. She bit her lip to keep from laughing out loud as she tore into the envelope. Its contents spilled out and into her hands.

It was an open-ended airline ticket to London.

With her jaw dropping to the floor and tears threatening to spill, Abby stood gripping Andrew's hand so tightly that he had to ask her to stop trying to cut off his circulation. Throwing herself into his arms, she placed her lips on top of his to thank him the best way she knew how, taking a moment to whisper in his ear the ways she would find to thank him at another, more opportune time.

Andrew put out his hands and stepped back from their embrace. "Abby, I'm not done yet. I still have one more gift to give you."

"Andrew! This is insane. I give you a hard time and you give me a ticket to London and there's still more?"

"Well, I was hoping you'd change your mind . . . if you didn't, I was going to have to return all of it before I left." Winking at Abby, he continued, "That's why that ticket is open-ended. See definition of 'refundable' in the airline dictionary."

Abby giggled and playfully swatted him. "Okay, mister. Good one."

Andrew then took a small box out of his pocket. It wasn't so small that it could be misconstrued for a ring box, but she knew it either held jewelry of some fashion or it was a joke. Tentatively, she took the small square box out of his hand and began unwrapping the paper around it.

Inside the box, Abby found the most delicate charm bracelet she had ever seen. Suspended on links of silver or pewter -- not that she could tell or even cared -- were two small palm trees growing from the same trunk with an emerald or some other green gemstone set inside, and another charm that was a heart with a red stone, possibly a ruby but more than likely a perfect imitation. Abby's breath was taken away as she picked up the fragile piece, which sparkled brilliantly in the sun, sending cascades of tiny lights like those on a Christmas tree floating around the pair.

"I saw it and thought of you. I was at Ricky's and Miss C. was selling them. She said she knew you and she thought the charm should actually be of a rum punch drink . . . not sure why, though." Abby still hadn't said anything. "Look, I know it's silly, and I'm pretty sure the stones are fake but . . . "

"It's beautiful," Abby whispered, interrupting his nervous prattling. She held the bracelet and her wrist out to Andrew. "Will you?"

He obliged, finishing off the moment with a soft kiss on the tip of her nose. Abby squeezed his hand and gazed into his eyes.

"So, we're going to do this?" Andrew asked.

Abby nodded. "You betcha."

She stood on her tippy-toes to give him a final kiss on the lips, long and slow. She wanted it to say Thank you, Trust me and I'm going to do the best I can.

Linking hands, they made their way inside for the impending meeting with Jack Rhys.

CHAPTER 16

ABBY STOOD ALONE OUTSIDE THE DOOR LEADING INTO THE dining room. She was pacing nervously, waiting for Leigh to join her so they could walk in together. She and Andrew had decided it was best to go in alone; for one, she didn't want to mix business with pleasure. And two, she didn't want to jeopardize his job if his boss, Jack Sr., thought they had something going on.

She was filled with nervous energy, knowing she was about to officially become the talking head for the inn. Knowing that she had the support of her family, Andrew and Maria behind her had made her all the more confident that this was the right decision.

She heard the soft tapping of feet on the floor behind her. Turning, she was greeted by the sight of a very refreshed and jubilant Leigh. Not like the Leigh she was accustomed to as of late, but Leigh from years past. This Leigh was one who liked to smile and thought frowning was for grumpy-farty old men.

She was almost skipping as she came to a halt next to Abby.

"Well, let's go tell these guys that we ain't selling. I already broke the news to our real estate agent, and now these folks are officially the last to know." Leigh smacked her sister's butt playfully as if they were about to "Play ball!"

Abby pushed open the doors to the dining room and stepped in. But the person sitting at the table wasn't the older man, Jack Sr., that she was expecting. No, the person sitting next to Andrew was very familiar. Too familiar, in fact. So familiar that she wasn't sure what was going on, but she was more than concerned that these two had been talking.

Abby could feel the color drain from her face as she stood across the room from Andrew's boss, Jack Jr.

"J.D.? What are you doing here?"

J.D.'s face lit up at the sight of Abby, almost as if he were backlit by a golden glow.

"Abby! I wanted to explain the other day . . . "

"You two know each other?" Abby heard the voices in unison echoing in the room, knew it was Leigh and Andrew, but couldn't shake the fact that the man she had been locking lips with the other day, the one person besides Andrew who physically made her crazy and made her question her own sexual sanity, was here in front of her . . . in her inn.

Her inn that he wanted to buy from her.

Abby and J.D. stared at each other a moment longer before she broke the gaze.

A little too much of that and everyone will wonder what the hell's going on, she thought.

Clearing her throat, Abby answered the question for Leigh and Andrew. "Yes. I know J.D. We've met on a few different occasions since I've been here." She turned to her sister, whose puzzled expression made her pause. "That's all. A little bit of a shock to see him here when I was expecting Jack Rhys."

"Well, I am Jack Rhys, Abby. J.D. to my family." His eyes were zeroing in on her lips and she could feel his heat even with a table separating them. "And to my close, intimate friends as well," he added.

"Well, I wouldn't go so far as intimate, but fine." Abby took a moment to regain her composure so as not to drag this out any further. Running her hand through her hair, she attempted to gather her thoughts but was interrupted by none other than J.D.

"That's a pretty bracelet you got there," he said, nodding at the charm bracelet. It had caught the sunlight as she was smoothing her hair back, causing the delicate twinkling to begin in the enclosed space.

"Thank you." Abby looked down lovingly at it.

"In fact, I almost got one just like it for my sister, Callie."

Abby worked overtime attempting a straight face. "Your sister's name is Callie?"

Andrew cocked his head as he spoke. "Yes. Well, her name is Colleen but I've always called her Callie. She was with me the other night. Do you remember seeing her? At the casino?"

"Oh." Abby's face was twitching in an effort to mask her surprise. Mystery woman is his sister? So, Callie was the woman he was meeting on Nevis, as well as the woman who was with him at the casino the other night. "I see. Come to think of it, there was a family resemblance...

Leigh grinned as she took Abby's arm, admiring the bracelet as well. "Well, this is absolutely gorgeous! Where did that come from?"

"Just someone very special," Abby said, hoping for a mysterious tone.

"Funny," J.D. began. "Andrew picked one of those up today for a lady friend, didn't you?" He turned to Andrew pointedly. "In fact, your words were that you were going to use it to lure her out of 'her cold, hard conch shell she chooses to live in,' I believe?"

Andrew's cheeks were a soft flushed pink as he realized he had been outed by his boss, not understanding that there was so much more subtext happening here. Subtext that didn't involve the bracelet. Or Andrew.

"Not that I meant you were cold and hard, Abby. In fact, just the opposite -- "Andrew stopped as soon as he realized he was revealing too much information. "Sorry. Carry on."

Abby took a deep breath, steeling herself for the next few moments. Her mission now was not just to tell J.D. they weren't selling the inn, but to get J.D. out of the house. And fast.

"Look, J.D., or Jack . . . I'm sorry to tell you this when you came here to buy the property, but we've decided not to sell. I hope that doesn't interfere with your plans for the rest of the evening."

J.D. kept his cool gaze on Abby, matching her faux-relaxed facial expression and her attitude of utter calm, which she had quickly regained. Abby was channeling her bosses of years past as she stood there with him staring at her. She knew she had to keep up her appearance as the cool business owner not just for him, but for Leigh as well.

The room was quiet. Abby wasn't sure what was going on, except for the fact that Andrew and J.D. were parked next to each other in her dining room. Both sets of lips had been on hers and both men had found ways to make her weak in the knees. Not that it mattered, but still. And now, no one was speaking. Not even Leigh. Abby wanted to swallow, but felt they'd all hear it and take it as a sign of weakness.

Just when she thought it couldn't go on any longer, J.D. cleared his throat and stood.

"Well, okay. I get it." He looked down at a folder that was on the table in front of him and he scribbled a number inside. He slid the folder over to Andrew, allowing him to see it. Andrew nodded his head in agreement.

"I'm going to double the offer."

Abby felt her heart drop in her chest. Are you kidding me? She wanted to slap him.

From behind her, Abby heard Leigh shuffle her feet. "I'm sorry. You want to double the offer?"

Keeping his gaze steady with Abby's, J.D. nodded. "Double. It's the only time I'll offer you that much."

Abby was flabbergasted. "Double. You want to pay double for this inn?"

J.D. tilted his head slightly to the right and smiled cryptically. "I do. I want La Cantina." It was only then that he tore his eyes from Abby's and focused on Leigh. "I told you double, and you have my word."

Leigh laughed, high and flitty. She grabbed Abby's arm. "Please excuse us for one moment. I just need to talk to my sister."

Abby felt as if she were rooted to the spot. It was as if she were in a dream, the way it felt when Leigh was tugging on her arm, signaling she wanted to speak with her privately, away from the stare of Jack Rhys, a.k.a. J.D., and his architect, Andrew. Abby finally gave way and allowed herself to be led into the kitchen.

"Double, Abby! Double! He wants to pay double." Leigh took Abby by both shoulders and sat her down on one of the barstools. "I'm going to ask you this only one time and this will be the last time. . . . Are you sure you want to do this? Take over the inn? Stay here on this island and not go back to Los Angeles?"

Abby sat for a second taking it all in. She knew she could just take the money and go. Go back to her apartment, her non-life in the city, her home full of broken memories and the sad air that still threatened to suffocate her on a daily basis since Matt. She could say "Yes, let's take it" and be gone, leave Maria and Ziggy here to tend to things and Cap'n Joe Cutty to his happy-hour parties of one. Yes, indeed, she could say yes and she, Ben and Leigh would all be the richer for it.

Yet when she thought of leaving the island, she was sad. She didn't want to say yes. She had to say no. The only thing she had now was this island and the inn. Abby knew in her heart that she could do this.

Grinning, she looked up at her sister and slowly began to nod her head.

"Are you saying yes to selling it?"

Abby shook her head. "No, I'm saying yes to staying here. I got this, Leigh. Let's tell him to leave. We're done. I have a business to run."

Leigh wrapped her arms around her little sister and hugged her close.

"Oh, Abs, I know you can do this. You know why?"

"Because I'm so freaked out I have no choice?"

Leigh laughed. "No, because you know you can do this." She began walking back to the dining room. She stopped at the doors and waited for Abby to join her.

Abby opened the doors and locked J.D. in her stare as she gave them their final answer.

"No, thank you, Jack. As I said, we're keeping the inn. It belongs to my family and we've decided to keep it." She tossed a small smile Andrew's way. "It's time I got to know it a little better."

J.D. pushed away from the table. "So be it. Can't say I didn't try." He put out his hand to Leigh. "You must understand, we Rhyses hate to lose. Anything."

Leigh took his hand and shook it, smiling. "I completely understand."

J.D. then put his hand out to Abby. "We like to win, at any cost." His smile was tight but his eyes were flirting. Abby sensed that all she had managed to do was to turn him on for the last half-hour.

"Well, J.D., it's been a pleasure. Again, I'm really sorry that we wasted your time."

His smile was almost a smirk as he held her hand for a moment too long.

"You didn't waste my time, Abby. I came here for Ricky's and your inn was brought to my attention, just a mere blip on the screen. Now it's front and center. I'll be watching it and you." He let go of her hand and started to walk past her, but stepped back, whispering, "I told you I didn't think we were done yet." J.D. then took a moment, allowing his eyes to rest seductively on Abby's lips as he brushed past her, making sure she felt the heat that she knew already existed between them.

And if she wasn't mistaken, it had gotten hotter.

J.D. paused at the door, turning back to the room to address Andrew, his tone taunting and his eyes watching Abby for her reaction. "Don't forget, you need to get back, Andrew. When's your flight?"

The realization hit Abby like a ton of bricks: J.D. must have known. He knew the whole time, she thought, narrowing her eyes and struggling to keep her composure. He knew that Andrew was here with me, so he decided to send him back!

She wanted to confront him, but knew now was not the time. Not here.

"Bollocks, Abby! I needed to be at the airport ten minutes ago! Do you mind . . . ?" he didn't need to finish, because she was already out the door and dashing to get Ziggy's keys from Maria.

As she bolted across the property to the maids' quarters, all she could think of was that Andrew was leaving her and she'd be left on this island, alone, with J.D. Rhys just down the road to torture her . . . if he felt the need.

CHAPTER 17

THE MORNING LIGHT WAS JUST BEGINNING TO FILL THE FRONT rooms of La Cantina. Abby had risen to another gorgeous day on St.Kitts and to another to-do list a mile long. Her schedule now required her to wake up with Maria at 6 a.m. so they could prep breakfast for the guests. Abby was making it a habit to eat with anyone staying there and to be visible in case the guests had any questions or needed suggestions or help organizing their day on the island.

This particular morning, Abby had given Maria some much-needed time off, which was a first. Even though the guests staying at the inn had asked to sleep in, Abby insisted on being there in the morning in case anyone's mind changed. She knew she could whip up a meal if needed.

Abby shuffled over to the check-in desk in the front hall with her coffee and settled in to go over the reservations for the week and organize any special accommodations. These mornings were like gold, silent starts to the day where she had a minute or two alone before the hustle and bustle began. Soon Ziggy would need his grocery list, more guests would arrive via a cruise ship and from the airport. To top it all off, she was organizing a poolside happy hour for the guests, a new tradition, complete with rum punch and conch fritters.

As Abby opened the drawer to pull out a pen, the white envelope with Andrew's handwriting on it caught her eye. She smiled to herself, remembering the moment he had given her the plane ticket for her flight to London. A hot, comforting warmth traveled through her body as she thought of him this morning.

It had been a few weeks since Andrew had rushed out the door, with Abby racing to get him to the airport for his plane back to London. Their goodbye had been hurried, but they had made up for it, logging several hours a few days a week on video chats. Abby was excited knowing he would be back in a few short weeks because he was needed for the beginning stages as the construction began on Ricky's. Since the Rhys family had decided on remodeling Ricky's versus tearing it down, it meant that Andrew's job would be a touch easier, but complicated nonetheless. Jack Sr. had asked that Andrew spend more time overseeing this project with J.D., and Andrew had quickly said yes. While Abby was thrilled that Andrew would be back for more time with her, she couldn't shake the nagging feeling she had in her gut that Jack would insist on turning their lives upside down if he saw the chance.

If he could do it once by sending Andrew home, he'll find a way to do it again, she thought as she lovingly stroked her airline tickets.

Abby had been thrilled with the tickets, as they would serve her a dual purpose when the time came: visiting her handsome boyfriend in London and meeting her father's lover and the mother of her half-brother, Carla Stenson. Abby sucked in a deep breath, feeling her stomach fill with excited butterflies. She wasn't sure when she would go yet, but she knew it would be soon. When the timing is right, she thought.

Abby sipped her coffee slowly, watching as the morning light stretched its golden fingers further inside the inn, welcoming the morning. The sun's rays hit the framed photo in front of her, which caught the light, begging to be seen. She smiled as she gazed lovingly at the picture that had been taken just a few days previously, before Leigh and Daryl had left to go home. Somehow they had all managed to pile in the photo together, after Ben had made several attempts at setting the camera on auto for a picture. Maria, Ziggy, Ben, Abby, Daryl and Leigh . . . they were all sitting on top of one another by the pool, laughing and hugging each other as they were toasting the inn and their family. Abby caught herself giggling at the memory.

In a few days' time, Will, Leigh's son who lived in Los Angeles, would be flying down with some of Abby's belongings and her cat, Giles. He would have with him packages she was ready to have in her possession again and most certainly needed. Will was going to spend some time with her and his Uncle Ben, getting to know him and helping Abby and Ziggy repaint the second floor of the inn. Yes, things were moving right along.

The voicemail light on the desk phone was blinking, teasing Abby to begin her day. As she pored over the reservations, her eyes kept being drawn back to the phone. She knew she should just get it over with, listen to the calls, and then she could move on to the next item up for business. While it was an easy task, taking down voicemails was the most mundane chore for her for some reason, but she knew she had to get it done.

She picked up the phone, plugging in the code to get into

the voicemail system, and began to take notes. One call was in regard to a guest coming in the next day who wanted to arrange a dive out in the Caribbean. Easy enough, she thought. I'll just call Cutty. The next caller was requesting a pickup at the airport and left flight details. It was the third call that made Abby's heart race so fast she thought for sure her head would explode. Just hearing the familiar voice on the other end of the line sent an odd mixture that felt like both ice and boiling water through her veins.

"Hello, La Cantina, and all of its amazing occupants -- but most importantly, hello, Abby. It's J.D. Don't worry, I'm not calling to make a reservation. I'm actually calling because I'm sitting here on the balcony of my hotel, watching the moon and its reflection as it dances over the sea." He took a moment to laugh at himself, then continued, "I can't believe I said that. That a moon dances. Anyway, Abby, you should be here on this balcony with me. I've been thinking about it more, and I still don't like losing. Not the inn and certainly not you. I'm not going anywhere anytime soon, you know. So be prepared, because I fully intend on winning you over." Abby wasn't positive, but she thought his words might have been slightly slurred. "Anyway . . . I, uh . . . I hope you're the one that gets this message, otherwise I may look like a fool, huh? I'll be seeing you around, Miss George. Sooner than you think."

And the call disconnected.

There were still a few more messages, but Abby was stuck somewhere between rattled and excited, so she absentmindedly placed the phone back on its base. She felt something soft, a furry winding around her ankles, and looked down to see one of Ben's cats dancing at her feet. "How is it he can make me feel like this?" She sat back and was speaking directly to the feline as if he had the answer she needed. "Like I need this right now."

Abby sat back and drank in her surroundings, observing La Cantina with new eyes. This time, as she took in the beautiful hand-carved pieces and the local art that had been placed lovingly on the walls, she was looking at her things. Her place. Not with wide-eyed wonder and a feeling of uncertainty, but with the keen eye of someone who owned the property. Her mind raced with ideas and plans for her future on the island as well as the future of the inn, knowing it was up to her to keep it going now.

Looking at the art on the walls, she giggled at the thought of having some of her old French liquor posters brought down from her apartment in Los Angeles and having Ziggy hang them on one of the walls in the main house. She was opting instead to put them in the pool house. Maria would never have appreciated that joke, anyway. Plus, with Ben leaving, Abby got the pool house as her own and she was looking forward to decorating it and staking her claim.

Abby's thoughts were interrupted by the phone ringing beside her. She sat up straight, smoothed back her hair and smiled as she realized she was ready to start the day.

"La Cantina . . . you need to speak to the owner? Yes, that's me . . . "

THE ABBY GEORGE SERIES

Thank you for reading *Rum Punch Regrets*, the first story in the **Abby George Series**. I hope you enjoyed it! If you did:

- Leave a review (it helps others find this book)
- Stop by my website & sign up for my newsletter at www.annekemp.com

The other Abby George stories:
Gotta Go To Come Back
Sugar City Secrets

Do you enjoy romance books set on tropical islands? Then you'll like these novellas. You'll even see some familiar faces pop up!

A Second Chance for Christmas
The Reality of Romance

facebook.com/missannekemp
instagram.com/annekempauthor
tiktok.com/annekempauthor
pinterest.com/annekemp

Printed in Great Britain
by Amazon

33878314R00162